Is CHRIST Allah, the God of Mohammed?

*Did Civilized European
Christians Invent Terrorism?*

Dr Ngozi Funmi Okeke

authorHOUSE®

AuthorHouse™ UK
1663 Liberty Drive
Bloomington, IN 47403 USA
www.authorhouse.co.uk
Phone: 0800.197.4150

Published by AuthorHouse 07/21/2017

ISBN: 978-1-5246-3748-4 (sc)
ISBN: 978-1-5246-3746-0 (hc)
ISBN: 978-1-5246-3747-7 (e)

Print information available on the last page.

CONTENTS

Civilized European Christians Invented Terrorism:

"Many Scots masters were considered among the most brutal, with life expectancy on their plantations averaging a mere four years. We worked them to death then simply imported more to keep the sugar and thus the money flowing. Unlike centuries of grief and murder, an apology costs nothing. So what does Scotland have to say?" Herald Scotland: Ian Bell, Columnist, Sunday 28 April 2013

"CHRIST is not mocked by any sense. He will not be mocked by counterfeit piety; He will not be mocked with idle resolution. CHRIST will not suffer His decrees to be invalidated; He will not leave His promises unfulfilled or His threats unexecuted. And this will easily appear if we consider that promises and threats can only become ineffectual by change of mind, or want of POWER. CHRIST cannot change His will. He, with the extra-terrestrial, self-sufficient, DIVINE, immortal and exceptional Y chromosome is not a man that He should repent. What CHRIST has spoken will surely come to pass as He will not want POWER to execute His purposes. He who spoke and the world was made could speak again and it will perish. CHRIST'S arm is not shortened that He cannot save neither is it shortened that He cannot punish." Dr Samuel Johnson, paraphrased

It is the absolute TRUTH that reasoning and vision are unbounded, if Christ's is infinite, He must be who He says He is. Had the Pharisees (The Anti-Christ Racist Freemasons of that era) understood genetics, particularly the exceptional, DIVINE, extra-terrestrial, self-sufficient and immortal Y chromosome of CHRIST or ALLAH or GOD, they mightn't have lynched Him. They did because they were ignorant. Their successors, the Anti-Christ Closeted Racist Freemasons seem shallower

"The supreme vice is shallowness" Oscar Wilde

DEDICATION

Some people secretly believe that some Anti-Christ, Closeted Racist Freemasons were instinctive, innate Slave Masters:

"It must be agreed that in most ages many countries have had part of their inhabitants in a state of slavery; yet it may be doubted whether slavery can ever be supposed the natural condition of man. It is impossible not to conceive that men in their original state were equal; and very difficult to imagine how one would be subjected to another but by violent compulsion. An individual may, indeed, forfeit his liberty by a crime; but he cannot by that crime forfeit the liberty of his children. What is true of a criminal seems true likewise of a captive. A man may accept life from a conquering enemy on condition of perpetual servitude; but it is very doubtful whether he can entail that servitude on his descendants; for o man can stipulate without commission for another. The condition which he himself accepts, his son or grandson would have rejected." Dr Samuel Johnson

During European Trade in millions of stolen human beings, members of the Ultra- Righteous Closeted Racist Freemasons were fed like battery hens with the yields of EVIL (millions of stolen and destroyed lives, including millions of kidnapped and carried children).

They do charitable works with the yields of merciless, racist evil. Charitable works without reparation are GRAND DECEIT.

The book is dedicated to all the victims of the Anti-Christ, Closeted Racist Freemasonry. What they want is for history to be rewritten in their favour and for blind merit, which they do not have control of – to be subjugated.

Some Anti-Christ, Closeted Racist Freemasons are deluded thugs; descendants of merciless, racist murderers, armed robbers and thieves: stealer, carrier and seller of millions of human beings, including millions of kidnapped and carried children.

INTRODUCTION

"The greatest enemy of knowledge is not ignorance; it is the illusion of knowledge." – Dr Stephen Hawking

Genetics is the Holy Grail.

Anti-Christ, Closeted Racist Freemasons seem to have the illusion of knowledge. Deluded, grossly overrated, self- aggrandised, closeted racist, latent but very potent white supremacists seem oblivious to the overriding importance genetics, particularly the exceptional, extra-terrestrial and immortal Y chromosome.

Reasoning and vision are unbounded. If Christ's is infinite, He must be who He says He is. The Divine Y chromosome is extra-terrestrial and immortal. Christ is extra-terrestrial.

No people will ever relinquish advantageous positions except by OVERWHELMING FORCE or in exchange for valuable consideration; substitution is likelier.

Europeans gang raped, partitioned and looted Africa, and decommissioned Natural Selection and damaged her inhabitants genetically.

"Moderation is a virtue only for those who are thought to have found alternatives." Henry Kissinger

Deluded Freemasons: motley assembly of exotic, Satanic Faiths that mixes terrestrial with extra-terrestrial. Mohammed is dead; Allah is imaginary.

Christ is an alien; He is immortal. The Divine Y chromosome is self-sufficient and immortal. Christ is genetically unrelated to Mary.

Nearly all Freemasons are genetic aliens (in Britain).Their unrighteous ancestors came to latch on to the yields of EVIL; millions of stolen and destroyed lives, including millions of kidnapped children. They were the BOKO HARAM of their era, albeit 'industrial scale' THIEVES: stealer, carrier and seller of millions of human beings (SLAVERY).

"It was in 1066 that William the Conqueror occupied Britain, stole our land and gained control by granting it to his Norman friends, thus creating a feudal system we have not yet fully escaped." Tony Benn

Normans stole from others what others had stolen from others. Genetically pure aboriginal Britons are extinct; all dispossessed, robbed and slaughtered. Tony Benn was dishonest or he was confused when he implied that he was genetically an Aborigine Briton.

Genetically pure Aborigine Britons are extinct. They were dispossessed and robbed of their land by a motley assembly of mainland Europeans - hereditary serfs or descendants of feudal agricultural labourers - who were hugely transformed by the gigantic gains of slavery. They have reinvented themselves.

According to the Organisation for Economic Cooperation and Development (OECD), young adults in the UK and the USA are amongst the least literate and numerate in the industrialised world.

According to OECD, on the merit based list of Literacy for people aged 16 – 24, USA was part of the bottommost; 20th out of 24. The USA was inferior to Finland, Japan, South Korea, Netherlands, Estonia, Australia, Sweden, Poland, Czech Republic, Germany, Austria, Slovak Republic, Denmark, France, Canada, Norway, Ireland, Spain, England/N Ireland, United States, Italy and Cyprus.

The quality of democracy is a function of the quality of the education of the public. More than that, it is a function of the genetic mix of the population. Randomness in genetic mix is inversely related to the quality of the genetic mix. Natural selection should guide genetic mix; it has been decommissioned.

"The best argument against democracy is a five – minute conversation with the average voter." Sir Winston Churchill

Harvard Professor, Dr Edward O Wilson believed that Natural Selection had been decommissioned, and irreversibly. Cambridge Professor, Dr Richard Dawkins believed that Natural Selection wouldn't have removed ignorance from the future generations even if it hadn't been decommissioned. Decommissioned Natural Selection has switched on unnatural extinction; it is accelerating.

"Wisdom alone is the science of other sciences." Plato

Genetics is the Holy Grail. Christ's Y chromosome is alien and immortal.

Education will ONLY polish what genetics present to it. The best education will not polish charcoal-brain.

According to OECD, on the merit based list of literacy for adults, the USA was 16th out of 22. The USA was inferior to Japan, Finland, Netherlands, Sweden, Australia, Norway, Estonia, Slovak Republic; Flanders (Belgium); Canada; Czech Republic; Denmark; South Korea; England/N Ireland and Germany

According to OECD, on the merit based list of numeracy for people aged 16 - 24, the USA was the last on a list of 24; 24th out of 24. The USA was inferior to Netherlands, Finland, Japan, Flanders (Belgium), South Korea, Austria, Estonia, Sweden, Czech Republic, Slovak Republic, Germany, Denmark, Norway, Australia, Poland, Canada, Cyprus, Northern Ireland, France, Ireland, England, Spain and Italy

According to OECD, on the merit based list of Numeracy for all adults, the USA was at the bottom of that list; 20th out of 22. The USA was inferior to Japan, Finland, Sweden, Netherlands, Norway, Denmark, Slovak Republic, Flanders (Belgium), Czech Republic, Austria, Germany, Estonia, Australia, Canada, South Korea, England/N Ireland, Poland, France and Ireland

So, millions of voters are morons. Shepherds know that sheep are morons. Sheep do not know that shepherds are morons too.

Sheep unnaturally shepherd sheep.

Genetics is the Holy Grail. Christ is exceptional only because of genetics. He is extra-terrestrial because the Divine Y chromosome is extra-terrestrial, and Divinity makes it self -sufficient. Purity will not mix impure. Mary's X chromosome was irrelevant.

New Pharisees: brainwash sheep. They aren't infallible geniuses. They concealed from sheep the fact that guns, not brains secured the past.

Freemasons think Judges (members) are infallible geniuses. Judges (members of the Freemasons) are their brains, cardinals and basis of their power. Judges have power, but it is not necessarily the truth that Judges are selected from amongst the brightest people in any society.

"I emphasis the point….." Judge Paulo Hayers, Badford County Court, 2027

Shocking!

"Why, that is, because, dearest, you are dunce." Dr Samuel Johnson

A fool's approval! If the Judge read his approved Judgement, he must be a fool. If he didn't, he must have lied.

Dr Stephen Hawkins implied that the least bright students in his school, not in his class, did biology. He implied that those who did law related subjects (humanities) were duller than those who did biology.

"In my school, the brightest boys did math and physics, the less bright did physics and chemistry, and the least bright did biology. I wanted to do math and physics, but my father made me do chemistry because he thought there would be no jobs for mathematicians." Dr. Stephen Hawking

CHAPTER 1

"Dr. Adosola Daramola, Born Again Parasite imported from Lagos, prays to her God; Anti-Christ, Closeted Racist Freemasons answer." Ngozi Okeke

"Truth, Sir, is a cow which will yield such people no more milk, and so they are gone to milk the bull." Dr. Samuel Johnson

Men aren't created equal, and they are not equal. Christ, with His extra-terrestrial Y chromosome was exceptional and different. He did not leave in a SPACECRAFT; the Divine Y chromosome did not arrive in a SPACECRAFT.

The principal purpose of the ANTI – CHRIST, essentially FREEMASONS, is to control the world without objective merit or the consent of the controlled. In order to do so, it deliberately plays down the overriding effect of genetics. FREEMASONS seem covenanted to obey Luciferian aliens. FREEMASONS are anti-merit. JUDGES (members) are their brains and Cardinals. The appointment of JUDGES is not based on measurable objective merit.

The implied assertion that homogeneity in the administration of the English law was based on other factors, which excluded merit – was dishonest or, at least, confused.

JUDICIAL DIVERSITY: ACCELERATING CHANGE. Sir Geoffrey Bindman QC; Karon Monaghan QC *"The near absence of women and Black, Asian and minority ethnic judges in the senior judiciary, is no longer tolerable. It undermines the democratic legitimacy of our legal system; it demonstrates a denial of fair and equal opportunities to members of underrepresented groups, and the diversity deficit weakens the quality of justice."*

Subjugated diverse merit in the administration of the law seems to be the Newest Apartheid; it paradoxically propagates and conceals racial bias in the administration of the English law.

SLAVERY was unprovoked unilateral war against unarmed and defenceless Africans by armed EVIL TERRORISTS, albeit highly enlightened, civilized and Christian Europeans.

The artificial wars in the African bush formented by EUROPEAN TERRORISTS were euphemism for organised theft of human beings.

European Christians who stole human beings, stole everything; those who stole human beings will steal anything: moveable and unmovable

Whenever European Christians, EVIL TERRORISTS slaughtered Africans, they dispossessed them, and wherever they robbed, they took possession.

The racial bias, which the Prime Minister lamented, is unlikely to be exclusive to the administration of criminal law.

"British Prime Minister attacks racial bias in Universities and Justice System. 'David Cameron has persuaded a leading labor MP to 'defect' by launching a Government investigation into why black people make up such a high proportion of the prison population. Mr. Cameron said Mr. Lammy would examine why blacks and ethnic minorities make up nearly a quarter of Crown Court defendant – compared to 14 percent of the population. He added: 'If you are black, you are more likely to be in a prison cell than studying in a University. And if you are black, it seems you're more likely to be sentenced to custody for a crime than if you are white. 'We should investigate why this is and how we can end this possible discrimination. That's why I have asked David Lammy to lead a review. Mr. Lammy who is a qualified barrister said: 'I am pleased to accept the Prime Minister's invitation." Mr. Paul Dacre, Daily Mail, 31.01.2016

"The Prime Minister, Mr. David Cameron noted that, extraordinarily, of the 2,500 students that were admitted to Oxford University in 2014, only 27 were blacks." Mr. Paul Dacre, Daily Mail, 31.01.2016

If admission to Oxford University were based on transparent objective merit, the tiny fraction of blacks who made the 'cut' may imply that blacks were created mentally inferior by Almighty God.

ANTI-CHRIST, CLOSTED RACIST, FREEMASONS were neck-deep in the merciless, sadistic commerce, which European trade in stolen AFRICANS was; then, ultra-righteous Freemasons were unrighteous, as they were fed like battery hens with unrighteous yields of the merciless, racist evil. The mercilessly evil, murderous commerce was purified Luciferian.

Today, righteousness without reparation is Luciferian righteousness.

The Grand Lodge of the Freemasons in London was built in 1717 with the yields of STOLEN LIVES and DESTROYED LIVES

At the very end of the 17th century and at the beginning of the 18th century, some overconfident, myopic fantasist Scots led by Mr. William Patterson embarked on a reckless and brainless adventure in Panama (Idiotic Darien Venture). When they failed as was glaringly foreseeable, and they brought their begging bowls to England (where else?), innocent Africans paid for the failures of the Scots with their lives, as their English cousins used the yields of stolen lives to prop up the dying or dead economy of Scotland. Scotland merged with England and together, they looted and destroyed Africa, and became immeasurably rich. Wherever they slaughtered Africans, they dispossessed them, and whenever they robbed Africa, they took possession. They were merciless Luciferians, armed robbers, and thieves. If God is just, they are in BIG trouble.

Some of President Trump's Scottish ancestors probably included Lord Richard Oswald – a Scottish Freemason and Grand – Merchant of stolen bodies.

Lord Richard Oswald was a fabulously wealthy Freemason. Lord Oswald, the son of a Caithness Kirk minister had about him of "an air of great simplicity of the purified higher upper class and honesty'". His friends James Boswell and Laurence Sterne also benefitted from the GIGANTICALLY PROFITABLE commerce in stolen lives.

Lord Richard Oswald was to his contemporaries, 'a wise, thoughtful man who embodied the Scottish virtues of frugality, sobriety, and hard work'; author Adam Hochschild confirmed this in his writing.

Lord Richard Oswald gave the false impression that he was a scholar of theology, philosophy, and history. He collected very expensive art, which included the works of Rubens and Rembrandt, and he gave handsomely to charity; as a Freemason, he was covenanted to do charitable works, which were always vulgar and indiscreet. Lord Richard Oswald learned his trade in Glasgow; he was selected by the Sovereign to represent Britain in negotiations with the Americans after their war of liberation. He was the cosmopolitan epitome of Enlightenment success; when he wasn't busy with selfless and charitable good works, Ultra – Righteous Freemason, Lord Richard Oswald waded in blood. The exact number of African deaths that could be laid at his door is impossible to calculate; he certainly had more BONES at his doorsteps than those that were at the doorsteps of POL-POT.

Lord Richard Oswald was the leading figure in Grant, Oswald & Co and had investments in each corner of the mercilessly evil and sadistic 'triangular trade'". The agents of Lord Richard Oswald kidnapped, stole, carried and sold thousands of defenseless, innocent Africans, although he never set foot on Africa.

Only a few decades after the spectacular failure of the Scottish brainless adventure in Panama, with the yields of merciless racist evil, which the merciless trade in millions of kidnapped and stolen Africans generated, Lord Richard Oswald bought Auchincruive House and 100,000 acres in Ayrshire in 1764. Writing in 2005, Hochschild believed that Lord Richard Oswald was $68 million (about £44m), which is very conservative as the very secretive Freemason was very secretive with his huge wealth. People saw a huge wealth and knew that he did BUSINESS abroad; they did not know what he actually did there.

Shepherds did not bring stolen Africans home; they carried millions of kidnapped and stolen human beings to The Americas and The West-Indies. Sheep believed their shepherds were paragons of wisdom and virtue who, like, Mother Teresa did virtuous works abroad; they did not know that their shepherds were human beings thieves, carriers, and sellers.

Ultra-righteous, closeted Racist Freemason, Lord Richard Oswald was remarkable; he was not extraordinary as there were other merchants of stolen bodies all over Britain who did better than him.

Glasgow and its merchants in sugar, tobacco, and human life were not the only ones who benefitted from the merciless, racist evil; there are loads of names and many monuments, which are the tell-tale signs of the merciless racist evil that European commerce in millions of kidnapped, stolen, carried and sold human beings was; monuments such as, Dennistoun, Campbell, Glassford, Cochrane, Buchanan, Hamilton, Bogle, Ewing, Donald, Speirs, Dunlop.

One clear way to understand what the merciless European merchants in stolen human beings wrought is to simply to take pleasure in the architecture of the cities of Britain today and one will be admiring the fruits of merciless, racist EVIL (slavery). Glasgow, London, Liverpool, Bristol and almost everywhere else have their stories to tell. Edinburgh's once-great banks grew from foundations built on millions of bones of stolen lives; millions of more bones than were at the doorsteps of Pol Pot.

The first Scottish venture into slavery set out from the capital in 1695, which was around the same time that the brainless adventure in Panama commenced. Montrose, Dumfries, Greenock and Port Glasgow each tried their hands in the merciless, racist and evil commerce. In the language of the present age, everyone was doing it, and they were all in it together. When commerce was coursing around the triangle, most of polite Scotland was implicated. Scotland that was rendered bankrupt only a few decades earlier, in 1700, in the aftermath of the Darien, Brainless adventure, was by the mid-1760s a country of big elegant townhouses and 100,000-acre estates. Theirs was an extraordinary reversal of fortune on the back of merciless, racist evil. Contrary to self-serving myth, the almost 'overnight' gigantic opulence did not happen because of "'frugality, sobriety, and hard work".

Certain things need to be remembered about Great Britain and slavery; the commerce in stolen lives was the 'GREAT' in Great Britain. The mercantile class, many of them got STINKING RICH: despite fortunes made from stolen lives, they were quick to demand compensation when slavery was ended in 1833.

Some Britons felt that what they were doing was wrong but the reward was so great, they allowed the merciless racist EVIL to go on for several continuous centuries of merciless, racist terrorism. There was a deep-rooted fear in Britain that the wheels of commerce would grind to a halt without slavery. Scottish economist, Adam Smith persuaded Britons that the gigantically profitable trade in stolen lives hampered freedom of enterprise; his argument that the SADISTIC, RACIST COMMERCE was no longer financially viable. Irrespective of those facts, European slave ships did not stop sailing to West – Africa until around 1888, and when the trade in stolen human beings finally ended, it was replaced with something as profitable if not as brutal. People grab was replaced by land, raw materials and natural resources grab, which goes on. Europeans will leave Africa only after they empty her of all her God granted riches.

"It did not become illegal to own a slave in Scotland until 1778. Until then it had been fashionable for wealthy families to have a young black boy or girl 'attending' on them. Scottish newspapers, such as the Edinburgh Evening Courant and the Caledonian Mercury from the 1740s to the 1770s, carried adverts offering slaves for sale or rewards for the capture of escaped slaves." National Library of Scotland

Some Scottish Christians invented BLACK paedophilia.

Iain Whyte, author of Scotland and the Abolition of Slavery, insists we have at times ignored our guilty past.

He said: *"For many years Scotland's historians harboured the illusion that our nation had little to do with the slave trade or plantation slavery. We swept it under the carpet."*

Scotland's wealth came from tobacco, sugar and cotton – from the slave plantations of the New World (Americas and the West Indies).

Jamaica, West Indies, Streets were to be found in a number of Scottish towns and cities.

Scotland was neck-deep in the EVIL commerce in millions of kidnapped and stolen human beings. The industries, which saw Scotland and much of the Great Britain flourish, were built on the back of slavery. Proceeds of centuries of merciless, racial hatred and fraud kick-started the industrial revolution in Great Britain and brought hundreds of British slave merchants and traders immeasurable wealth.

Anti- Christ, Closeted Racist Freemasons (Satanic Network) are everywhere. Like the Pharisees, they control almost everything except intellect. Ignorant fools, without objective basis, they award they award themselves the monopoly of knowledge.

In Scotland, for example, there were familiar names such as Scot Lyle of Tate and Lyle fame whose fortune was built on gigantic yields of the EVIL commerce in millions of kidnapped and stolen human beings.

Lord Ewing, a Closeted Racist, Anti-Christ Freemason from Glasgow was the richest sugar producer in Jamaica. He was a very generous man and gave handsomely to charity, as Freemasons were obligated to do.

"The Good Samaritan had money." Mrs Thatcher

Mrs Thatcher, like the scripture that she quoted must have referred to virtuous money. Christ referred to virtuous money when He asked the wealthy Pharisees to sell all he had, give the proceeds to the poor and follow him.

Anti-Christ, Closeted Racist Freemasons do charitable works but almost always with the yields of EVIL.

Anti-Christ, Closeted Racist Freemason, Mr Jim-Will- Fix-It, fixed it for many; he did not fix anything for anyone for nothing. Seemingly guarded by the Anti-Christ, Closeted Racist Freemasons, he died with his secrets; all for one, one for all. Not all Masons will die with their secrets because what Christ wants, Christ will get. What Christ wants; Christ already has.

Genetics is the Holy Grail.

Like the Pharisees, deluded Anti-Christ, Closeted Racist Freemasons are oblivious to the glaringly overriding importance of genetics.

Reasoning and vision are unbounded; only FOOLS and Anti-Christ, Closeted Racist Freemasons seem to have not worked that glaring fact out. If the reasoning and vision of Christ is unbounded and infinite, He must be who He says He is.

Deluded, Satanic and EVIL Anti-Christ, Closeted Racist Freemasons are ignorant of the exceptional, extra-terrestrial Y chromosome. In their scatter-head motley assembly of exotic faiths, they brainlessly branded terrestrial with extra-terrestrial, and mortal with immortal.

Prophet Mohammed his dead; Christ is immortal and extra-terrestrial. He left, not in a spacecraft; He left an immortal helper.

Anti-Christ, Closeted Racist Freemasons: ignorant fools seemingly propped up by gigantic yields of millions of stolen and destroyed lives.

The stunning Inveresk Lodge in Edinburgh, Scotland, which is now open to the public, was bought by Mr James Wedderburn and Anti-Christ, Closeted Racist Freemason with money earned from three decades in Jamaica, West Indies, as a merciless, racist owner and exploiter of millions of kidnapped and stolen Africans.

Many Churches in Great Britain were built with the yields of millions of stolen and destroyed lives. For example, the Scottish Wee Free Church was founded using profits and donations from the slave trade. So many schools in Great Britain have dark histories, which are linked to several centuries of merciless and evil commerce in millions of stolen human beings, including millions of kidnapped and stolen children. To give only a couple of examples, Bathgate Academy in Scotland was built from money willed by John Newland, a renowned slave master and Dollar Academy, also on Scotland has a similar foundation.

For several centuries, the goods and profits from West Indian slavery were unloaded at Kingston docks in Glasgow, Scotland. Leith in Edinburgh and Glasgow were popular ports from which ambitious Scottish men sailed to make their fortunes as merciless and evil slave masters. The government of Great Britain decided that £20m, a gigantic sum, could be raised to fund the expected financial losses that were expected to follow abolition

In his 2010 book, The Price of Emancipation, Mr Nicholas Draper reckons Glasgow's mob got £400,000, which in modern terms, is equivalent to hundreds of millions of pounds.

"There was a feeling in Scotland that something was wrong, which is not to say we didn't let it go on for 300 years. But there was a deep-rooted fear in Britain that the wheels of commerce would grind to a halt without slavery. It was only when economists like the Scot Adam Smith suggested slavery hampered freedom of enterprise that the argument took hold that it was no longer financially viable." Herald Scotland: Ian Bell, Columnist, Sunday 28 April 2013

Compensation cases demonstrated that the Scots were not a mere accomplice of England in the merciless, racist evil; they were neck deep in it. According to Mr. Draper, a country with 10% of the British population accounted for at least 15% of absentee slavers. More than 30% of Jamaican plantations were run by Scots. For all the pride taken in the abolitionist societies of Glasgow and Edinburgh, the slave-holders did not suffer because of abolition. They were handsomely "compensated".

The American South is commonly accepted as the benchmark barbarism. Few realize that the behavior of Scots busy getting rich in the slave-holders'' empire was by far more evil– than the worst of the cottonocracy of the American South. One needed only to count the dead bodies; there were millions of more bones than those at the doorsteps of Pol-Pot.

"I know of no evil that has ever existed, nor can imagine any evil to exist, worse than the tearing of eighty thousand persons annually from their native land, by a combination of the most civilised nations inhabiting the most enlightened part of the globe, but more especially under the sanction of the laws of that Nation which calls herself the most free and the most happy of them all." Prime Minister William Pitt the Younger

At 80,000 stolen lives carried per annum over several centuries; there would be millions of unfortunate souls. For every African successfully carried, about eight died in the African bush, as the carrying trade involved fierce resistance. European armed only a few Africans, and they artificially fomented wars, which were Euphemisms for organized, armed theft of human beings. So, millions of Africans perished in the African bush during the merciless sadistic evil, which the European merciless but gigantically profitable commerce in stolen human beings was.

Genetic damage is the most enduring residue of European trade in stolen Africans. European trade in stolen Africans wiped out a significant proportion of the brightest African genes or the-shepherd-genes.

On the plantations of the Americas and West – Indies where millions of kidnapped and stolen Africans were incarcerated at gunpoint, the brightest Africans were rebellious and they objected to the terroristic tyranny of indefinite slavery; they were summarily deselected. De-selection of the brightest genes weakened the genetic pool of the enslaved Africans. Militant kidnapped Africans were summarily deselected because they demanded liberty.

"Give me liberty or give me death." Patrick Henry

The less militant but very bright amongst the kidnapped and stolen Africans refused to breed on stolen land and under, indefinite enforced, hard labor. The genes were lost for eternity; the common genetic pool was diluted and weakened.

Of the mentally weaker remainder, the civilized, European Christians selected the prettiest amongst the African girls and boys – for their own personal use. The prettiest amongst the duller of the kidnapped and stolen Africans became Mulato – slave-babies' factory. The rest of the Africans were systematically paired up and deliberately bred for labor.

Again, the almost irreversible genetic damage is the most enduring residue of European commerce in millions of kidnapped and stolen human beings, including millions of stolen children of Africa.

In the American South, slaves were valuable and bred. Scots worked slaves to death, and personally bred Mulattos by raping some of the Africans; their possessions. For their immediate labor needs, the civilized European Christians used the proceeds of EVIL (sugar and cotton) to import more stolen human beings to keep more sugar and more money flowing.

Liverpool, London and even the Church of England have apologized for the years of slave trading.

Apology without equitable reparation is FROTH with no beer.

Writer Chris Dolan and theologian Dr Robert Beckford stated that Africa deserved an apology for the merciless evil that Europeans served on her.

Africa desires and deserves equitable reparation.

CHAPTER 2

"The great question that has never been answered, and which I have not yet been able to answer, despite my thirty years of research into the feminine soul, is 'What does a woman want?" Sigmund Freud

"Women, not all, are glorified prostitutes and thieves." Anonymous

"I was born here." Adosola Daramola

"The best opportunity of developing academically and emotional." JUDGE PAULO HAYERS, APPROVED JUDGEMENT

Imbecile barrister; descendant of human being thieves and owners

Selfish and myopic, Luciferian and Satanic Europeans destroyed Africa seemingly irreversibly. Europeans were the original terrorists; they invented anarchical, industrial-scale theft of human beings, which is the mother of all terrorism.

Signs of the Anti-Christ, Closeted Racist Freemasons: Ignorance and incompetent lies. Some Judges are the Cardinals and brains of the Anti-Christ, Closeted Racist Freemasons.

What if art were to competently imitate life and Professor Richard Boris Hill, an Anti-Christ, Closeted Racist Freemason, were to emerge on November 18, 2045, in a Court drama in Bedford, Middlesex, Massachusetts, and the following dialogue occurred.

Like Mr. Bill Cosby, Dr. Yinka African Bombata was hunted in the future by the alleged deeds of the past: The retrospective case concerned a Negro Dentist in Bedford, Massachusetts, in 2045. Professor Richard Boris Hill was hired by Middlesex County (Bedford) as an expert witness in its case against Dr Yinka African-Bombata (Negro Dentist).

THE REVIEW OF THE PAST IN THE FUTURE:

November 18, 2045, Court Room 7:

Chief Justice, Dr. Shiv Chicken-Massala India: Good morning everyone again. Mr. Hut, Counsel for Bedford, Massachusetts would you like to carry on with your witness, please.

Mr. Hut, Counsel for Bedford, Massachusetts: Your Honour, yes. Mr. Moore, counsel for Dr. Yinka African Bombata indicated to me that he wants to raise a matter with you before we go too much further.

Chief Justice, Dr. Shiv Chicken-Massala India: Mr David Moore, the ball is in your Court.

Mr Moore, Counsel for Dr Yinka African Bombata: Thank you, Sir. Can I take the Committee to head of Charge 13, please, and can I tell the Committee that heads of Charge 13 (b) and (c) are now admitted?

PAUSE:

Subjugated diverse merit in the administration of any LAW is likelier to paradoxically propagate and conceal RACIAL BIAS in the administration of the LAW.

Dr Yinka African Bombata was the ONLY African in the process.

"Now admitted" was a spin, which seemed designed to paint a false picture.

Mr Moore was engaged by Dr Yinka African Bombata's defense Union. Mr Moore was alleged to be a member of the Anti-Christ, Closeted Racist Freemasons. He unrelentingly LIED under oath

Some Blacks secretly believe that subjugated diversity in the administration of any LAW is the Newest Apartheid; it is as EVIL and less sincere.

Chief Justice, Dr Shiv Chicken-Massala India: Thank you very much, Mr Moore. Yes, Mr Hut, what do you have in response?

Mr Hut, Counsel for Bedford, Massachusetts: Your Honour, thank you very much. I now call Professor Richard Boris Hill. The Committee may be assisted by having head of Charge 13 before them when you hear this evidence because this is very much the evidence which goes to the matters which remain in dispute under head of Charge 13.

Chief Justice, Dr Shiv Chicken-Massala India: Are we referring to any of the bundles, Mr Hut?

MR HUT: Your Honour, you shall be, yes, I am grateful. You will require just Volume 1 of your three volumes.

PAUSE:

"Thank you very much, your Honour." Mr Hut, Counsel for Bedford Massachusetts

"I am very grateful to you, your Honour." Mr Hut, Counsel for Bedford Massachusetts

"Your Honour, you are very kind." Mr Hut, Counsel for Bedford Massachusetts

"Some people think that incompetence is the same thing as sincerity." Quentin Crisp, paraphrased

Incessant fake or schooled courtesy is deceit.

Homogeneity in the administration of the LAW is an instrument of WAR.

Chief Justice, Dr Shiv Chicken-Massala India: Thank you. Shall we just keep one on the witness table and get rid of the other two, please.

PAUSE:

Professor Richard Boris Hill swore to tell the truth, as follows: "I swear by the name of Almighty God to tell the truth, the whole truth and nothing but the truth."

Professor Richard Boris Hill was Cross-examined by MR HUT, Bedford's Counsel

Chief Justice, Dr Shiv Chicken-Massala India: Thank you. Good morning, Professor Richard Boris Hill.

(Professor Richard Boris Hill and Chief Justice, Dr Shiv Chicken-Massala India were allegedly (only rumour) members of the Anti-Christ, Closeted Racist Freemasons.

Professor Richard Boris Hill: Good morning.

MR HUT: Mr Hill, my name is Andrew Hut. I am going to ask you some questions, first of all, on behalf of Bedford, Massachusetts.

Professor Richard Boris Hill: Right.

MR HUT: This is quite a difficult room in terms of layout, so if you can try and address your answers to the Committee; I will not think you are being rude. When I have finished, Mr Moore, who sits to your left, will ask you some questions on behalf of Dr Yinka African Bombata. You are Professor Richard Boris Hill. Is that right?

Professor Richard Boris Hill: That's correct, yes.

MR HUT: Your professional address is c/o Bedford Primary Care Trust, Gilbert Hitchcock House, 221 Kimbolton Plaza, Bedford, Massachusetts. Is that right?

Professor Richard Boris Hill: That's correct.

Mr Hut: And you are a part time Dental Practice Adviser for the Bedfordshire Primary Care Trust.

Professor Richard Boris Hill: That's correct.

MR HUT: Can you tell the Committee what is a Dental Practice Adviser and what does a Dental Practice Adviser do?

Professor Richard Boris Hill: There is no strict definition of Dental Practice Adviser. A Dental Practice Adviser essentially carries out activities on behalf of the PCT to whom he or she advises. It can be obviously practice visits, inspections, that type of activity. It will be activities such as organising the emergency dental service locally; it will be advising practitioners on such matters as infection control and, as we have done so in Bedfordshire, writing documents on things like Health & Safety at work, this type of activity. Also part of my role has been, not so much today but has been involved in developing continuous professional development courses. We have organized them over the years on things like infection control, for example, the relationship within a practice between different practitioners and such other matters.

PAUSE:

Purified ROT!

Tortuous gibberish by a direct descendant of THIEVES: stealer, carrier, and seller of human beings.

Gentlemen, you are now about to embark on a course of studies which will occupy you for two years. Together, they form a noble adventure. But I would like to remind you of an important point. Nothing that you will learn in the course of your studies will be of the slightest possible use to you in after life, save only this, that if you work hard and intelligently you should be able to detect when a man is talking rot, and that, in my view, is the main, if not the sole, purpose of education."

John Alexander Smith, Professor of Moral Philosophy, Speech to Oxford University students, 1914

MR HUT: You have mentioned that within your role is to carry out practice inspections and visits. Is that to ensure that dentists are complying with their General Dental Services Terms of Service?

Professor Richard Boris Hill: Yes. It is essentially that they comply with those Regulations.

PAUSE:

Professor Richard Boris Hill of Bedford employed the World's language like an imbecile.

"The best opportunity of developing academically and emotional."
JUDGE PAULO HAYERS, APPROVED JUDGEMENT

A fool's approval! Semi-illiterate waste of money fake JUDGE; he sat on bones of STOLEN LIVES, in a magnificent building that destroyed lives yielded (future Condominium); virtue shan't sustain the yields of vice, HABAKKUK

Had he been BLACK, he'd not be a JUDGE

MR HUT: You are also in practice as a general dental practitioner yourself. Is that correct?

Professor Richard Boris Hill: That's correct.

MR HUT: At a practice in Hertfordshire.

Professor Richard Boris Hill: Yes.

MR HUT: How many days of your working week do you spend doing that?

Professor Richard Boris Hill: Usually two, occasionally two and a half.

MR HUT: And obviously, therefore, you are a qualified dentist, a Bachelor of Dental Surgery. Is that right?

Professor Richard Boris Hill: That's right.

MR HUT: And I think you also have a qualification in Bachelor of Laws.

Professor Richard Boris Hill: That's correct.

PAUSE:

Envy is a thief!

In 2045, experts suggested that if, as alleged, Professor Richard Boris Hill is a Lawyer and he swore by the name of Almighty God never to tell lies, why did he unrelentingly deviate from the truth under oath?

Professor Richard Boris Hill seemed to be a member of the Anti-Christ, Closeted Racist Freemasons

MR HUT: In terms of the Dental Practice Adviser, can you help the Committee with this: is it a role akin to a policeman or is it a role more akin to support?

Professor Richard Boris Hill: No, it's more to do with support. I would like to divorce it really from the Dental Reference Service. The Dental Reference Service is more of a policing activity whereas the Dental Practice

Adviser acts very much as a link, a bridge, if you like, between the Primary Care Trust and the practitioners there in the field. So, consequently, it is more support. Obviously you will report back to the PCT and the managers at the PCT to inform them of what's happening up there, but when I was first appointed (and I'm going back now to 1991 when it was then the Family Health Service Authority) I was told by the then General Manager that my role was essentially pastoral.

PAUSE:

What a brainless, tortuous gibberish by the Professor!

In 2045, experts suggested that there could be no divorce where there had never been a marriage or union of any kind. The Professor employed the English language like an imbecile.

The Professor implied that he was told about his role after he had been appointed. Reductio Ad Absurdum

Those who are regularly spun are oftener amongst the dullest adult population in the industrialized world.

Like the Pharisees, Anti-Christ, Closeted Racist Freemasons seem oblivious to the notion of infinite vision and reasoning power. Had the Pharisees understood the exceptional nature of the Divine and extraterrestrial Y Chromosome, they mightn't have lynched Christ.

MR HUT: Thank you. Now, as you know, you have been asked to assist with your involvement with Dr Yinka African Bombata who originally had a practice situated at 21 Grove Place in Bedford.

Professor Richard Boris Hill: Yes.

MR HUT: I think it is right to say that you first met Dr Yinka African Bombata in your professional capacity as a Dental Practice Adviser from around 1994 onwards. Is that right?

Professor Richard Boris Hill: That's correct.

PAUSE:

In 2045, experts concluded that 'since 1994 backward is nonsensical'; 1994 onwards is dishonest in fact and nonsensical in style.

In 1994, Dr Yinka African Bombata had only seen Bedford on maps; he had never been there.

Homogeneity or subjugated diverse merit in the administration of the LAW is the NEWEST APARTHEID

Anti-Christ, Closeted Racist Freemasons run the legal system for the benefit of imbeciles (adults with the basic skills of a child)

MR HUT: I see you have got your statement there.

Professor Richard Boris Hill: Yes.

MR HUT: If you do need to refresh your memory from your statement, do please ask and then we can discuss it.

Professor Richard Boris Hill: Sure.

MR HUT: To avoid the temptation put it to one side.

Professor Richard Boris Hill: Yes, put it on one side.

MR HUT: It is very important that the Committee hear your evidence as you give it rather than as influenced by your statement. Between 1994 and 1997 you were working as a Dental Practice Adviser for Bedfordshire Health. Is that correct?

Professor Richard Boris Hill: That's correct.

PAUSE:

In 2045, experts concluded that Mr Hut (Bedford's Counsel): semi-illiterate racist; ultra-righteous descendant of human being THIEVES: stealer, carrier, and seller of human beings.

"It is very important that the Committee hear your evidence as you give it rather than as influenced by your statement. Between 1994 and 1997 you were working as a Dental Practice Adviser for Bedford Health. Is that correct?"

What the white cretin, propped up by the yields of millions of STOLEN and DESTROYED LIVES (MR HUT), could not think:

Professor Boris Richard Hill earlier stated that he secured employment in 1991 and he has been in the same employment since that time.

"When I was first appointed (and I'm going back now to 1991 when it was then the Family Health Service Authority) I was told by the then General Manager that my role was essentially pastoral." Professor Richard Boris Hill

What does the cretin counsel mean by: "Between 1994 and 1997 you were working as a Dental Practice Adviser for Bedford Health. Is that correct?"

Oyinbo olodo!

White skin seemed to conceal DARK BLACK BRAIN.

TRUST FUND: Gigantic yields of millions of STOLEN and DESTROYED LIVES seemed to have distorted the realities of some people.

A genetic ROMANIAN with camouflage English name; his ancestors changed their name and righteously blended with the yields of merciless EVIL.

"I emphasis the point....." JUDGE PAULO HAYERS, APPROVED

Chips and Fish Judge: intellectually impotent nonentity; semi-illiterate, closeted racist, Freemason Judge of Imbeciles (adults with the basic skills of a child).

https://www.youtube.com/watch?v=BlpH4hG7m1A&feature=youtu.be

An important OBJECTIVE of FREEMASONS is to pass LIES to the next generation as the TRUTH.SLAVERY turned DALITS to MAHARAJAHS.

Pharisees were DECORTICATE imbeciles; they didn't discern the overriding importance of GENETICS, which was beyond their control; Anti-Christ Closeted Freemasons are shallower.

FREEMASONS ARE DECORTICATE imbeciles; they don't discern the overriding importance of GENETICS, which is beyond their control

The PRINCIPAL basis of the POWER of the FREEMASONS is MONEY. The foundation of the MONEY is EVIL (SLAVERY); what else?

EUROPEAN CHRISTIANS: Wherever they slaughtered, they dispossessed. Whenever they robbed, they took possession. LUCIFER KILLS AND ROBS

The selection and initiation SATANIC rituals of the FREEMASONS don't eliminate LUNACY; it turns sane men to LUNATICS! HABAKKUK

MR HUT: That is what it was called then anyway.

Professor Richard Boris Hill: Yes, it was called that.

MR HUT: Dr Yinka African Bombata being a single handed practitioner. Is that right?

Professor Richard Boris Hill: Correct.

MR HUT: And in that time you undertook routine practice inspections of his practice and offered him professional advice and support.

Professor Richard Boris Hill: That's correct, yes.

MR HUT: Just one issue perhaps you could clarify for the Committee at this stage before we go too much further. Is there a technical difference between an inspection and a visit?

Professor Richard Boris Hill: It's difficult to say. I think there's an overlap between the two. I think you would visit a practice and you would offer advice, but I suppose you would never be failing to look and consider all the various information that comes to your attention.

I would go as far as to say there's an overlap.

MR HUT: An overlap. All right. Would it be fair to say – and please contradict me if this is a wrong way of looking at it – a visit is something a little less formal and more pastoral than an inspection?

Professor Richard Boris Hill: Yes, certainly so.

MR HUT: Thank you. I think it is right that you visited Dr Yinka African Bombata's practice on 22 January 1996.

Professor Richard Boris Hill: Yes.

MR HUT: We have a copy of your practice inspection report at our divider 12 in the file that is just in front of you. Everybody has got that. With all the documents that we are going to look at together, Mr Hill, and indeed any documents that you are shown or taken to by the defence or by the Committee, do feel free to take as much time as you would like to read the document to refresh your memory. Do not feel rushed in any way in answering if you want to check what the documents say. It is right, is it, that the particular reason for conducting this visit was because there had been some complaints about Mr Bamgbelu's practice?

Professor Richard Boris Hill: That's correct.

MR HUT: As a consequence, you went along to the practice on 22 January 1996 and you compiled this report accordingly. Is that right?

Professor Richard Boris Hill: That's correct.

MR HUT: Let us just take a moment to look at it, if we can.

"Following the receipt of complaints regarding the above named practice, a visit was made on Monday 22nd January. The complaints mainly concerned practice furnishings.

Entry to the practice is through a lobby leading into a hall and reception area. These areas were considered to be in a poor decorative state with little information to guide the new patient.

The waiting room is off the hallway and has recently been improved. The practitioner stated that he intended to further improve this room by purchasing several plants. Patient accommodation here was considered to be satisfactory

Problems were identified with the surgery:

1. Carpet on floor in the clinical area. This would make the removal of spilt mercury virtually impossible leading to a serious health hazard."

Just pausing there, can you elaborate on your concern there?

Professor Richard Boris Hill: Yes, if you have a carpet rather than linoleum flooring, what will happen, of course, is that particles of mercury if they are spilt, and they can be spilt very easily, will evaporate, so causing perhaps a hazardous state to occur.

PAUSE:

Ignorant FOOLS!

What they want is superiority that was based on superior skin color that they neither made nor chose; descendants of agricultural laborers from mainland Europe who were immeasurably transformed by the GIGANTIC YIELDS of millions of STOLEN and DESTROYED LIVES; the intellects of the wretched SERFS and their descendants seemed untouched.

Like the Pharisees, they hate the supremacy of color blind natural talent because they do not have any control of it.

Genetics is the Holy Grail! Had the Pharisees realized this fact, they mightn't have lynched the Messiah. They would have realized the overriding importance of the exceptional, extra-terrestrial and immortal Y chromosome.

The Anti-Christ, Closeted Racist Freemasons control everything except intellect. They are quick to remind cretins about their charitable works. Deluded charitable workers who sit on bones of stolen and destroyed lives, more bones than the millions of skulls that were at the doorsteps of Pol-Pot, want to rewrite history; descendants of wretched Serfs have latched on to the yields of merciless, racist EVIL (millions of STOLEN and DESTROYED lives).

"History shall favor me because I shall write it." Sir Winston Churchill

Homogeneity or subjugated diverse merit in the administration of the LAW is the NEW APARTHEID; it is not as brutal as the real apartheid but it is less sincere; it insincerely propagates and paradoxically conceals white supremacy.

Anti-Christ, Closeted Racist Freemasons bargain unsolicited vulgar indiscreet charitable works for CONTROL; seemingly immortal, illegal (unelected) POWER and CONTROL; the people did not employ them and the people cannot sack them – a very BAD deal.

What white supremacists privileged dullards could not think. More than a decade after Dr Yinka African Bombata started work at the practice, Mr Hut on behalf of Bedford, Massachusetts charged him with allegations that he was unaware of, and which he had never been tried for or allowed to defend himself against.

Only about two weeks after Dr Yinka African Bombata started at the practice following the receipt of alleged complaints, Professor Richard Boris Hill carried out a visit on Monday 22nd January. The complaints mainly concerned practice furnishings.

On September, 18, 2045, Mr Hut (Counsel for Bedford) stated that in 2008, it was found that in January 1996, only a couple of weeks after Dr Yinka African Bombata started at the practice, the entry to the practice was through a lobby leading into a hall and reception area. Mr Hut stated that the areas were considered to be in a poor decorative state with little information to guide the new patient. He also said that the waiting room is off the hallway and has recently been improved. The practitioner stated that he intended to further improve this room by purchasing several plants. Patient accommodation here was considered to be satisfactory.

On 18 November 2045, Mr Hut, Counsel for Bedford, stated that in 2008, it was detected that in 1996, Dr Yinka African Bombata stated he was going to purchase several plants to improve the waiting room.

In 1996 and 2008, some lawyers smoked cheap, impure weed and talked rot, and in 2045, some lawyers will smoke cheap impure weed and talk rot; descendants of human being THIEVES, and HEROIN DEALERS!

How could several plants improve the room?

Brainless nothing! Semi-illiterate racists! Righteous descendants of THIEVES: stealer, carrier, and seller of millions of human beings, including millions of kidnapped and carried children (the BOKO HARAM of their era), HABAKKUK

On November 18, 2045, Mr Hut stated that in 2008, the following problems were identified in 1996:

Carpet on floor in the clinical area. This would make the removal of spilt mercury virtually impossible leading to a serious health hazard." Just pausing there, can you elaborate on your concern there?

Professor Richard Boris Hill: Yes, if you have a carpet rather than linoleum flooring, what will happen, of course, is that particles of mercury if they are spilt, and they can be spilt very easily, will evaporate, so causing perhaps a hazardous state to occur.

MR HUT: The Committee is made up of lay and dental members. Is mercury something which is routinely present in a dental practice?

Professor Richard Boris Hill: Yes, most practices will use it in a machine called an amalgamator where they will pour into one particular compartment mercury and in another compartment the alloy that is mixed to make the amalgam itself. Some practices use capsules which are a much more, if you like, safer way, I suppose, of preventing mercury spillage. But mercury is spilt even with the most careful operators and if you have a little bubble of mercury spilling, it can cause that effect.

MR HUT: Thank you. Turning back to your report:

"2. Very poor quality of cabinetry. As they are not specifically designed for clinical use, efficient surface disinfection may be a problem." Again, can you explain a little more your concern there, Mr Hill.

PAUSE:

In 2045, experts concluded that in order to corroborate the incompetent mendacity of Ms Wollaston Bishop's–Cathedral, privileged dullards went back over a decade to dig up rot. Their own kindred, a white woman had worked at the practice for years with the same furnishings and equipment that she bought. Dr Yinka African Bombata took over and HELL BROKE loose, but the racist insanity was delayed for more than a decade.

Digging up racist rot was possible because of the imbalance in the administration of the Law, which homogeneity caused.

Subjugated diverse merit in the administration of the Law is the New Apartheid; not as EVIL but less sincere.

The stereotypical BLACK man is very dirty.

In 2045, Mr Hut stated that in order to corroborate the allegations by Ms Bishop's – Cathedral in 2007, Bedford went back to 1996 to exhume allegations that were never rebutted at the material time.

Professor Richard Boris Hill: I think Dr Yinka African Bombata had bought the practice from the practitioner who founded it a few years earlier. We felt that the quality of the furnishings which she had actually put in were perhaps not entirely suitable and, of course, to be entirely fair to Mr Yinka African Bombata, he had only really taken the practice over and so there was a need for him to get that all sorted out. It was really recommendation.

PAUSE:

Comments in the present about a future Occurrence:

Homogeneity or subjugated diverse merit in the administration of the Law is the Newest Apartheid; it propagates and conceas RACIAL BIAS.

In 2045, Dr Yinka African Bombata contradicted Professor Richard Boris Hill when he confirmed that he was visited by Professor Richard Boris Hill only two weeks after he commenced work at the practice, which meant that Professor Richard Boris Hill lied when he stated that Dr Yinka African Bombata took over at the practice a few years prior to his visit of January 1996.

The statement by Professor Richard Boris Hill is factually untrue. Scatter-head rubbish! Superior white skin seemed to conceal dark black brain.

The law seemed paralyzed. Homogeneity is not random. Subjugated diverse merit is the new apartheid.

Descendants of aliens with camouflage English names whose ancestors came to latch on to the yields of millions of stolen and destroyed lives.

MR HUT: What are the issues about suitability of that sort of cabinetry and furniture. What are the concerns? You mention there "surface disinfection".

Professor Richard Boris Black: If it's perhaps something like cabinetry which is, how shall we describe it, B&Q type of material, you can have little grooves, little marks where mercury can go. You can find it very difficult, because it's not an entirely smooth surface, to actually disinfect that surface.

MR HUT: Thank you.

PAUSE:

The privileged dullards employed their own language like DAME FAKA PATIENCE GOODLUCK- JONATHAN or MODA FAKA from OKRIKA.

In 2045, experts were of the opinion that the cabinetry, which Professor Richard Boris Hill described were present during the several years that his white kindred Ms Ballister ran the practice.

"3. A Kavoklave was present and was the only prescribed method of sterilisation present in the surgery. Most leading authorities agree that Kavoklave is appropriate only as a 'back-up'. Conventional autoclaves such as an SES 2000 or Little Sister are recommended."

Again, can you elaborate on this finding?

Professor Richard Boris Hill: The problem with the original Kavoklaves that I have found was that you could break into the cycle before sterilisation was complete. I am sure that Kavoklave would argue themselves that they are perfectly suitable and they do the job, but that was my concern about them. I find that the SES Little Sister is a far better machine.

PAUSE:

Comments in the present about a future occurrence.

"Most leading authorities agree that Kavoklave is appropriate only as a 'back-up'."

In 2045, experts discerned brainless nonsense by a closeted racist imbecile that was used to mesmerize closeted racist imbeciles that sat before him. The statement is meaningless. When the white man is intellectually challenged by a mere black man, which he had been brought up to believe is inferior, in order not to lose face, he tells naked lies; homogeneity in the administration of the law allows the dishonesty.

Professor Richard Boris Hill did not name a single one of the 'most leading authorities'.

Reductio ad absurdum! Brainless Nonsense!

"The problem with the original Kavoklaves that I have found was that you could break into the cycle before sterilisation was complete. I am sure that Kavoklave would argue themselves that they are perfectly suitable and they do the job, but that was my concern about them. I find that the SES Little Sister is a far better machine."

Brainless tortuous gibberish! The statement does not make sense. Homogeneity or subjugated diverse merit in the administration of the law allows for legal hooliganism.

In 2045, Professor Richard Boris Hill made comments about the comments he made in 2008 about the autoclave that Dr Yinka African Bombata used for about two months in 1996.

Crass!

In 2045, Professor Richard Boris Hill confirmed that he included Kavoklave in his 2003 and 2004 reports of Dr Yinka African Bomabata's surgery. In 2045, it became apparent that the 2004 reports were later withdrawn, albeit more than four years after the alleged visit of July 2004.

Some people used guns to impose their will on unarmed and defenceless Africans over several centuries of merciless racist tyranny. Part of The resultant effect of the merciless racist tyranny is that an imbecile white man became a professor in Bedford, Massachusetts.

Gigantic yields of millions of stolen and destroyed lives immeasurably improved the standard of living of agricultural laborers and their descendants; it left their intellects untouched.

In 2045, Professor Richard Boris Hill alleged that in 2003, Dr Yinka African Bombata had a Kavoklave autoclave has a back-up. He lied.

If they needed anything, they fabricated it. Homogeneity, the subjugation of diverse merit in the administration of the LAW is the NEW APARTHEID; it propagates and paradoxically conceals racial bias in the administration of the LAW.

In 2045, Professor Richard Boris Hill alleged that in 2004, Dr Yinka African Bombata used only Kavoklave autoclave. The report was later withdrawn, albeit more than four after the alleged visit.

In 2045, homogeneity or subjugated diverse merit in the administration of the law is the NEW APARTHEID; it conceals and paradoxically propagates racial bias in the administration of the English law.

"75 to 90 percent of American trial lawyers are incompetent, dishonest, or both." Charles E. Corry, Ph.D.

MR HUT: Thank you. You go on to report:

"It was considered that sufficient and appropriate dental instruments were present in the surgery to allow compliance with the terms of service in this respect.

X-ray equipment was satisfactory and regularly maintained. Cross infection control procedures were considered satisfactory and the practice complies with the regulations relating to the storage collection and disposal of clinical waste."

Then over the page you make some Recommendations:

"In the opinion of the Dental Adviser, action needs to be taken as follows:

1. Decoration of entrance, hallway and reception areas with appropriate signposting.

2. Removal of carpet in surgery. Replacement by linoleum.

....

4. Purchase of an appropriate autoclave ....

6. In the longer term, it is recommended the surgery should be re-

designed and re-fitted."

You then conclude:

"It therefore cannot be said that the practitioner meets with requirements of paragraphs 33(1) and 33(3) of the terms of service. It is suggested that regular visits be made to the practice and appropriate support and advice given to ensure complete compliance with terms of service."

Professor Richard Boris Hill: That is correct.

PAUSE:

Comment in the present about a future occurrence:

Number 3 was redacted from the list ONLY because privileged dullards did not know the meanings of 'latter' and 'former'.

No 5 was redacted to fool the fools before them. Those regularly spun are amongst the dullest adult populations in the industrialised world.

White Skin concealed Dark Black Brain (DBB)!

MR HUT: Is this an example then of the pastoral rather than the policing side of things?

Professor Richard Boris Hill: Yes, it's recommendation and the recommendation will then be made back to the then Health Authority in the hope that some financial support could be forthcoming. This obviously depended upon the financial state of the Health Authority at the time and what funds were available.

MR HUT: If we go over to divider 13, please, so the next divider. We have there I think your exhibit RWH2, which is a letter of 2 February 1996. This is a letter that you wrote to Dr Yinka African Bombata after that particular visit. Is that correct?

Professor Richard Boris Hill: That's correct.

MR HUT: We can see the address there.

"Dear Dr Yinka African Bombata,

Thank you for the opportunity for me to visit your practice last week.

I am sure you are aware that a number of improvements are needed. The areas

I have identified which should be promptly addressed are ...."

and you set the three out there, the decoration, the issue about the carpet, to be replaced by linoleum or similar and disinfection of the autoclave.

"I do hope that this does not appear to be too prescriptive. We wish to give you all necessary support and advice to enable your practice to be successful.

I will contact you in a few weeks to see how you are progressing.

Yours sincerely."

Again, Professor Richard Boris Hill, the sentiments you express in the penultimate paragraph, "I do hope this does not appear too prescriptive" and "We wish to give you all necessary support and advice to enable your practice to be successful", is that a genuine sentiment behind the task that you were undertaking?

Professor Richard Boris Hill: Yes, very much so.

MR HUT: If we could then forward, please, to 2006(sic). It is right, I think, that on

15 April 2006(sic) you carried out a follow up visit to Mr Bamgbelu's practice and you noted some improvements being made. Is that right? We will look at the report in a moment.

Professor Richard Boris Hill: 1996, I think.

MR HUT: 1996, I am sorry. There is an error in your statement. You are quite right,

15 April 1996. If we go to divider 14, you notice some improvements.

Professor Richard Boris Hill: Very much so.

MR HUT: If we look then at the report, the visit on, as you say, 15 April 1996:

"The visit was a follow up from an earlier inspection where several deficiencies were identified. The practitioner was asked to address these matters with urgency." Just breaking off there, in terms of impressing upon Dr Yinka African Bombata the urgency of your observations and the remedies that you felt were necessary on the last occasion, how did you express the urgency? Was that orally or in writing?

Professor Richard Boris Hill: That would have been orally, yes.

PAUSE:

She-she man looking man, Professor Richard Boris Hill's mouth of a fellow who had taken so much stuff in orally.

MR HUT: On the last occasion.

Professor Richard Boris Hill: Yes.

MR HUT: Turning back to the note:

"It was noted that a new autoclave had been purchased [and you give the details]. This was present in the surgery and replaced the Kavoklave which was now being used as a back up machine. The waiting room and reception areas have been decorated and improved. There appears to be a greater degree of efficiency in the practice.

The carpet in the surgery has been removed from around the chair and linoleum placed. This will prevent problems with mercury spillage.

Further hand pieces and syringes have been purchased so improving cross infection control measures.

The practitioner will be carrying out further practice improvements in the near future, e.g. a further surgery will be equipped.

At the time of inspection, the practice premises can be considered to be

satisfactory ...."

according to the relevant paragraphs of the terms of service.

Professor Richard Boris Hill: Yes.

PAUSE:

Comment in the present about a future occurrence:

On 18 November 2045, Professor Richard Boris Hill stated that in 1996, Dr Yinka African Bombata had a new autoclave and the Kavoklave was used as a back-up. On the same day, Professor Richard Boris Hill stated that on July 22, 2004, Dr Yinka Black had only a Kavoklave autoclave. He seemed intellectually disorientated and mentally imbalanced. The 2004 reports were withdrawn, albeit more than four years later.

Homogeneity or subjugated diversity in the administration of the law is the NEWEST APARTHEID; it conceals and paradoxically propagates racial bias in the administration of the law.

MR HUT: After that visit it is right, I think, that you carried out another visit in 1996. Is that right? You went back in July again.

Professor Richard Boris Hill: Yes.

MR HUT: The reason that you went back was because you were asked to by senior colleagues of yours at the Bedfordshire Health. Is that right?

Professor Richard Boris Hill: Yes. I was requested by the Director of Operations and the Clinical Services Manager.

MR HUT: They had received further complaints about Dr Yinka African Bombata practice. Is that correct?

Professor Richard Boris Hill: I believe that to be the case.

PAUSE:

Blatant persecutory Negrophobia!

In 2045, experts confirmed that Mr Hut and Professor Richard Boris Hill unrelentingly LIED under oath.

MR HUT: So as a consequence of that you were asked to make regular visits to Dr Yinka African Bombata practice to offer peer support and to ensure that improvements were being maintained.

Professor Richard Boris Hill: That's correct.

MR HUT: Again, in this sense, Mr Hill, and I am sorry to return to a theme, but are these visits or inspections? Is this pastoral or policing?

Professor Richard Boris Hill: These are pastoral. You need to ensure that continued progress is being made, but it is essential pastoral. What would also happen in these circumstances (and this was agreed by both the Director of Operations and the Patient Services Manager at the time) was that they would monitor any further level of complaints and continue this as an ongoing process, in which time I would make some visits to the practice, pastoral visits, and obviously if there was a change in the situation then they would make the decision on how to progress it.

PAUSE:

Comments in the present about a future occurrence:

In 2045, Professor Richard Boris Hill stated that in 1996, he was a 'pastor'.

Anti-Christ, Closeted Racist Freemasons went back to 1996 to exhume mummified racist forgeries and used them to corroborate the allegations by Ms Bishop's Cathedral of 2007; all became an issue in 2045.

THE LEGAL ADVISED (MR ACROMEGALY DICK-HEAD MASON): Can I just interrupt? It is noticeable – and it is this issue you have been asking questions about – that the document behind divider 12 was headed "Report of Practice Visit", the document behind divider 14 was headed "Report of Practice Inspection" and yet the word "visit" is used in the body. Professor Richard Boris Hill has dealt with it to a certain extent, but the words to an outsider appear to be almost interchangeable at that point and it might be that you want to explore that a little more.

MR HUT: Yes, I am grateful.

THE LEGAL ADVISER (Mr Acromegaly-Dickhead Mason): It seems to me an important issue that there the words appear to be almost interchangeable. It might help the Committee to explore that issue a little at this stage because they do appear to interchangeable.

MR HUT: I am grateful, Sir, thank you.

PAUSE:

Comments in the present about a future occurrence:

Some lawyers try to use excessive courtesy to conceal mediocrity and crookedness.

"I am very grateful Sir."

"Thank you very much Sir."

"You are very kind Sir."

"75 to 90 percent of American trial lawyers are incompetent, dishonest, or both." Charles E. Corry, Ph.D.

THE CHAIRMAN (Dr Shiv Chicken-Massala India): That would be useful to the Committee because I had noticed that earlier on.

MR HUT: Professor Richard Boris Hill, in a sense you have heard the observation made that the term "visit" and "inspection" appear to be used ----

Professor Richard Boris Hill: Interchangeably.

MR HUT: ---- interchangeably. Perhaps you can take us back to basics again, first of all, the difference between the two. Is there a difference and perhaps you could explain it and your rationale.

Professor Richard Boris Hill: I don't think there is a difference. I think within the literature and amongst Dental Practice Advisers we tend to use the word interchangeably anyway. It's perhaps, you know – I think it probably does go more than semantics and it's perhaps an area that we should perhaps in future be a little more careful about, about actually calling something a visit or an inspection.

MR HUT: Would it be fair to say then that so far as the 22 January 1996 attendance (I will use a different word for now) by you at the surgery, although it has been called in inspection could just as easily be called a visit without any injustice to the meaning behind it?

Professor Richard Boris Hill: Yes, I would not disagree. I would not disagree with that.

MR HUT: So the 22 January is just as fairly described as a visit rather than an inspection.

Professor Richard Boris Hill: That's correct.

MR HUT: Thank you. Similarly, in 1996 and 1997 the attendances (I use it neutrally again for now) that you undertook, could they just as fairly in your perspective be described as visits rather than inspections?

Professor Richard Boris Hill: I think I would call those visits and as we note from this particular document of 29 July 1996, it is headed "Practice Visit". I think that is probably more accurate.

MR HUT: Thank you. So certainly as far as you are concerned, you would have no quarrel in describing what has been called an inspection as a visit.

Professor Richard Boris Hill: No.

MR HUT: Sir, that may well assist for the purposes which I understand the Committee were concerned.

PAUSE:

Comments in the present about a future occurrence:

The Anti-Christ, Closeted Racist Freemasons, at least, in part, seem to be an Organised Racist Crime (ORC). Some people secretly believe that some members of the KKK, BNP and other white supremacists organizations may be hiding inside the belly of the Anti-Christ, Closeted Racist Freemasons.

Reasoning and vision are unbounded; if Christ's is infinite, He must be who He says He is.

When someone properly explains GENETICS to the Anti-Christ, Closeted Racist Freemasons they are likelier to disband.

THE CHAIRMAN (Dr Shiv Chicken-Massala India): This relates to Charges 7 and 8, does it not?

MR HUT: Yes.

THE CHAIRMAN (Dr Shiv Chicken-Massala India): At the start Mr Morris made the point that the charges would be admitted if the word "visit" was used and "inspection" was taken out. I shall leave that to you, Mr Hurst, to amend if you wish.

MR HUT: Sir, for my part I feel I have sufficient grounds upon which to make the appropriate application to amend at the appropriate stage. I do not propose to take it any further with this witness.

(To the witness) Thank you very much, Professor Richard Boris Hill, for helping us with that. I am sorry to talk around you, but it is just a technical issue which had arisen. We are back then with you being asked to return to Dr Yinka African Bombata practice at Grove Place, a visit which you undertook on 29 July 1996. Is that right?

Professor Richard Boris Hill: That's correct.

MR HUT: The concerns that you were asked to address related to such things as the consulting room door being left open, again appearance and standards at the premises and issues of uniform.

Professor Richard Boris Hill: The 29 July?

MR HUT: Yes, that is right, the issues that you were being asked to look at.

Professor Richard Boris Hill: Yes.

MR HUT: Questions about gloves not being worn by assistants, standard of hygiene and so on; those are the sorts of things which had caused concern. So you went back on 29 July. We have your report at divider 15 and we can see there – and do not worry about the blanking out, they are things which are not relevant to this hearing:

"Report of Practice Visit

A visit took place at the surgery of Dr Yinka African Bombata of 21 Grove Place, Bedford on Monday, 29 July 1996.

This was part of an ongoing visiting programme that had originally identified deficiencies with the practice. These had mostly concerned infection control and cleanliness issues.

The practitioner has now addressed these issues and the practice now appears to meet paragraphs 33(1) and 33(3) of the GDS terms of service."

Is that right?

Professor Richard Boris Hill: That's correct.

MR HUT: On that visit you had in mind issues about infection control and cleanliness. Is that right?

Professor Richard Boris Hill: Yes, these were factors that we had identified in the early stages, obviously and were ones that we wanted to focus upon.

MR HUT: In the course of that visit you would have looked at those areas and you satisfied yourself that Dr Yinka African Bombata had addressed them appropriately.

Professor Richard Boris Hill: Absolutely. Absolutely.

MR HUT: Then you continued to be involved with Dr Yinka African Bombata You obviously write to him, although we do not have a copy of the letter in the file, after your visit of July 1996 confirming your findings. Is that right?

Professor Richard Boris Hill: I would have done, yes.

MR HUT: Yes, normal practice. You said that you were going to return on 25 November 1996. Is that right? I do not think it is in dispute. You wrote to him saying that you would return on the 25 November.

Professor Richard Boris Hill: I can't remember without looking.

MR HUT: I am sure it is not in dispute. Dr Yinka African Bombata then wrote back to you and, again, this is not in our bundle, saying he was happy for that visit to take place.

Professor Richard Boris Hill: That's correct, yes.

MR HUT: I think it is fair to say that you have looked, but you cannot find any stand alone record now of a visit on 25 November 1996.

Professor Richard Boris Hill: No, there is no record.

MR HUT: Is it possible that you did visit but there is no record or does the record suggest that you simply would not have visited?

Professor Richard Boris Hill: It's possible – I have thought about that one – it was delayed, but there's no record there.

MR HUT: You have no particular memory of a November visit.

Professor Richard Boris Hill: No, it's too long ago. My memory doesn't go back that far.

MR HUT: What we do have a record of though, is a visit on 21 April 1997. Is that right?

Professor Richard Boris Hill: Yes, that's correct.

MR HUT: On that visit you went to 21 Grove Place again and if we look at our divider 19 I think we should have a copy of that visit.

Professor Richard Boris Hill: Yes.

PAUSE:

Comments in the present about a future occurrence:

In 2045, Closeted Racist, Privileged Dullards seemed to be throwing flares about a hearing in 2008, which concerned alleged incidents in 1996.

If you could see the Anti-Christ, Closeted Racist Freemason, they'd lynch you.

Those regularly spun are amongst the dullest adult populations in the industrialised world.

Homogeneity or subjugated diverse merit in the administration of the law is the New Apartheid.

MR HUT: What that does say is that this followed on from a previous visit in November 1996.

Professor Richard Boris Hill: Yes.

MR HUT: Does that help you in trying to identify whether the missing documentation for November 1996 does not necessarily mean that the visit did not take place?

Professor Richard Boris Hill: Looking at this, without the benefit of obviously any papers, you can't confirm it but I would expect it did because if we look at the content of the second paragraph, we'd obviously discussed the matter of funding. So I think as a corollary of that first paragraph that pointed to the previous visit, then I very much doubt if without the visit we could have discussed the issue of he Financial Incentive Scheme.

MR HUT: Thank you. You go on to say:

"The practitioner has now fitted a new surgery to replace the previous one. The new equipment meets with the Terms of Service ...."

and you give the paragraphs.

"Payment will now be made to him under the Financial Incentive Scheme."

Professor Richard Boris Hill: Yes.

CHAPTER 3

PAUSE:

Comments in the present about a future occurrence:

Anti-Christ, Closeted Racist Freemasons seemed to run the show for the benefit of imbeciles.

Those needed to be spun by the Anti-Christ, Closeted Racist Freemasons were:

Chief Justice: Dr Shiv Chicken-Massala India

Judge 1: Professor B.D.A. Midgeto Austria

Judge 2: Dr Flat-Fat-Ass Irish-Dunce

Judge 3: Dr King-Prawn Fried-Rice Dogeater

Judge 4: Ms Typically English-Mademoiselle Always-dull

Independent Legal Assessor: Mr Acromegaly-Dickhead Mason

If the Anti-Christ Closeted Racist Freemasons are very clever as they seem to ostensibly imply, why are the sheep they shepherd amongst the dullest in the industrialised world?

Very often, two or more people on the high table will be in the loop of the Closeted Racist Evil.

Parts of the administration of the law seemed akin to organised RACIST CRIME.

MR HUT: Thank you. In addition to the documented visits that we have looked at here, did you also visit on other occasions less formally?

Professor Richard Boris Hill: Yes. Dr Yinka African Bombata was very, very cooperative and positively welcomed visits at short notice, in effect no notice at all. I know that he was determined to improve and progress his practice and he was very much open and hoping to improve.

I discussed the matter with senior managers at the Health Authority and they were happy for an informal pastoral approach to go ahead, you know, put the formality aside and progress it this way. As I said, they would continue to monitor any complaints or any change of pattern to complaints over that period of time.

MR HUT: So you were in that pastoral role, supporting Dr Yinka African Bombata and assisting him. Other areas in which you helped or provided support were things like identifying training needs, administration and that sort of thing.

PAUSE:

Comment in the present about a future occurrence:

Gigantic yields of millions of stolen and destroyed lives seemed to have distorted the realities of some people. They artificial create jobs for themselves at the expense of BLACKS.

The greatest FEAR of some white people is to be intellectually defeated by Africans.

Professor Richard Boris Hill: Administration was a major part. I know that he had some problems with staffing issues, with the staff that left and, you know, recruitment was a problem.

MR HUT: You have explained Dr Yinka African Bombata's attitude at the time; you have described it as being very cooperative.

Professor Richard Boris Hill: Absolutely.

Q. And you would sometimes turn up with no notice at all.

Professor Richard Boris Hill: Yes, or a telephone call, maybe even the next day or that evening, that type of thing. There were never any problems; I was never stalled. He was always open to a visit which showed I think very good faith on his part.

MR HUT: Thank you. If I can take you now forward, please, to April 2003 and our divider 20. First of all, before we look at the documentation, perhaps we can deal with it in this way: by the time of 2003 the Trust insofar as the dental practice was concerned, was it undertaking any sort of design review of the practices in the area? Was there a programme undertaken?

Professor Richard Boris Hill: I was not aware of anything, no; nothing that I was informed of.

PAUSE:

Comments in the present about a future occurrence:

People whose mothers and fathers had very strong views about education wouldn't immortalize rot for eternity. Mr. Hut talked ROT. He seemed to be a hereditary rot talker. He seemed mentally malformed and subhuman.

MR HUT: Can you recall whether you visited Dr Yinka African Bombata in 2003?

Professor Richard Boris Hill: Yes.

MR HUT: Can you remember why it was that you visited?

Professor Richard Boris Hill: A routine visit.

MR HUT: As a consequence of your routine visit would you have produced a report?

Professor Richard Boris Hill: There was a Department of Health, if you like, form which was filed, but not a written report. We had moved away from that. We wanted to standardise the issue.

PAUSE:

Comments in the present about a future occurrence:

Professor Richard Boris Hill was asked a simple question. He did not give a straight answer. "Not a written report." The standardised report was written.

The 'meat' of the matter in 2045 was that in November 2008, the seemingly racist thugs knew that their own kindred did not disclose any report about the alleged visit in 2003 to Dr Yinka African Bombata.

Dr Yinka African Bombata was charged with the content of a report that he had never seen almost six years after the alleged visit and report.

Homogeneity in the administration of the English LAW is an instrument of RACIST WAR

IN 2045, experts concluded that Mr Hut and Professor Richard Boris Hill unrelentingly LIED under oath.

The soft underbelly of the Anti-Christ, Closeted Racist Freemasons is the intellect of the individual member.

In 2045, it was apparent that the 2003 report was a retrospective fabrication, which was created with the implicit order of the ANTI-CHRIST, CLOSETED RACIST FREEMASONS.

Parts of the administration of the LAW seemed akin to organised RACIST CRIME.

MR HUT: If we look at our divider 20 and turn over in that divider to the document, have you seen this document before, Mr Hill?

Professor Richard Boris Hill: I have.

MR HUT: Can you tell the Committee what it is?

Professor Boris Richard Hill: It's a practice visiting protocol, I would describe it as, produced by the Department, I believe along with the then General Dental Services Committee, which would reflect the type of issues and the type of requirements that would be expected in a standard general dental practice.

MR HUT: Is this your handwriting?

Professor Boris Richard Hill: Yes, this is.

PAUSE:

Comments in the present about a future occurrence:

2045: In November 2008, Professor Richard Boris Hill stated that he created a handwritten report in 2003. He also said that in he did not make written records in 2003.

Life is GRAND, isn't it?

Parts of the administration of the LAW seemed akin to organised RACIST CRIME.

Homogeneity; subjugated, diverse merit in the administration of the LAW is the NEW APARTHEID; it conceals and paradoxically propagates racial bias.

MR HUT: Can you identify for us in the document a date?

Professor Boris Richard Hill: The date is under "Date of Visit", p.1, Part A, 2/4/03.

MR HUT: So you are looking in that first box under Part A?

Professor Boris Richard Hill: That's right.

MR HUT: We see Bedford PCT; then the name of the practice, Gray Friars Dental Practice. Is that right?

Professor Boris Richard Hill: That's correct.

MR HUT: The address here is a new address from the previous one. Is that right?

Professor Boris Richard Hill: Yes.

MR HUT: 52 Bromham Drive.

Professor Boris Richard Hill: Yes.

MR HUT: "Practice Visitor(s)" says "Richard Hill"; it gives your designation and then you deal with some "Practice Data", as we see there. You have ticked the "Location" box "High Street"; then "Exterior Condition" as "Good"; "Professional Name Plate" is ticked; and then "Practice Information Leaflet" is ticked. You then talk about the "Principal Dentist" under "Part time" as "Dr Yinka African Bombata". Is that right?

A. That's correct.

Q. Why would Dr Yinka African Bombata be recorded as part time in that column?

A. Because we were aware he was working at other premises outside the PCT area.

Q. From whom would you have got that information?

Professor Richard Boris Hill: That would have come from the Contract Department.

PAUSE:

Comments in the present about a future occurrence:

In 2045 and prior to that date, Dr Ugly-Ass Racist-Cougar (Territorial Defence) implied that she was not told by Bedford's Contract Department that Dr Yinka African Bombata served patients at two locations and, therefore did not work full time at any location. She lied under oath. Congressman Cameron Davidson implied that she was likelier to be jailed had she been BLACK.

In 2045, Dr Muscular Ugly-Ass Racist-Cougar admitted that she stated the following facts decades earlier.

In 2045, Dr Muscular Ugly-Ass Racist-Cougar confirmed that she spoke with Dr Yinka African Bombata on 23.08.2006, 09.02.2007 and 15.02.2007; this fact was corroborated by her contemporaneous records.

CHAPTER 4

European psychosis: seemingly mental imbalance and intellectual disorientation caused by the gigantic yields of millions of stolen and destroyed lives, which included millions of kidnapped, carried and sold children.

Some people are living a lie; it is glaringly obvious that 'things' shan't endure. Virtue shan't sustain the yields of vice, HABAKKUK

Reasoning and vision are unbounded; if Christ's is infinite, He must be who He says He is. If He is who He says He is, He must be Allah, the God of Mohammed.

In 2045, Dr Muscular Ugly-Ass Racist-Cougar confirmed that on August 15, 2006, Mr John Harper, a Bedford apparatchik stated the following, which he, also conveyed to Mrs Do-Little Fake-Ass, Dr Soft Ugly-Ass Wrinkling-Cougar, and Professor Richard Boris Hill:

"Dear all, Dr Muscular Ugly-Ass Racist-Cougar has been in touch a few times as her colleagues had highlighted issues from a similar practice in a nearby town, not far from Bedford, and they would like to review report etc etc prior to visiting. Mrs Do-Little Fake-Ass prioritised Dr Yinka African Bombata's surgery. Dr Muscular Ugly-Ass Racist - Cougar also wanted to know if there has been a dental inspection there at all and I did not know the answer........ Cue Professor Richard Boris Hill, have you carried out an inspection at this practice, please could you advise Dr Muscular Ugly-Ass Racist-Cougar when she contacts you, and would it be possible to see our reports so we can be more proactive with any other queries"

PAUSE:

If, in 2045, Dr Muscular Ugly-Ass Racist-Cougar stated that she was aware that on August 15, 2006 that Dr Yinka African Bombata worked part time in Bedford and at another nearby Town, she must have lied or was pathologically confused (Alzheimer's disease) when she stated that in a conversation, about a week later (August 23, 2006), she was not aware of the fact that Dr Yinka African Bombata worked part time in Bedford and at another Practice in another nearby town?

Latent, progressive dementia or Alzheimer's disease is considerable more common than ordinarily realised.

In 2006, Dr Muscular Ugly-Ass Racist-Cougar was in her seventh decade. In 2045, the wrinkling, ugly missing – link was in her eleventh decade.

In 2045, Dr Muscular Ugly-Ass Racist-Cougar confirmed that under oath on November 19, 2006, she stated the following:

"One of the other things that he did also comment to me was in one of my telephone conversations with him he did tell me that he had had a surgery inspection within the previous year, which was something I was not aware of. As things developed I think, in fact, at that point he was referring to his other practice. At that point I did not know. When I ring dentists I do not know all the details about their contracts and practices. The Reference Service now does. It has access to a dentist's full details, and we can look up and see what the commitments are. At that stage, other than telephone calls to find out what dentists' other commitments were and what other practice contracts were, and it was not something you would routinely do. There was too much else to get on with rather than take time to make telephone calls."

In 2045, Dr Muscular Ugly-Ass Racist-Cougar, also stated that on November, 19 2008, she stated as follows:

"I was clear about that, that was the telephone number that I had telephoned where I had spoken to Mr Bamgbelu. I had telephoned and sent correspondence to that address, so as far as I knew, and I had explained I would be coming to the practice and at that point he had not said: "Well, I do have another practice". He had not said, with us talking about I think needs, whether there would be a surgery free for me to examine the patients. because we were trying to impinge as little as we could, and if a dentist had more than one surgery in the practice and one would be empty on the day of the visit, we would say well fine. I would either work in one surgery to see four patients and say, "Please do not bring people in specially, make it people that you are going to see that day either for a check up or for some fairly simple treatment anyway. Once you have finished, perhaps they could come through to the other surgery and see me". At least dentists could then get on with treating other patients during that half day rather than having, in the case of a single handed surgery dentist, but obviously once they had finished with the patient they would then have to leave the surgery empty for me to spend my 15 minutes with the patients afterwards. So I do remember talking to him and saying: "Do you have a spare surgery?" He didn't, he said there were several surgeries. There was only one which was fully equipped, the others were partially shut down because there was nobody else working there. I remember ascertaining that probably one of those surgeries would be adequate for the dental facilities I needed to do my patient examinations."

MR HUT: The fact that he was deemed to be part time at this practice.

Professor Boris Richard Hill: Yes.

MR HUT: If we turn over the page, we see a box which is headed "Facility"; there are a number of designations there, four columns, "Standard of cleanliness", "Standard of décor", "Type and condition of flooring" and "Notes".

Professor Boris Richard Hill: Yes.

MR HUT: It seems you have written "Satisfactory" against the "Standard of cleanliness" for each of the areas. Is that right?

Professor Boris Richard Hill: That's correct, yes.

MR HUT: Then "Standard of décor" says "Satisfactory" and "Type and condition of flooring", does that say "Linoleum"?

Professor Boris Richard Hill: Linoleum/tiling. I suppose you could describe it as a composite material.

MR HUT: So that we are clear, in order to complete this box was it necessary for you actually to visit the practice?

Professor Boris Richard Hill: Yes.

MR HUT: This is not something you could gain from records at the offices?

Professor Boris Richard Hill: No, because this was a new address. This was not the previous address, which was Grove Place. This was in a new building.

PAUSE:

Comments in the present about a future occurrence:

2045:

The suggestion by Mr Hut in 2008 that the fact of a report is the evidence of a visit seemed based on incompetent reasoning. It seemed baselessly assumed that the content of the report was accurate. In 2008 and, certainly, in 2045, reports could be fabricated.

In 2045, Mr Hut knew that the 2004 reports by Professor Richard Boris Hill were fabricated and withdrawn more than four years later in 2008.

LUCIFERIANS! Semi-illiterate Racists; righteous descendants of THIEVES: stealer, carrier, and seller of millions of human beings, including millions of kidnapped and carried children.

Imbecile Counsel, he sat on bones of stolen and destroyed lives; more bones than the millions of bones that were at the doorsteps of Pol-Pot, HABAKKUK

NEWEST APARTHEID: Homogeneity in the administration of the LAW; subjugated, diverse merit in the administration of the LAWS in Bedford, Massachusetts

MR HUT: Then "Part C, Quality Assurance – GDS Terms of Service requirements".

A number of questions are answered there. Can you just take us through the questions, explain their purpose and the answers and who gave you the answers.

Professor Richard Boris Hill: Yes. "Quality Assurance", this is part of the Clinical Governance issue. Practitioners are required to put up a little note in the waiting room saying, "This practice complies with Clinical Governance", i.e. for example CPD, x-ray matters, complaints system, consistent quality of treatment and meets with General Dental Council guidelines. It is simply that; you display those.

MR HUT: Is it that you would only be able to answer that question again by a visit?

Professor Boris Richard Hill: Yes.

MR HUT: It is not a matter of record.

Professor Boris Richard Hill: No, no, it is not something that you would look back through records on. In fact, that requirement was something that was rather more recent than the original inspections, the previous inspections; it wasn't a requirement at that stage. The Clinical Governance agenda developed mostly sort of late nineties into the early part of two thousands. So it was really a recognition of that and the fact that practitioners were participating in Clinical Governance.

MR HUT: The second question:

"Does the dentist show an awareness of the Disability Discrimination Act?"

Can you read out your answer.

Professor Boris Richard Hill: It says:

"Yes, no disabled access …." because the surgery was upstairs. It was not possible because of the width of the stairs to actually fit a stair lift. The DDA says what changes are reasonable and in this case it wasn't reasonable to put a stair lift in which would have occupied, you know, virtually the width of the stairs.

PAUSE:

Privileged dullards employed the world's language like decorticate morons!

MR HUT: There is a little bit more to the sentence.

Professor Boris Richard Hill: Yes. I will interpret my scrawl for you: "…. but the GDP has domiciliary equipment for home visits if necessary."

And that would, in my opinion, be sufficient to comply in a practice where disabled access was not possible. If the practitioner was willing to visit a home of a patient that required domiciliary treatment and they had the necessary equipment, that's fine; or perhaps in more extreme circumstances, the practitioner would then liaise with a nearby practice and either treat the patient there or refer the patient to be treated. The third route, obviously in those situations, is with the community service which would have domiciliary equipment to deal with it. But as far as that requirement is concerned, certainly the practice as far as I was concerned because of its location and because of his willingness to actually do home visits complied.

Q. From where would you have got information that the practitioner has domiciliary equipment to pay a visit?

Professor Boris Richard Hill: It would have been by word of mouth.

PAUSE:

Comments in the present about a future occurrence:

2045:

If a company buys its worker a car, it'd be absurd to know about this fact through – 'word of mouth'.

Homogeneity; subjugated, diverse merit in the administration of the LAW is the NEWEST APARTHEID; it makes the buffet of mendacity possible.

Those regularly spun by privileged dullards are amongst the dullest adult population in the industrialized world.

In 2045, experts concluded that the 2003 report was a retrospective forgery.

Q. And from whose mouth? I am sorry to be specific.

Professor Richard Boris Hill: From the practitioner.

Q. You then deal with "Effective infection control" and we see a number of ticks there. I am not going to go through each box. "Autoclave" is ticked, but there is manuscript note. Can you tell us what that says?

Professor Richard Boris Hill: I've put down here "plus Kavoklave as back up." That's no criticism whatsoever.

MR HUT: No criticism.

Professor Richard Boris Hill: Not at all.

PAUSE:

Comments in the present about a future occurrence:

JUDGE LYNCH: Extra-legal 'VIOLENCE'.

BEDFORD: "I emphasis the point...." JUDGE PAULO HAYERS, APPROVED

A FOOL'S APPROVAL

https://www.youtube.com/watch?v=BlpH4hG7m1A&feature=youtu.be

Anti-Christ, Closeted Racist Freemasons 'FRY' the brains of the sheep they shepherd and turn them to a PRIVATE ARMY (ZOMBIES)

DUNCE, BEDFORD JUDGE! He sat on a CHAIR that people couldn't and didn't buy. STOLEN lives yielded his COURT. Righteous HYPOCRITE!

Parts of the administration of the law seemed akin to organized, RACIST CRIME (legal terrorism).

In 2045, Professor Richard Boris Hill stated that in 2008, he was happy about the fact that Dr Yinka African Bombata allegedly had a Kavoklave autoclave as a back-up in 2003. The scatter-head, cretin Professor of incompetent lies immortalised incompetent mendacity a year later when he stated that in a 2004 report, he stated that a Kavoklave should not be used. Professor Richard Boris Hill seemed to have had modular education as he stated something completely different, only a year later.

"Record of Practice Visits-Bedford PCT. Dear John, Please find attached the record of practice visits that you were chasing up. Sorry for the delay! As you can see, the great majority of practices are not a cause for concern. However, we will need to focus particularly on the Dr Yinka African Bombata and the alpha practices. Perhaps also beta practice in delta and the gamma practice are worthy of closer attention. Regards, Richard."

RECORD OF PRACTICE VISITS: BEDFORD, MASSACHUSETTS. Surgeon: Dr Yinka African Bombata: ADDRESS: Grey Friars Dental Practice 52 Bromham Drive Bedford. Visit Date: JULY 2004. Assessment Date: November 2045. CONCERNS: No risk assessment, no CoSSH, A Kavoclave type autoclave was present in the surgery. This type of autoclave should not be used as the cycle can be broken into before sterilisation is complete. No other member of staff were present at the visit so could not be questioned as regards the methods of cross infection control used by practice. - Bedford's report of July 2004

OUTSTANDING ISSUES: Even though the necessary documents have now been seen. I continue to have concerns as to the cross infection control procedures in the practice. - Bedford's follow up report of undisclosed date

CHAPTER 5

2045:

"A Kavoclave type autoclave was present in the surgery. This type of autoclave should not be used as the cycle can be broken into before sterilisation is complete." Professor Richard Boris Hill, July 2004

"I've put down here "plus Kavoklave as back up." That's no criticism whatsoever." Professor Richard Boris Hill, November, 2008

If a car tire is good enough to be used as a spare, it must be roadworthy.

The mother and father of Professor Richard Boris Hill mightn't have had very strong views about education; he seemed to be a genetic dunce. He could not have been taught critical reasoning as a subject at home (by his closeted racist, plebeian mother, and father) or at school.

Professor Richard Boris Hill, like his mother and father, and his teachers at school, seemed not to realize that reasoning and vision are unbounded.

Genetics is the Holy Grail. Reasoning and vision are unbounded; if Christ's is infinite, He must be who He says He is. Had the Pharisees known that, they mightn't have lynched Him. The Divine Y chromosome is exceptional, extra-terrestrial and immortal

Mohammed and all prophets and messengers of prophets and Gods – are all dead or will all die. The fellow (CHRIST) with the extra-terrestrial,

Divine and immortal Y chromosome is exceptional; He alone lived and will never die. He alone is GOD or Allah; He is the God of Mohammed.

Professor Richard Boris Hill seemed to be a thuggish dunce. He seemed intellectually disorientated and mentally imbalanced.

In 2045, he stated that in 2003, he found Kavoklave autoclave in the surgery of Dr Yinka African Bombata, which he allegedly used as a back-up. He said it was perfectly alright to use Kavoklave autoclave as a back-up. Only a year later, the brainless Professor, hereditary English, somersaulted and said the opposite, which was that it was wrong to use Kavoklave.

SHOCKING!

"Why, that is, because, dearest, you are a dunce." Dr Samuel Johnson

Subjugated, diverse merit (HOMOGENEITY) in the administration of the English LAW is the NEW APARTHEID.

Anti-Christ, Closeted Racist Freemasons seem to run the legal system for the benefit of millions of adults with the basic skills of a child.

MR HUT: Various other boxes are ticked.

Professor Richard Boris Hill: Yes.

Q. Then over the page another long column of matters. We have "Not applicable" about gas cylinders and then towards the bottom, just below the second of our two ring binder holes, we see "Risk Assessment" and "COSHH Assessments". What are these?

Professor Richard Boris Hill: These are documents which relate to the safety or the safe handling of material. The two really overlap. "Risk Assessment", you are talking about all the materials that you use in a practice, mercury, filling materials, whatever, and then you do an appraisal of the risk to health. Now, it's sufficient for the practitioners who purchase the necessary sheets from various sources – the BDA do a very good document on that matter, but it's being aware and knowing exactly, you know, the risk factors that are there. It's not a clinical point in the sense that it's going to affect front line treatment or anything like that.

Q. Various other matters are ticked which we can see.

Professor Richard Boris Hill: Can I just return to the gas cylinders?

Q. Yes, please do.

Professor Richard Boris Hill: This is a point – and this is not to do with the case – that has caused some degree of perhaps confusion. Some practitioners looked at this and said, "Ah, does it relate to the oxygen cylinder that I use in my practice for emergencies?" The way in which we've interpreted this is for such things as, for example, where somebody would be carrying out relative analgesia, which is a form of sedation, that type of thing and, of course, the great, great majority of practices nowadays do not perform that type of activity. The more specialist ones will, but 99 per cent. of practices that we visit, that is not applicable, so just to clarify that point really more than anything.

Q. Thank you. Over the page we see, again, a number of ticks there. There is nothing particular that you want to take us to on that page, I take it?

Professor Richard Boris Hill: No, there's nothing. It perfectly well complies.

Q. Perfectly well complies.

Professor Richard Boris Hill: Yes, it's not a problem at all.

Q. Page 5 of the document (p.6 within that divider) is called "Part D Feedback".

Professor Richard Boris Hill: Yes.

Q. Everything is blank save for "Essential action points" about the risk assessment documentation.

Professor Richard Boris Hill: Yes, it's just a question of acquiring those papers. That's it. You know, as I said, it's not in the sense that it affects day to day clinical practice directly, front line practice, treating a patient in the chair. It's not, if you like, a cross infection control issue which are the ones that we take most seriously.

Q. It then says "To be competed by", which presumably should read "To be completed by" and then Principal. Is that your handwriting?

Professor Richard Boris Hill: Yes.

Mr Hut: Can you remember how it was determined in your mind that the Principal would be the person to complete that action point?

Professor Richard Boris Hill: We just mention the matter on the visit, that's all. It's a question of mentioning it. I mean, clearly where there are serious problems, you know, where there are a number of serious issues which impact directly on patient welfare and patient safety, things, for example, like autoclave is inefficient or it hasn't been serviced or where we believe that there's a problem with the radiography equipment, those types of thing, then what will happen is that my Dental Contracts Manager will write to the practitioner and outline these things that need to be put right and given a date to do so. In the most serious cases, we will then return to the practice quickly and if we feel that there is a significant patient safety issue, then it's a matter which I will then discuss with a senior manager. If necessary, it's a matter we will deal with through the Health & Safety executive, as we have done on at least one occasion.

PAUSE:

Comments in the present about future occurrences:

2045:

If the principal must complete a task, he must know about the task.

"Can you remember how it was determined in your mind that the Principal would be the person to complete that action point?" Mr Hut, November 2008

The seemingly, retrospectively fabricated report of 2003 was concealed from Dr Yinka African Bombata. He knew about the report after he had been charged with its content about six years after the alleged visit.

Life is GRAND, isn't it?

Parts of the administration of the LAW seemed akin to organized RACIST crime.

Homogeneity or subjugated diversity in the administration of the LAW is the NEWEST APARTHEID; it conceals and propagates racial bias.

In 2045, Professor Boris Richard Hill stated that in 2003, there was no concern, which corroborated the fact that Dr Yinka African Bombata was not given any report, and he was charged with the content of the retrospectively 2003 almost six years later and before the report was disclosed to the lone Negro in their midst; merciless, legal terrorism and spineless cowardice.

"Had there been any problem, I would be asked by the PCT to visit the practice and carry out a formal inspection in that situation. That's normally along with a colleague, so it's a proper and formal procedure. But I have no record of being told that there were any concerns." Professor Richard Boris Hill, commenting in 2045 about a court incident in November, 2008

MR HUT: Can I then take you forward nearly but not quite four years to February 2007. We will deal with the run up to that but just, first of all, do you remember undertaking a practice inspection of 52 Bromham Road on 22 February 2007?

Professor Richard Boris Hill: Yes.

Q. And you carried that out with a colleague called Stephanie Twidale. Is that right?

Professor Richard Boris Hill: Yes.

Q. Have I pronounced her name correctly?

Professor Richard Boris Hill: Stephanie Twidale is the Dental Reference Officer of then Dental Practice Board. My role was supportive.

Q. Can you remember when you were first asked to accompany Stephanie Twidale to undertake that practice inspection?

Professor Richard Boris Hill: A date?

Q. Time of year? The year, first of all. How long before approximately February 2007 would you have been aware that you were to be asked to do this?

Professor Richard Boris Hill: I would say it was probably in the autumn, sometime in the autumn, when it was flagged up.

Q. Of the preceding year.

Professor Richard Boris Hill: Of the preceding year. I can't be entirely certain about that date because it was not something – I wasn't emailed or I wasn't sent any documentation. I was just asked by the Consultant in Dental Public Health would I undertake the visit along with the Dental Reference Officer.

Q. Just looking at that a little bit more closely, can you remember what the practice inspection was to address? What sort of inspection was it to be?

Professor Richard Boris Hill: It's part of a routine process. Since the new contract came into effect which was in April 2006 ----

PAUSE:

Comments in the present about a future occurrence:

2045:

In 2045, Professor Richard Boris Hill stated that the inspection of Dr Yinka African Bombata's surgery in February 2007 was a ROUTINE INSPECTION. Seemingly, guided and guarded by the ANTI-CHRIST, CLOSETED RACIST FREEMASONS, Professor Richard Boris Hill lied unrelentingly under oath. Parts of the administration of the LAW seemed mediocre, Negrophobic and DISHONEST.

It was alleged that Professor Richard Boris Hill was a member of the ANTI – CHRIST, CLOSETED RACIST FREEMASONS; their people are everywhere and they control everything except intellect, which is exclusively Christ's or Allah, and only He could grant it.

Christ is Allah; the God of Mohammed and every other living and dead thing; only He (Christ) is immortal, even demons expire.

In 2045, the privileged dullard, Anti-Christ, Closeted Racist Freemason Professor Richard Boris Hill could not think the following, as his semi-illiterate, closeted racist Mother and Father did not teach him critical reasoning and/or did not send him to schools in Bedford where critical reasoning was taught as a subject. In August 2006, Mr John Harper, a Bedford, closeted racist apparatchiks asked Professor Richard Boris Hill for reports, which took him three weeks to retrospectively create. On September 6, 2006, he released a report laden with stereotypically Negro cross-infection issues. The report of July 22, 2004, and follow-up of undisclosed date were FORGERIES.

In 2045, Professor Richard Boris Hill did not to detect the absurdities in his brainless construction. If he had cross –infection issues in July 2004 and the cross were still there at a later undisclosed date, if he disclosed these facts about two years later, the situation is not routine; cross-infection is an emergency. The fact that the emergency was concealed implied that it wasn't a real emergency, but a racist fabrication. The fact that the brainless creation was withdrawn confirmed that it was an incompetent white supremacists construction.

Anti-Christ, Closeted Racist Freemasons create White Supremacist imbeciles and they turn them to a Private Army. If the Anti-Christ Closeted Racist Freemasons are as clever as they ostensibly imply, why are the sheep they shepherd among the dullest in the industrialized world?

Homogeneity or subjugated diverse merit in the administration of the English LAW is the NEW APARTHEID; it conceals and paradoxically propagates racial bias.

What the ANTI-CHRIST, CLOSETED RACIST FREEMASONS want is a control that is not based on objectivity. Their people are everywhere and they control everything except intellect.

If some of one's ancestors were EVIL TERRORISTS: stealer, owner, carrier, and seller of millions of stolen human beings, including millions of kidnapped and carried children (the BOKO HARAM of their era), it'd be naïve not to expect mendacity to be part of one's genetic inheritances.

Reasoning and vision are unbounded; if Christ's is infinite, He must be who He says He is. Had the Pharisees realized that fact (the Anti-Christ, Closeted Racist Freemasons of another era), they mightn't have lynched Him.

Christ is Allah; the God of Mohammed and all living and dead Prophets, and all dead and/or imaginary GODS. The Divine Y chromosome is self-sufficient, exceptional, extra-terrestrial and immortal.

What is Freemasonry for? It is intellectually flawed and Satanic. The rumor in 2045 is that Professor Richard Boris Hill is a member of the Anti-Christ, Closeted Racist Freemasons.

In 2045 and prior to that year, it is not the TRUTH that black people are equal under the LAW. Only visible chains have been removed; the

TRUE chains will never be voluntarily removed. Substitution is likelier. Substitution is 'pretend emancipation'; CRUEL DECEIT.

"Moderation is a virtue ONLY for those who are thought to have found alternatives." Henry Kissinger, paraphrased

No people will voluntarily relinquish advantageous positions except by force or in exchange for valuable consideration.

"All have taken what had other owners and all have resorted to arms rather than quit the prey on which they had fastened." Dr Samuel Johnson

MR HUT: Is that the General Dental Services contract?

Professor Richard Boris Hill: Yes, I will refer to it as new GDS, if you like, for the purposes of clarity – is that the system of monitoring by the Dental Practice Board for the Primary Care Trusts changed. If we remember what happened before, patients were selected at random or sometimes targeted by the Board and they were examined by a Dental Reference Officer normally in a dedicated centre and that was it. The purpose of it, yes, it was a certain amount of Quality Assurance, but there was also a large probity element in that, making sure that what had been claimed for had been done. Now, with the new contract, the new GDS, it changed to the extent that there was a greater degree of monitoring, a more Clinical Governance Quality Assurance role was introduced. So it was really very much a sort of three pronged approach towards it. Firstly, there would be a practice visit. I will call this one an inspection. I will clarify it in those terms because the Dental Reference Officer's visit is an inspection; it has a more policing function. Secondly, there would be four patients which the practitioner would themselves choose based upon the complexity of the treatment. Treatments are in three bands, what we can describe, I suppose, as simple, intermediate and more advanced, Bands 1, 2 and 3. There would be one Band 1, two Band 2s and a Band 3 selected; the practitioner would choose those and those patients would then be inspected by the Dental Reference Officer, not my function at all. The third one would be a record check, eight records selected by the Dental Practice Board to be checked by the Dental Reference Officer. Then the practitioner would have feedback on all of this. There would be a report compiled for each practice which would then relate to each performer within the practice and so the provider, which is, if you like, the principal of the practice, shall we say for want of a better word, would then get the feedback and they could make any necessary changes. So we are moving from a situation which was perhaps more probity based to one which is more Quality Assurance and, if you like, to use for a better phrase, bottoming up, raising standards in a more consensual fashion. So this inspection was, if you like, just one of the three, but my involvement in the other ones, I wouldn't necessarily have any involvement in the other two parts of it.

PAUSE:

Comments in the present about a future occurrence:

Brainless, tortuous gibberish by a white supremacist descendant of merciless EVIL TERRORISTS: stealer, carrier, and seller of millions of stolen human beings, including millions of kidnapped and carried children - Habakkuk

"The great enemy of the clear language is INSINCERITY (DISHONESTY). When there is a gap between one's real and one's declared aims, one turns as it were instinctively to long words and exhausted idioms, like a cuttlefish squirting ink. In our age, there is no such thing as 'keeping out of politics'. All issues are political issues, and politics itself is a mass of lies, evasions, folly, HATRED, and schizophrenia. When the general atmosphere is bad, language must suffer." George Orwell

MR HUT: So necessarily then, when it comes to what you are actually going to look at when you turn up at the relevant surgery, you are going to be looking at an inspection of the premises as they are, how they appear and whether they meet the relevant standards.

Professor Richard Boris Hill: That's correct. I mean, I must say that the ambit of the Dental Reference Service inspection is far, far greater than the Dental Practice Adviser sheet, as we can see from the documents; it goes much, much further. I mean, our visits, and I will use that terminology correctly, our visits are normally about 30 to 45 minutes, whereas a Dental Reference Officer visit is going to be much longer. I think in the case of 22 February 2007, it was something like five hours and that seems to be, from what I have heard, quite normal.

Mr Hut: You were asked to assist Dr Muscular Ugly-Ass Racist-Cougar and obviously she is going to give her evidence after you, so she will be able to give evidence as to things from her perspective, but did you understand why you particularly had been asked to assist Dr Muscular Ugly-Ass Racist-Cougar?

Professor Richard Boris Hill: No. It is, as I mention in my statement, unusual for a Dental Practice Adviser to attend on a DRO visit. I was simply asked and part of my contract is to act in accordance with the wishes of the senior managers of the PCT.

PAUSE:

Comments in the present about a future occurrence:

In 2045, Professor Richard Boris Hill stated that in 2006, he did not know why he was asked to assist Dr Muscular Ugly-Ass Racist-Cougar with the inspection of Dr Yinka African Bombata Surgery in 2007.

In 2045, presented with the facts, Professor Richard Boris Hill seemed to agree that he lied criminally under oath!

Criminally DISHONEST, mediocre, and RACIST legal system (PART).

Subjugated, diverse merit (HOMOGENEITY) in the administration of the LAW is the NEW APARTHEID; it conceals and paradoxically propagates racial bias.

"Subject DRS visit to Dr Yinka African Bombata. Dear Dr Muscular Ugly-Ass Racist-Cougar, Just to confirm that I have spoken with Professor

Richard Boris Hill and he will join you for the DRS visit on Thursday 22nd February to Dr Yinka African Bombata Bedford Practice, commencing at 9 am. We will endeavour to share any issues that the PCT may have with you PRIOR to the 22nd. Kind regards." Dr Ugly Soft-Ass Wrinkling-Cougar, November 30, 2006

In 2045, on being presented with the facts, Professor Richard Boris Hill agreed that on November 30, 2006 when Dr Ugly Soft-Ass Wrinkling-Cougar contacted he and Dr Muscular Ugly-Ass Racist-Cougar, the reports of July 22, 2004 and the follow up of undisclosed date were the ONLY available reports, and he was asked by his superiors, which included Dr Ugly Soft-Ass Wrinkling-Cougar and Mrs Do-little Fake-Ass, to discuss the issues on them with Dr Muscular Ugly-Ass Racist-Cougar prior to the visit of February 22, 2007.

"But did you understand why you particularly had been asked to assist Dr Muscular Ugly-Ass Racist-Cougar?" Mr Hut

"No!" Professor Richard Boris Hill

He lied under oath; a criminal! Anti-Christ, Closeted Racist Freemason, seemingly, guided and guarded by the Criminal Battalion of the merciless, racist, Satanic Network.

Some people secretly believe that if some LAWMAKERS demand and accept BROWN ENVELOPES, some Judges who interpret the LAWS must do it too.

If the security guards of a shop steal from the shop, it will be naïve not to expect some of the shop workers and customers to do it too.

In 2045 and prior, Professor Richard Boris Hill seemed to lack both integrity and knowledge; he seems to be a RACIST NEW PHARISEE or ANTI-CHRIST, CLOSETED RACIST FREEMASON; their people are everywhere and they control everything except intellect.

"Integrity without knowledge is weak and useless, and knowledge without integrity is dangerous and dreadful" Dr Samuel Johnson

Anti-Christ, Closeted Racist Freemasons: Self-appointed and Self-Styled enlighten shepherds of the whole people; they wear VULGAR CHARITY as a cloak of deceit. They swear never to tell lies, but they lie that they do not lie, - Songs of David 144 paraphrased

Reasoning and vision are unbounded, if Christ's is infinite, He must be who He says He is. Had the Pharisees (the Anti-Christ, Closeted Racist Freemasons of their era) realized the fact, they mightn't have lynched Him.

Q. But you had had dealings with Professor Yinka African Bombata before.

Professor Richard Boris Hill: Yes, as with every other practice within the PCT.

Q. Although these are not within the Committee's bundle, is it right that you were asked by a colleague at the PCT to provide your previous practice inspection reports or visit reports so that Ms Twidale would have them in advance. Is that right?

Professor Richard Boris Hill: I don't think so, no. I think that's a wrong reading of it. I don't think that we did anything of the sort. I don't think she read any of those – in my knowledge, according to my knowledge, I don't believe there was any of that. It would come as a surprise to me if it was. I think, after all, you would not wish to go into a Dental Reference practice in any way prejudiced. You want to go in with an open mind and you need to see things as they are, not from what you have read.

PAUSE:

2045: Homogeneity or subjugated diversity in the administration of the LAW is the NEWEST APARTHEID; it conceals and paradoxically propagates racial bias. Professor Richard Boris Hill was a criminal; he unrelentingly lied under oath. Had he been BLACK, he'd have been jailed.

Parts of Bedford's legal system seemed mediocre, Negrophobic, and criminally DISHONEST.

In 2045, Professor Richard Boris Hill stated that Dr Muscular Ugly–Ass Racist-Cougar did not read any report (note the word, 'read') prior to visiting the surgery of Dr Yinka African Bombata. Professor Richard Boris Hill said they did not do anything of the sort. In 2045, he stated that prior to that year Dr Muscular Ugly-Ass Racist-Cougar did not read the fabricated reports of 2004. He implied that reading the report would prejudice the inspection. Professor Richard Boris Hill implied that he and Dr Muscular Ugly-Ass Racist-Cougar inspected the surgery of Dr Yinka African Bombata with open mind and as they needed to see things as they were and not from what you had read.

Intellectually impotent NONENTITY!

Intellectually disorientated and mentally imbalanced!

Purified ROT!

Subjugated, diverse merit (HOMOGENEITY) in the administration of the English LAW is the NEW APARTHEID;

In 2045, Mr Harper, a Bedford's apparatchik, affirmed that his statement of August 15, 2006 was unambiguous:

"Dear all, Dr Muscular Ugly-Ass Racist-Cougar has been in touch a few times as her colleagues had highlighted issues from a similar practice in a nearby town, not far from Bedford, and they would like to review report etc etc prior to visiting. Mrs Do-Little Fake-Ass prioritised Dr Yinka African Bombata's surgery. Dr Muscular Ugly-Ass Racist - Cougar also wanted to know if there has been a dental inspection there at all and I did not know the answer........ Cue Professor Richard Boris Hill, have you carried out an inspection at this practice, please could you advise Dr Muscular Ugly-Ass Racist-Cougar when she contacts you, and would it be possible to see our reports so we can be more proactive with any other queries"

In 2045, Dr Ugly Soft-Ass Wrinkling-Cougar seemed to confirm that her statement of November 30, 2006 corroborated the earlier statement by Mr Harper:

"Subject DRS visit to Dr Yinka African Bombata. Dear Dr Muscular Ugly-Ass Racist-Cougar, Just to confirm that I have spoken with Professor Richard Boris Hill and he will join you for the DRS visit on Thursday 22nd February to Dr Yinka African Bombata Bedford Practice, commencing at 9 am. We will endeavour to share any issues that the PCT may have with you PRIOR to the 22nd. Kind regards." Dr Ugly Soft-Ass Wrinkling-Cougar, November 30, 2006

In 2045, Mrs Do-Little Fake-Ass seemed to seamlessly corroborate the statements by Mr Harper and Dr Ugly Soft-Ass Wrinkling-Cougar, when on November 20, 2008 she contradicted Professor Richard Boris Hill.

****

2045, RETROSPECTIVE REVIEW OF NOVEMBER 2008:

Mr Moore: Good morning, Mrs Dowling. Can I just go back to a few things you said yesterday. You were talking about a rolling inspection every three years, I think by the Dental Reference Service?

Mrs Do-Little Fake-Ass: That is correct, yes.

MR DAVID MOORE: Now that had not been in place prior to 2006, had it?

Mrs Do-Little Fake-Ass: It was not in the same format prior to 2006, the DRS. As I understand it they have been reviewing the practice visits that they undertake, and they have changed since the introduction of the new contract to include the premises inspection as well as checks on patients.

MR DAVID MOORE: But as far as Dr Yinka African Bombata and his Bedford practice is concerned, had there been any DRS inspections of his premises before Dr Muscular Ugly-Ass Racist - Cougar went in 2007?

Mrs Do-Little Fake-Ass: Not of those premises, no.

PAUSE:

"Not of those premises, no," – reasonably implies that there had been DRS inspection at other premises.

They seemed uninterested in the truth and are absolutely incapable of academic law.

Mrs Do-Little Fake – Ass studied very soft Business Studies at a Sports' University, in Loveborough where the majors were cheap gals and beer.

MR DAVID MOORE: You mentioned also yesterday that there had been concerns raised, both in Bedford and a nearby town, about Dr Yinka African Bombata's practices in those respective areas. The other area we know about because we have heard evidence about the inspection, the visit that took place there. I just want your help as far as Bedford is concerned. I think at that stage when those were raised let's take it in stages. Can I just first of all take you to a document D2 which...

CHAIRMAN (Dr Shiv Chicken Massala India): I do not think that the committee has that document. Have you got that?

Mrs Do-Little Fake-Ass: Yes I have.

MR. MOORE: I think this was an e mail you received in 2005 from Sue Gregory, a colleague of yours at Bedford, is that right?

PAUSE:

Part of the administration of the LAW is akin to organised RACIST CRIME.

Homogeneity or subjugated, diverse merit in the administration of the LAW is the NEW APARTHEID; it conceals and paradoxically propagates racial bias.

The mother and father of Mr Moore couldn't have sent him to schools where critical reasoning was taught as a subject. Neither the email nor the alleged concerns were shared with Dr Yinka African Bombata, which reasonably implied that like the the 2004 reports, they were forgeries. In 2005, the 2003 and 2004 reports were live and valid, and they must have been recorded in the NHHHS Data Base, which allegedly recorded the visit, not the actual inspection.

Mrs Do-Little Fake-Ass: That is correct, yes. She's the Consultant Dental Public Health at Bedfordshire.

MR DAVID MOORE: And talks of Vicky Harrison from Northamptonshire telephoning you with some continuing concerns about Mr. Bamgbelu's other practice on her patch: "Most of these relate to cross infection control and include disposing of clinical waste. I know that we had a number of concerns about his practice in Bedford, and he had both money and support to get things right. Please let me know about any outstanding concerns and when his practice was last inspected". I think at that stage your understanding was that those concerns were ones that were raised way back in 1996, and sort of led to visits from Mr. Hill which was sorted out I think by the end of 1996/7?

Mrs Do-Little Fake-Ass: As far as I am aware, yes, it was 95/96; it was prior to my involvement with the PCT.

PAUSE:

Privileged dullards within one of the least literate countries in the industrialised world seemed incapable of academic law. Dr Yinka African Bombata was not in Bedford in 1994. He was registered by Bedford on December 18, 1995 and he started work there on January 8, 1996.

Privileged dullards talk rot. Homogeneity or subjugated, diverse merit in the administration of the LAW (NEW APARTHEID) is their shield.

MR DAVID MOORE: Now, I do not think much happened as a result of that inquiry until 2006, August, is that right?

Mrs Do-Little Fake-Ass: I believe that is correct, yes.

PAUSE:

Privileged dullards who expend their entire professional lives on daily dialogues with imbeciles are likelier to become dull.

In 2045, it became apparent that if there were concerns in 2003 and 2004 and they did not start to do something about it until 2006, the alleged concerns must have been forgeries.

The 2004 reports were forgeries, which were later withdrawn, and the 2003 reports were never disclosed to Dr Yinka African Bombata. They were disclosed to him in October 2008 after he had been charged with the content of the report that had not been disclosed to him six years after the reports were created.

In 2045, many people agreed that parts of the administration of the LAW were mediocre, Negrophobic and dishonest; managed mediocrity and chaos.

MR DAVID MOORE: Because we then got another e mail dated it's D4.

CHAIRMAN (Dr Shiv Chicken Massala India): Do you have a copy for Mrs Do-little Fake-Ass (Handed).

MR. MOORE: Again, from Dr Soft Ugly – Ass Wrinkling - Cougar in August 2006 no, sorry, John Harper 2006. John Hooper is another colleague at Bedford, is that correct?

Mrs Do-Little Fake-Ass: That's correct; he was one of the managers in my team.

MR MOORE: Referring to, "Dr Muscular Ugly-Ass Racist-Cougar" calling us a few weeks ago and she wanted to know if there had been a dental inspection there at all (I think that's Bedford) and I didn't know the answer. Cue Professor Richard Boris Hill, have you carried out an inspection at this practice. Please could you advise Stephanie when she contacts you". That is the next time this matter arose, is that right?

Mrs Do-Little Fake-Ass: That is correct, yes.

CHAPTER 6

Like the Anti-Christ, Closeted Racist Freemasons (New Pharisees or Mediocre Mafia) and the Pharisees (old), before them, privileged dullards seemed oblivious to the fact that reasoning power and vision are not bounded. Had the Pharisees realised that fact, they mightn't have lynched Christ for disclosing the picture that his unbounded mind painted.

"I emphasis the point.........." Judge Paulo Hayers, Approved Judgement

A fool's approval

Organisation for Economic Cooperation and Development (OECD) implied that his children should be duller. If the Judge couldn't spell, his children might not be able to read, and they wouldn't know that their father (a Judge) couldn't spell.

Ignorance is BLISS!

"I do not approve of anything that tampers with natural ignorance. Ignorance is like a delicate exotic fruit; touch it and the bloom is gone. The whole theory of modern education is radically unsound. Fortunately in England, at any rate, education produces no effect whatsoever. If it did, it would prove a serious danger to the upper classes, and probably lead to acts of violence in Grosvenor Square." Oscar Wilde

Reasoning and vision are unbounded, if Christ's is infinite, He must be who He says He is.

Mohammed and all Prophets and Messengers are all dead or will all die. The fellow with the extra-terrestrial, Divine Y chromosome is exceptional and immortal. He is Allah or God; the God of Mohammed.

MR DAVID MOORE: And then I think in response to that, do we get an e mail from Richard Hill, which we have behind tab 21 in volume 1.

Mrs Do-Little Fake-Ass: Sorry, can I have the tab again.

MR DAVID MOORE: Tab 21. From Richard Hill 6 September 06 to you and others at Bedford; record of practice visits, and we have the entry on that schedule for July 2004, all right?

Mrs Do-Little Fake-Ass: Yes.

MR DAVID MOORE: And did you, as part of his process then well, I can see the concerns that were raised in that column: no risk assessment, no COSSH, Kavoclave type autoclave, why that shouldn't be used, no other members of practice staff present at visits, and could not be questioned regarding cross infection control by the practice. But did you, as part of this process, receive a copy of what was purported to be the visit record for that date 22 July 04?

PAUSE:

In 2045, it became apparent that Kavoklave was the artificial tool of EVIL in 1996, 2003, 2004 and 2008, which closeted racist privileged dullards used to corroborate the 2007 lies of Ms Wollaston Bishop's Cathedral.

HOMOGENEITY or subjugated, diverse merit in the administration of the LAW is the NEW APARTHEID; it conceals and paradoxically propagates racial bias in the administration of the LAW.

Mrs Do-Little Fake-Ass: Not at that time, but we did get copies of the reports and for these visits at a later date. We had been requesting them.

PAUSE:

In 2045, it became apparent that one could not be requesting reports that were in the Practitioner's file and were accessible. Professor Richard Boris Hill unrelentingly and criminally lied under oath, including when he stated under oath that the reports were in the practitioners file and accessible to Bedford's apparatchiks.

In 2045, in Bedford, it was reported that some decades prior, a Negress, Judge Constance Briscoe attempted to mislead the Police; she was jailed. In Bedford, Judge Paulo Hayers unrelentingly deviated from the truth under oath, Professor Richard Boris Hill fabricated reports and lied under oath; Ms Wollaston Bishop's Cathedral unrelentingly lied under oath, Dr Muscular Ugly-Ass Racist-Cougar unrelentingly lied under oath, Dr Soft Ugly-Ass Wrinkling – Cougar unrelentingly lied under oath. Selective justice is an injustice.

Semi-illiterate Racists; ultra-righteous descendants of evil terrorists and human being thieves: stealer, owner, carrier, seller and exploiters of millions of stolen human beings, including millions of kidnapped and carried children (the Boko Haram of another era).

MR DAVID MOORE: That is D5, if you can have a look at that, please. (Handed)

Mrs Do-Little Fake-Ass: Thank you (Perused document).

MR DAVID MOORE: And I think if I can take you to the feedback, final page, page 5, summary of these concerns: "The practice uses a Kavoclave type autoclave. This is not acceptable. There is also a large turnover of staff and I am not satisfied that staff training is at an acceptable level and have concerns over the cross infection control procedures", and the essential action points set out there. So you would have received that, and that would have informed your concerns at that time about that practice?

Mrs Do-Little Fake-Ass: This report was received at a later time. I did not receive it until 2004.

PAUSE:

Scatter head Mrs Do-Little Fake-Ass. The soft under belly of some privileged dullards, including the Anti-Christ Closeted Freemasons is the intellect of the individual member.

Europeans cowardly used guns to dominate, loot, and destroy unarmed AFRICA; a brainless genetic ROMANIAN is a Judge in England

In 2045 and prior to that year, it became apparent that the 2004 reports were created in 2006 and released on September 6, 2006. Mrs Do-Little Fake-Ass did not realise that a report that was fabricated in 2006 could not exist in 2004.

Mrs Do-Little Fake-Ass: imbecile, sensuous looking but tasteless creepy, racist dunce; a descendant of merciless, racist murderers and human being thieves.

In 2045, it became apparent that Mrs Do-Little Fake Ass must have smoked something years prior, as if she could not request in 2006, the creation of the report she had in 2004.

We are all victims of the past; we are the evidence of it. Some people secretly believe that gigantically profitable European trade in millions of stolen human beings, including millions of kidnapped and carried children (BOKO HARAM of that era), unnaturally Decommissioned Natural Selection. It immeasurably improved the standard of living but seem to leave the intellect of the individual Serf and their descendants untouched. Those who inherited the intellects of Serfs and who would have worked with forks and spades on the estates of the upper classes and their Lordships are now something GRANDER than their Natural Talent. Had Natural Selection not been unnaturally decommissioned, hereditarily dull people would work on farms.

MR DAVID MOORE: No.

Mrs Do-Little Fake-Ass: But what I also I received was part of the decision making process, and prioritising the practice for an inspection by the DRS.

PAUSE:

Brainless gibberish!

Mrs Do-Little Fake-Ass talked a lot of nonsense under oath interspersed with keywords. She fooled only the foolish; all of whom were kindred. Bedford is the Serengeti of imbeciles.

Homogeneity or subjugated, diverse merit in the administration of the LAW is the NEW APARTHEID; it propagates and paradoxically conceals racial bias.

"But what I also I received was part of the decision making process, and prioritising the practice for an inspection by the DRS." Mrs Do-Little Fake-Ass

The statement is meaningless!

Those regularly spun by privileged dullards are amongst the dullest adult population in the industrialised world.

Shepherds know that their sheep are morons. Sheep do not know that their shepherds are morons too.

MR DAVID MOORE: And would those concerns, informed in part by that report, have been fed through to Dr Muscular Ugly-Ass Racist-Cougar prior to her conducting her inspection in February 07?

Mrs Do-Little Fake-Ass: I can't remember if I passed them on. I think Richard Hill would have shared those issues with Stephanie as part of the discussion prior to the visit, and that is part of the reason why Richard went with Stephanie to undertake the visit with her.

PAUSE:

In 2045 and prior, it became apparent that Mrs Do-Little Fake-Ass might have passed the fabricated reports of 2004 to Dr Muscular Ugly-Ass Racist Cougar. The probability that Mrs Do-Little Fake-Ass passed the reports of 2004, which Professor Richard Boris Hill fabricated, to Dr Muscular Ugly-Ass Racist- Cougar was exceedingly high for the following reasons:

Dr Muscular Ugly-Ass Racist-Cougar asked to see previous reports prior to visiting the surgery of Dr Yinka African Bombata. Closeted, white supremacists are oftener overexcited when they is the opportunity to persecute and destroy some BLACKS; it is almost genetic. Some of their ancestors were merciless, racist murderers, armed robbers and thieves.

"Many Scots masters were considered among the most brutal, with life expectancy on their plantations averaging a mere four years. We worked them to death then simply imported more to keep the sugar and thus the money flowing. Unlike centuries of grief and murder, an apology costs nothing. So what does Scotland have to say?" Herald Scotland: Ian Bell, Columnist, Sunday 28 April 2013

In 2045, Dr Soft Ugly-Ass Wrinkling-Cougar seemed to reaffirm that in November 2006, she offered to share concerns with Dr Muscular Ugly-Ass Racist-Cougar through Professor Richard Boris Hill.

In 2045, Mrs Do-Little Fake-Ass confirmed that the reports were requested and she might have shared the concerns in them with Dr Muscular Ugly – Ass Racist- Cougar, but she certainly expected Professor Richard Boris Hill who fabricated reports to do so.

In 2045, Dr Muscular Ugly-Ass Racist-Cougar or somebody else confirmed that Dr Muscular Ugly-Ass Racist-Cougar had several discussions with Mr Harper, Dr Soft Ugly-Ass Wrinkling –Cougar and Mrs Do-Little Fake-Ass about the reports of 2004, which were fabricated by Professor Richard Boris Hill; they were withdrawn more than four years later.

MR DAVID MOORE: It would have made a lot of sense for the information in that report to have been passed on and fed through as necessary preliminary material prior to inspection?

Mrs Do-Little Fake-Ass: Yes, it would have been.

MR DAVID MOORE: And do you appreciate that now, very recently, Mr. Hill has realised that that report, relating to Dr Yinka African Bombata's practice, in fact was an error, in as much as the concerns in it related to wholly different matters?

Mrs Do-Little Fake-Ass: No, I was not aware of that.

PAUSE:

In 2045, Mrs Do-Little Fake-Ass seemed to agree that it's improbable and implausible that she was unaware of the fact that Bedford's Professor Richard Boris Hill had withdrawn the fabricated reports of 2004, a month earlier. The reports were withdrawn, but its effects remain.

Mrs Do-Little Fake-Ass studied Business at a 5th Rate University (not an IVY LEAGUE). If you remove the catalyst the reaction it caused will not be reversed; she seemed too dull to discern that fact.

MR DAVID MOORE: It was a bad question because there were two questions in one, so perhaps I ought to go back and break it down. First of all, did you provide the previous reports of your visits in advance of the practice inspection in February?

Professor Richard Boris Hill: I'm not aware of them being provided for that purpose.

PAUSE:

"I'm not aware of them being provided for that purpose." Professor Richard Boris Hill

Professor Richard Boris Hill: incompetent mendacity by a descendant of merciless racist murderers, cowards, armed robbers and human being thieves (stealer, carrier and seller of millions of kidnapped human beings, including children (the BOKO HARAM of their era), HABAKKUK

Some genetic Europeans were the world champions at using guns to mercilessly slaughter unarmed and defenceless Africans. Those who like gun fights should go and use guns to evict Mr Putin from Crimea.

A legal system that admits fabrications and tolerates unrelenting dishonesty under oath is backwards, racist and evil.

Professor Boris Richard Hill unrelentingly deviated from the truth under oath; homogeneity in the administration of the law is the shield of racist mendacity.

In 2045, Mr John Harper will confirm that his statement of August 15, 2006 confirmed that Professor Richard Boris Hill unrelentingly lied under oath.

In 2045, Dr Soft Ugly-Ass Wrinkling-Cougar confirmed that her statement of November 30, 2006 was the evidence that Professor Richard Boris Hill was a racist criminal who unrelentingly lied under oath.

In 2045, Dr Muscular Ugly-Ass Racist-Cougar confirmed that in 2006, she made the following statements:

"Having discussed with the Bedford Authority they told me that Mr Hill had made previous visits not that long before from which there had been some queries, and they felt perhaps it would be sensible for Mr Hill to come along as well with me to be a second person and follow up on his previous visits to the practice."

"Then I know it came through that Richard Hill had been in before about six months ago."

Dr Muscular Ugly-Ass Racist-Cougar LIED and her incompetent mendacity confirmed the incompetent mendacity of her kindred, Professor Richard Boris Hill.

In 2045, Dr Muscular Ugly-Ass Racist-Cougar confirmed that she had several discussions with Bedford apparatchiks about the fabricated reports of 2004.

MR DAVID MOORE: Well, again, is it that you provided them and then we can discuss what the reason was?

Professor Richard Boris Hill: They were provided but then, again, they would be within the practitioner's file so there would be ready access to them.

PAUSE:

Brainless nonsense!

If any report in any year was in the files and accessible, those who need the reports would not ask for them, and it wouldn't take several weeks to re-create them.

Parts of the administration of the LAW in Bedford seemed akin to organized crime; they're mediocre, Negrophobic and DISHONEST.

MR DAVID MOORE: So you did provide them but for the purpose ----

Professor Richard Boris Hill: Indirectly, I would say. I do not recall whatsoever being asked to do so for the purpose of the visit.

THE CHAIRMAN (Dr Shiv Chicken Massala India): I think what is trying to be established is did you provide them or are you saying that the PCT would have had access to them anyway?

Professor Richard Boris Hill: Yes, the PCT would have access.

PAUSE:

In 2045, experts were able to detect that Dr Shiv Chicken Massala India was a LUNATIC!

If others requested for reports that you provided, it simply meant they had access to them because you provided them, and, only after you provided them.

Dr Shiv Chicken Massala India seemed intellectually disorientated and mentally imbalanced.

"If a madman were to come into this room with a stick in his hand, no doubt we should pity the state of his mind; but our primary consideration would be to take care of ourselves. We should knock him down first, and pity him afterwards." Dr Samuel Johnson

THE CHAIRMAN (Dr Shiv Chicken Massala India): So the PCT could have provided them.

Professor Richard Boris Hill: That's right. They would have access to them.

PAUSE:

In 2045, experts realised that you could only have access to what you did not have and requested only after your request had been granted and you had been provided with what you did not have and had sought.

Just as Lucifer created Anti-Christ, Closeted Racist Freemasons, they create imbeciles and turn them into a private army.

Many privileged dullards were not taught critical reasoning at School.

In 2045, Mr John Harper reaffirmed that he did not have access to them (reports) and he confirmed that Professor Richard Boris Hill lied when he said that he did. Had he had access to reports, he would not have asked for them on August 15, 2006 as he did in statement below.

"Dear all, Dr Muscular Ugly-Ass Racist-Cougar has been in touch a few times as her colleagues had highlighted issues from a similar practice in a nearby town, not far from Bedford, and they would like to review report etc etc prior to visiting. Mrs Do-Little Fake-Ass prioritised Dr Yinka African Bombata's surgery. Dr Muscular Ugly-Ass Racist - Cougar also wanted to know if there has been a dental inspection there at all and I did not know the answer........ Cue Professor Richard Boris Hill, have you carried out an inspection at this practice, please could you advise Dr Muscular Ugly-Ass Racist-Cougar when she contacts you, and would it be possible to see our reports so we can be more proactive with any other queries"

In 2045, Dr Ugly Soft-Ass Wrinkling-Cougar implicitly confirmed that her statement of November 30, 2006 corroborated Mr Harper's statement of August 15, 2006:

"Subject DRS visit to Dr Yinka African Bombata. Dear Dr Muscular Ugly-Ass Racist-Cougar, Just to confirm that I have spoken with Professor Richard Boris Hill and he will join you for the DRS visit on Thursday 22nd February to Dr Yinka African Bombata Bedford Practice, commencing at 9 am. We will endeavour to share any issues that the PCT may have with you PRIOR to the 22nd. Kind regards." Dr Ugly Soft-Ass Wrinkling-Cougar, November 30, 2006

"I can't remember if I passed them on. I think Richard Hill would have shared those issues with Stephanie as part of the discussion prior to the visit, and that is part of the reason why Richard went with Stephanie to undertake the visit with her." Mrs Do-Little Fake-Ass:

THE CHAIRMAN (Dr Shiv Chicken Massala India): The question was did you provide them specifically.

Professor Richard Boris Hill: For that purpose?

THE CHAIRMAN (Dr Shiv Chicken Massala India): Yes.

Professor Richard Boris Hill: No, is the answer to that.

PAUSE:

In 2045, it was apparent that Professor Richard Boris Hill an alleged Freemason unrelentingly LIED under oath; a criminal act.

Members of the Anti-Christ, Closeted Racist Freemasons are everywhere and they control everything except intellect, which is exclusively Christ's and only He could grant it.

Reasoning and vision are unbounded, if Christ's is infinite, He must be who He says He is. Had the Pharisees (The Anti-Christ Closeted Racist Freemasons of their era) understood the fact that the Divine Y chromosome was exceptional, extra-terrestrial, self-sufficient and immortal, they mightn't have lynched Him.

THE CHAIRMAN (Dr Shiv Chicken Massala India): Not for that purpose, did you provide them at all? Were you asked for them?

Professor Richard Boris Hill: I provided all inspection sheets previously, but not for that purpose – well, as a matter of routine. I mean, part of the reason why we do so was obviously because there was going to be a Health Care Commission inspection or visit to the PCT which is done on a regular basis. But I was not aware of those being passed to the Dental Reference Officer. They may have been, I don't know, but I was not aware of that.

PAUSE:

In 2045, some commentators stated that several decades prior, a JUDGE in the older Europe, JUDGE CONSTANCE BRISCOE misled the POLICE and she was jailed.

Seemingly, guided and guarded by the Anti-Christ, Closeted Racist Freemasons, Professor Richard Boris Hill unrelentingly lied under oath. Has he been BLACK, he'd have been jailed.

HOMOGENEITY: subjugated, diverse merit in the administration of the LAW is the NEW APARTHEID; it conceals and propagates racial bias.

MR HUT: So you are not aware of the reason, but you did provide ----

Professor Richard Boris Hill: No, but they were provided as part of the routine monitoring, that's all. But, as I said, they might have been shown to the Dental Reference Officer. I'm not aware of it.

PAUSE:

Some Anti-Christ, Closeted Racist Freemasons, seemingly racist forgeries that go wrong; Professor Richard Boris Hill unrelentingly lied under oath.

In 2045, it seemed apparent that the reports that took Professor Richard Boris Hill about three weeks to incompetently fabricate were not provided as part of the routine monitoring. Professor Richard Boris Hill lied under oath (a criminal act) when he stated that the reports that he maliciously fabricated might have been shown to the Dental Reference Officer but he was not aware of it.

Again, in 2045, it was very obvious that Mr Harper and Dr Soft Ugly-Ass Wrinkly-Cougar statements of several decades earlier confirmed that Professor Richard Boris Hill unrelentingly lied under oath.

"Dear all, Dr Muscular Ugly-Ass Racist-Cougar has been in touch a few times as her colleagues had highlighted issues from a similar practice in a nearby town, not far from Bedford, and they would like to review report etc etc prior to visiting. Mrs Do-Little Fake-Ass prioritised Dr Yinka African Bombata's surgery. Dr Muscular Ugly-Ass Racist - Cougar also wanted to know if there has been a dental inspection there at all and I did not know the answer…….. Cue Professor Richard Boris Hill, have you carried out an inspection at this practice, please could you advise Dr Muscular Ugly-Ass Racist-Cougar when she contacts you, and would it be possible to see our reports so we can be more proactive with any other queries." Mr John Harper

"Subject DRS visit to Dr Yinka African Bombata. Dear Dr Muscular Ugly-Ass Racist-Cougar, Just to confirm that I have spoken with Professor Richard Boris Hill and he will join you for the DRS visit on Thursday 22nd February to Dr Yinka African Bombata Bedford Practice, commencing at 9 am. We will endeavour to share any issues that the PCT may have with you PRIOR to the 22nd. Kind regards." Dr Ugly Soft-Ass Wrinkling-Cougar, November 30, 2006

Anti-Christ, Closeted Racist Freemasonry seem to be the refuge of some half-educated school dropouts, some plebeians, some policemen and others who seem to have informal access to some JUDGES.

Parts of the administration of the administration of the law seemed akin to organised, racist crime.

MR HUT: We can ask her later.

Professor Richard Boris Hill: It's not a matter that I actually discussed with her either.

PAUSE:

In 2045, it was apparent that Professor Richard Boris Hill could not discuss with Dr Muscular Ugly-Ass Racist-Cougar if she stated under oath decades earlier that she did not have any contact with Professor Richard Boris Hill.

Those regularly spun are amongst the dullest adult populations in the industrialised world.

2045: Retrospective review of a singular encounter in Bedford in 2008:

MR DAVID MOORE: This is a report by Richard Hill dated 22 July 2004. Might you have seen that before the inspection?

DR MUSCULAR UGLY-ASS RACIST-COUGAR No, I have never seen this before.

PAUSE:

Gigantic yields of millions of stolen and destroyed lives, including millions of kidnapped and carried children seemed to have distorted the realities of some people.

In 2045, Professor Richard Boris Hill seemed to confirm that the reports he fabricated decades earlier consisted of about four separate sentences.

It was brainless to suggest that seeing a report with three sentences was the only way of knowing about the report.

The duller the public the easier it becomes for them to be manipulated.

Some people secretly but sincerely believe that if the bottom of a whole were to descend to the basement, the top of that whole should automatically fall to the bottom from whence the former bottom vacated. There will be change but there wouldn't be relative change as the distance between the basement (former bottom) and the bottom (former top) will remain unchanged. The former top stubbornly refuses to accept that it is the new bottom because it is oblivious to the notion of relativity.

CHAPTER 7

"Sometimes people don't want to hear the truth because they don't want their illusions destroyed." Friedrich Nietzsche

If the bottom of a whole falls into the basement and if the top of that whole automatically falls to the bottom from whence the former bottom vacated, there will be change but there will be continue to be harmony as there wouldn't be relative change because the distance between the basement (former bottom) and the bottom (former top) will remain unchanged. Ignorant former top stubbornly refuses to admit that it is the NEW BOTTOM.

Contrariwise, if the bottom of a whole were to fall to the basement and the top of that whole refuses to automatically fall to the bottom from whence the former bottom vacated, there will be disharmony and fracture as the distance between the basement (former bottom) and the top will be increased by the space occupied by the former bottom. If the former bottom is oblivious to the fact that it is the NEW BASEMENT, it may associate the disharmony and fractured relationship with the top, with insanity.

"MURRAY: 'It seems to me that we are not angry at a man for controverting an opinion which we believe and value; we rather pity him.'

JOHNSON: 'Why, Sir; to be sure when you wish a man to have that belief which you think is of infinite advantage, you wish well to him; but your primary consideration is your own quiet. If a madman were to come into this room with a stick in his hand, no doubt we should pity the state of his mind; but our primary consideration would be to take care of ourselves. We should knock him down first, and pity him afterwards." Dr Samuel Johnson

Dr Samuel Johnson implied that one would always be stronger than an armed mad man. He was wrong. Had he been alive today, he would have changed his mind, as he would have realised that lunatic terrorists strike before they could be knocked down. Therefore, only the immortal could make rules or provide guidance for people to follow, as they are in the position to make amends.

"If the facts don't fit the theory, change the facts." - Albert Einstein

Indefinite potential change desires immortality.

Prophet Mohammed is dead. Christ is Allah, his God. Christ's extra-terrestrial, self-sufficient and immortal Y chromosome makes Him exceptional. All Prophets and Messengers are dead or will die. All their Gods were imaginary or imaginary or dead. Only Christ has lived and His immortal.

Christ alone could make Laws; Christ alone is the Good Shepherd. He doesn't need to change His mind because His reasoning and vision are unbounded and infinite. He left a 'HELPER' to clarify His Laws

"CHRIST is the mocked by any sense. He will not be mocked by counterfeit piety; He will not be mocked with idle resolution. CHRIST will not suffer His decrees to be invalidated; He will not leave His promises unfulfilled or his threats unexecuted. And this will easily appear if we consider that promises and threats can only become ineffectual by change of mind, or want of POWER. CHRIST cannot change His will. He with the extra-terrestrial, self-sufficient, DIVINE, immortal and exceptional Y chromosome is not a man that He should repent. What CHRIST has spoken will surely come to pass as He will not want POWER to execute His purposes. He who spoke and the world was made could speak again and it will perish. CHRIST'S arm is not shortened that He cannot save neither is it shortened that He cannot punish." Dr Samuel Johnson, paraphrased

MR DAVID MOORE: Sir, you will recall Professor Richard Boris Hill's evidence was that this is a report mistakenly attributed to Dr Yinka African Bombata practice when it in fact relates to something that was a mistake?

THE CHAIRMAN (Dr Shiv Chicken Massala India): Was this where there was a lot of cancellations? I remember something in evidence.

PAUSE:

"Was this where there was a lot of cancellations? I remember something in evidence." Dr Shiv Chicken Massala India

"I do not want to talk grammar. I want to talk like Dr Shiv Chicken Massala India." George Bernard Shaw

The statement by Mr David Moore was unrelated to the response that Dr Shiv Chicken Massala India, gave. The fellow was so dull, he could be mad but he couldn't have acquired such a very high level of dullness from nature; he must have been born with it.

MR DAVID MOORE: Professor Richard Boris Hill said yesterday that while he made an error and he thought there had been an inspection on 22 July 2004, and in fact that was not right, it referred to another practice. In chatting with Professor Richard Boris Hill, presumably you did before going round did he mention any previous inspections that he had done?

PAUSE:

In some Jurisdictions, only members of the Anti-Christ Closeted Racist Freemasons and those who could afford to bribe JUDGES tell lies under oath.

Mr David Moore unrelentingly lied under oath. He invited Professor Richard Boris Hill to lie immortally under oath that his fabricated reports were genuine and belonged to another practice; they weren't because they couldn't be.

MR DAVID MOORE: In chatting with Professor Richard Boris Hill, presumably you did before going round did he mention any previous inspections that he had done?

DR MUSCULAR UGLY-ASS RACIST-COUGAR: I never spoke to Richard Hill, nor had I ever met him before we arrived at the practice together. It was a classic two people standing outside a building saying: "Are you? Oh yes, right fine" we had never met and we did not speak beforehand. The only people I spoke to beforehand would be Mr John Harper and some e-mail correspondence with John, with Mrs Do-Little Fake Ass and with the Consultants in public health, Dr Soft Ugly-Ass Wrinkling -Cougar. I didn't actually have any contact with Professor Richard Boris Hill at all.

Dr Muscular Ugly-Ass Racist-Cougar unrelentingly lied under oath with the confidence that her kindred sat beside and before her. She confessed that she had several indirect contacts with Professor Richard Boris Hill, and he confirmed that he had direct contact with her. Descendants of aliens, likelier Eastern Europeans with camouflage English names, which their ancestors used to latch on to the yields of millions of stolen and destroyed lives.

THE LEGAL ADVISER (Mr Acromegaly Dick-head Mason): Mr Morris, can you make it absolutely clear for everybody that I think you are referring to the document behind divider 21, and it is the Schedule Record of Practice which is the second part, is that right?

MR DAVID MOORE: That is right, sir.

THE LEGAL ADVISER (MR ACROMEGALY DICK-HEAD MASON): Sorry, do I look behind it?

MR DAVID MOORE: Yes, if you look behind tab 21. Richard Hill sent an e-mail to his colleagues at the PCT, Bedford PCT.

THE LEGAL ADVISER (MR ACROMEGALY DICK-HEAD MASON): It is page 3 behind page 21, I think you have said. There is a table and there is a reference there which I think you suggested to Mr Hill was not actually a report of Dr Yinka African Bombata's practice, is that right?

MR DAVID MOORE: That is right. It was a report, we have the report here.

PAUSE:

Anti-Christ, Closeted Racist Freemasons are everywhere and they control everything except intellect. They secretly agree to everything in their grand lodges that STOLEN and DESTROYED lives yielded, and things are then played out in the open as if they were live and real.

THE LEGAL ADVISER (Acromegaly Dick-Head Mason): So the Committee understand what the status of D5 is?

MR MOORE: It is my fault, I should have clarified this with Professor Richard Boris Hill yesterday, but D5 is a report drafted by Professor Richard Boris Hill in error, which he accepted yesterday, in error attributing it as an inspection of Dr Yinka African Bombata's practice at Bromham Drive, Bedford. When, in fact, it was not, and the substance of the contents were from another practice.

PAUSE:

2045: It was his fault, of course it was! Mistakes do happen, don't they?

NEW APARTHEID: Subjugated, diverse merit in the administration of the English LAW; HOMOGENEITY

There couldn't be another practice because Professor Richard Boris Hill implied that he fabricated the reports, which based on all available evidence were incompetent fabrications.

THE LEGAL ADVISER (MR ACROMEGALY DICK-HEAD MASON): Was there a visit to another practice?

MR DAVID MOORE: That is how he put it yesterday.

PAUSE:

In 2045 or prior, Professor Richard Boris Hill and/or the facts revealed that he did not voluntarily state that he visited another practice in Bedford on July 22, 2004; Mr David Moore invited him to agree that he did, and he did, under oath.

THE LEGAL ADVISER (MR ACROMEGALY DICK-HEAD MASON): Effectively, so that the address is incorrect because it is a different surgery, is that right?

MR MOORE: The address is incorrect, the name of the practitioner is incorrect?

THE LEGAL ADVISER (MR ACROMEGALLY DICK-HEAD MASON): The name of the practitioner is incorrect?

PAUSE:

Things are agreed in secret prior to hearings, they are then played out in the open as if they are live and real; incompetent art incompetently imitates life.

MR DAVID MOORE: Yes. He listed, when being chased for previous inspections he listed it in that schedule, and he accepted yesterday that there was no such visit in 2004.

PAUSE:

In 2045, it became apparent that there was no such visit in 2004 because there couldn't be any such visit as the reports were fabricated.

THE CHAIRMAN (DR SHIV CHICKEN MASSALA INDIA): This was not put to Mr Hill yesterday.

MR DAVID MOORE: The actual report was not, but we went through the schedule, but for completeness I should have put it to him yesterday. (To the witness) You have not seen that before and you did not have any discussion with Mr Hill about it?

Dr Muscular Ugly-Ass Racist- Cougar: None at all.

PAUSE:

In 2045 and prior, those regularly spun are amongst the dullest adult populations in the industrial world.

'You have not seen this before.'

Seeing a report with only about four sentences isn't the ONLY way of knowing about such a report.

"And you did not have any discussion with Professor Richard Boris Hill about it?"

How could Muscular Ugly-Ass Racist Cougar have discussions with Professor Richard Boris Hill when she stated under oath that she did not have any contact with him at all?

"I never spoke to Richard Hill, nor had I ever met him before we arrived at the practice together. It was a classic two people standing outside a building saying: "Are you? Oh yes, right fine" we had never met and we did not speak beforehand. The only people I spoke to beforehand would be John Hooper and some e-mail correspondence with John Harper, with Mrs Do-Little Fake-Ass and with the Consultants in public health, Dr Soft Ugly-Ass Wrinkling Cougar. I didn't actually have any contact with Richard at all." Dr Muscular Ugly-Ass Racist-Cougar

Dr Muscular Ugly-Ass Racist-Cougar LIED; she unrelentingly LIED under oath.

Negress, Judge Constance Briscoe misled the Police; she was jailed.

Parts of the administration of the LAW seemed akin to organized RACIST crime

MR DAVID MOORE: The question you posed as reported in D4, an e-mail from John Hooper, whether or not there had been a dental inspection before, you never got an answer to?

DR MUSCULAR UGLY-ASS RACIST-COUGAR: I got an answer at some stage, but I can't remember exactly where. The question I was asking at that point from John Hooper in the very early stage was quite simply: "Do you just need the SP2?" In other words patients and record card examinations carrying out, in other words is that the reason why you have brought this forward for an urgent visit as opposed to a routine visit which could have taken a year for me to get round to it with the workload we had at that stage or: "do you need anything else in particular? If it is anything to do with the practice, do you need me to do a surgery inspection. Is that part of what you are looking for me to do?" I eventually got an answer that said: "Yes, please we would like a surgery inspection". At the point at which I was informed that Richard Hill had been there some months before hand and had some concerns. I don't think that at that stage, but I am relying on memory here, my memory is it came in when the decision was made that Richard Hill would be the person to accompany me on the visit. As the PCT would rather he did it as he had been there before, rather than the consultant who was in public health, as they felt it was not appropriate for her and while there was a second DRO going to accompany me. That is my memory of it.

PAUSE:

In 2045, Dr Muscular Ugly–Ass Racist- Cougar would have agreed that she was a 'rotter' BLOWER.

"At the point at which I was informed that Richard Hill had been there some months before hand and had some concerns." Dr Muscular Ugly-Ass Racist-Cougar

Professor Richard Boris Hill later confirmed that Dr Muscular Ugly-Ass Racist-Cougar had 'lost it'. The last time Professor Richard Boris Hill visited the surgery of Dr Yinka African Bombata was several years earlier in 2003.

The NEWEST APARTHEID: Subjugated, diverse merit in the administration of the LAW.

HOMONEITY in the administration of the LAW is an instrument of WAR.

****

MR HUT: Thank you. Now obviously during the course of the run up to the visit of 22 February there was some communication between you and Stephanie Twidale.

PROFESSOR RICHARD BORIS HILL: Yes.

PAUSE:

2045: Professor Richard Boris Hill confirmed that he had contacts with Dr Muscular Ugly-Ass Racist-Cougar; the fact fitted seamlessly with Mr John Harper's statement of August 15, 2006, and that of Dr Soft Ugly –Ass Wrinkling Cougar of November 30, 2006, and that of Mrs Do-Little Fake-Ass of November 20, 2008. These statements, together, confirmed that Dr Muscular Ugly-Ass Racist-Cougar was a criminal who unrelentingly LIED under oath.

"The only people I spoke to beforehand would be Mr John Harper and some e-mail correspondence with John, with Mrs Do-Little Fake Ass and with the Consultants in public health, Dr Soft Ugly-Ass Wrinkling -Cougar. I didn't actually have any contact with Professor Richard Boris Hill at all." Dr Muscular Ugly–Ass Racist-Cougar

What was the point of the legal system that allowed only white people to tell lies under oath?

Criminally DISHONEST, mediocre, and RACIST legal system (Part).

Newest Apartheid: Subjugated, diverse merit in the administration of the LAW; it propagates and conceals racial bias.

MR HUT: And obviously she can explain her involvement with Dr Yinka African Bombata, so I am not going to ask you to report on what you heard from her. Simply that by the time you were going to conduct the inspection on 22 February 2007, is it right that you understood that the patient examination element would not be part of the inspection for that day for various reasons which Dr Yinka African Bombata had explained to Stephanie Twidale?

Professor Richard Boris Hill: Yes.

MR HUT: She can deal with that side of things.

Professor Richard Boris Hill: I was aware of that, but I didn't see it as a problem.

Q. You did not see it as a problem.

Professor Richard Boris Hill: No.

Q. Thank you. I think it is right that you have explained in your statement that you did not carry out any preparation for the inspection on 22 February. Is that right?

Professor Richard Boris Hill: No. I was emailed a copy of the inspection sheet, the ambit of the inspection.

Q. Is that the pro forma?

Professor Richard Boris Hill: That's a blank sheet, the pro forma which the Dental Reference Service use. I just familiarized myself with it. I didn't need to do any further work on that. It was a question of understanding each requirement, reading it through and then attending the practice visit. I don't remember any communications with Stephanie Twidale ahead of it sort of discussing any issues. We just met at the practice.

PAUSE:

In 2045, analyst confirmed that 'I do not remember' isn't the evidence of the fact that the incident that couldn't be remembered did not happen.

"I don't remember any communications with Stephanie Twidale ahead of it sort of discussing any issues. We just met at the practice." Professor Richard Boris Hill

The statement by Professor Richard Boris Hill was inconsistent with his assertion that he had contacts with Dr Muscular Ugly-Ass Racist-Cougar prior to the inspection of Dr Yinka African Bombata's surgery on February 22, 2007; he corroborated Dr Muscular Ugly-Ass Racist-Cougar's assertion that they did not have any contact prior to inspecting Dr Yinka Africa Bombata's surgery on February 22, 2007. He lied, and he did incompetently, as he had told Mr Hut that he had contact with Dr Muscular Ugly-Ass Racist-Cougar prior to the inspection of Dr Yinka African Bombata's surgery on February 22, 2007

MR HUT: Thank you. Now obviously during the course of the run up to the visit of 22 February there was some communication between you and Stephanie Twidale.

PROFESSOR RICHARD BORIS HILL: Yes.

MR HUT: Just so that we can square off what you did do, if we can look at our divider 21, we have an email from you to Mr Hooper, Charlotte Dowling and Sue Gregory attaching your Record of Practice Visits. Is that right?

Professor Richard Boris Hill: That's right, yes.

PAUSE:

NEWEST APARTHEID: subjugated, diverse merit in the administration of the English LAW; it conceals and paradoxically propagates racial bias.

In 2045, some scholars argue that what Mr Hut did not say was that no one asked Professor Richard Boris Hill for a synopsis of reports and the report of July 22, 2004, and follow-up of undisclosed date for Dr Yinka African Bombata were incompetent fabrications, which were withdrawn with further fabrications more than four years after the alleged visit.

Q. And you provide a synopsis over the page. Is that right?

Professor Richard Boris Hill: That's correct, yes.

Q. It is within divider 21.

Professor Richard Boris Hill: That's fine.

Q. So you have an email and then behind the email at p.3 we have a landscape document (side on in other words) headed "Record of Practice Visits".

Professor Richard Boris Hill: Yes.

Q. We see Dr Yinka African Bombata is on the first one and then there are a number of others.

Professor Richard Boris Hill: Yes.

PAUSE:

Without transparent equality under transparent LAWS, only the visible chains are off; the TRUE CHAINS will never be voluntarily removed.

In 2045, experts confirmed that Professor Richard Boris Hill was asked to provide reports by Mr John Harper and he asked for only Dr Yinka African Bombata's reports.

Some white people derive so much pleasure from intellectually defeating black people. In 2045, it was apparent that Mr Hut was intellectually disorientated, mentally imbalanced, racist and dishonest.

Q. Have you got that page, Mr Hill?

Professor Richard Boris Hill: Yes, I have the page, p.5.

Q. No, p.3 at the bottom. Go back two pages in your bundle.

Professor Richard Boris Hill: Yes, got it.

Q. Page 3 and then in landscape we have what I think you have described as a synopsis of your visits. Is that right?

Professor Richard Boris Hill: Correct.

Q. You have explained your understanding of why you were asked to do that and the limitations that should be applied to it.

Professor Richard Boris Hill: Yes.

PAUSE:

"You have explained your understanding of why you were asked to do that and the limitations that should be applied to it." Mr Hut

Anti-Christ closeted racist Freemasons agree to things in secret, they are then played out in the open as if they were live and real; incompetent art incompetently imitates life.

In 2045, experts argued that Professor Richard Boris Hill did not give a truthful explanation about why he was asked to provide reports; he lied and lied incompetently. He lied to a receptive audience of his own kindred in a mediocre Negrophobic charade.

HOMOGENEITY or subjugated diverse merit in the administration of the LAW is the NEWEST APARTHEID.

Seemingly, organized racist crime by privileged dullards; they delude themselves that they are clever and associate the yields of several centuries of merciless RACIST EVIL (TRUST FUND); stealing, carrying and selling millions of kidnapped human beings, with personal intellect and industry, Habakkuk

In 2045, some experts came to the conclusion that Mr Hut was spinning morons in a racist charade where the verdicts had been prior agreed in the Anti-Christ, Closeted Racist Freemason LODGES. Things are played out in the open as if they were live and real; incompetent art incompetently imitates life; a very elementary legal process within one of the least literate countries in the industrialized world.

MR HUT: Dr Muscular Ugly-Ass Racist-Cougar was the lead in the 22 February inspection. Is that correct?

PROFESSOR RICHARD BORIS HILL: That's correct.

PAUSE:

In 2045, experts concluded that Dr Muscular Ugly-Ass Racist-Cougar was not good enough; she seemed as thick as a ton of planks. Her wrinkling white skin concealed her dark black brain; semi-illiterate racist, a ultra-righteous descendant of THIEVES: stealer, carrier, and seller of millions of unarmed and defenseless human beings, including millions of kidnapped and stolen little African children. Some European pedophiles bought and used some of the prettiest stolen African boys and girls; some of them escaped from captivity. All of the escaped children were caught by the civilized the European Christian pedophiles; their life expectancy was only a few months.

"It did not become illegal to own a slave in Scotland until 1778. Until then it had been fashionable for wealthy families to have a young black boy or girl 'attending' on them. Scottish newspapers, such as the Edinburgh Evening Courant and the Caledonian Mercury from the 1740s to the 1770s, carried adverts offering slaves for sale or rewards for the capture of escaped slaves." National Library of Scotland

MR HUT: You were supporting her.

Professor Richard Boris Hill: Yes.

PAUSE:

In 2045, experts came to the conclusion that Dr Muscular Ugly-Ass Racist-Cougar was the hired closeted racist ASSASSIN. She was so dull, she couldn't have acquired such a high level of dullness from NATURE; she must have been born dull.

"I emphasis..." JUDGE PAULO HAYERS

Semi-illitcrate RACIST! Righteous DESCENDANT of THIEVES: stealer, carrier, and seller of human beings.

Some people hate BLACKS with merciless, sadistic passion.

In 2045, it became apparent that Dr Muscular Ugly-Ass Racist-Cougar was hired to create an inspection report and link it to the inspection report of 2003 and the reports of 2004. She was rubbish! The fact that she had anything to do with Dr Yinka African Bombata's career was the evidence that he had under-achieve in life; Dr Muscular Ugly-Ass Racist-Cougar was incompetent and incapable. The 2003 report was a fabrication because it was revealed to Dr Yinka African Bombata almost six years after the alleged visit. Dr Yinka African Bombata was charged

In 2045, some real professors confirmed that Professor Richard Boris Hill was a cretin; he detected a Kavoklave autoclave in Dr Yinka African Bombata's surgery in 2003, which he alleged he used as back-up, which he said was perfectly reasonable. A year later, in 2004, he stated that he saw only a Kavoklave, which he was unhappy with as it should not be used. He was confused. He seemed incapable of academic law. White skin seemed to conceal dark black brain.

They were all white, and they were all DISHONEST and/or dull.

Newest Apartheid: Subjugated, diverse merit in the administration of the English LAW; it propagates and conceals racial bias.

Dr Muscular Ugly-Ass Racist Cougar was hired to link the fabrications of 2003 and 2004 together and create a new one, which should fit seamlessly with it.

The white collar racist removes his mask only when he believes that there's a cover.

Dr Muscular Ugly–Ass Racist-Cougar was selected, not because of her intellect; her RESUME was a byword for mediocrity, she was selected because she was a very well connected soldier – a Territorial Army Officer.

In 2045, experts concluded that she was correct to describe her inspection of February 22, 2007 as a follow-up of the fabricated visits and reports of 2003 and 2004.

SHOCKING!

"Why, that is, because, dearest, you are a DUNCE." Dr Samuel Johnson

So, in 2045, it became apparent that the 'MEAT' was the follow-up of the follow-up of the fabricated reports of July 22, 2004.

"Having discussed with the PCT they told me that Professor Richard Boris Hill had made previous visits not that long before from which there had been some queries, and they felt perhaps it would be sensible for Professor Richard Boris Hill to come along as well with me to be a second person and follow up on his previous visits to the practice."

"Then I know it came through that Richard Hill had been in before about six months ago." Dr Muscular Ugly-Ass Racist-Cougar

The statement is immortalized dishonesty, and the grammar was very poor.

"I do not want to talk grammar. I want to speak like a lady." George Bernard Shaw

"I spoke to Dr Soft Ugly-Ass Wrinkling-Cougar, Consultant in Dental Public Health at the Bedfordshire PCT to impart the information and was informed that Richard Hill, Dental Practice adviser to Bedfordshire PCT, had carried out a previous Surgery inspection at Bromham Drive that had raised some concerns." Dr Muscular Ugly-Ass Racist -Cougar

She lied under oath; a criminal! Her kindred were before and beside her. Homogeneity or subjugated, diverse merit in the administration of the law is the NEWEST APARTHEID; it conceals and paradoxically propagates racial bias.

Anti-Christ, Closeted Racist Freemasons create imbeciles and they turn them into an instrument of EVIL. Like the Pharisees, they control everything except intellect.

Reasoning and vision are unbounded; if Christ's is infinite, He must be who He says He is. Had the Pharisees understood the significance of the DIVINE, extra-terrestrial, immortal and exceptional Y – chromosome, they mightn't have lynched Christ.

Prophet Mohammed is DEAD. All prophets and messengers are dead or will die. Prophet Mohammed and all prophets and messengers of alleged Deity are terrestrial. Only Christ is extra-terrestrial and immortal; only Christ is God. Christ alone is Allah, the immortal, extraterrestrial GOD of Prophet Mohammed and all Prophets and messengers.

Deluded privileged dullards isolate a single Negro in a mediocre, mendacious and unbalanced legal process, and they 'WIN' with their skin color rather than their brains.

European trade in millions of kidnapped and stolen Africans was imposed with guns, not brains.Genetic damage is the most enduring effect of the chronic terrorism;

Q. As you went round on the inspection did you discuss matters between you, that is between you and Stephanie Twidale as you went round?

Professor Richard Boris Hill: Yes. I mean obviously, you know, she would lead on the inspection, ask the questions, ask to see the various literature that is required under the ambit of that particular inspection and quite a lot of the things are self evident once you have seen the documentation. There are certain things that we might have a word over before it was actually entered onto the sheet and that was really it; the terms of it is quite self explanatory.

Q. In terms of note taking you made no separate note. Is that correct?

Professor Richard Boris Hill: No, I didn't. No, I didn't.

Q. As I say, Stephanie Twidale will be able to speak to the notes that she made. Do you remember what time you arrived on 22 February?

Professor Richard Boris Hill: I think it was shortly after 9 a.m.

Q. You met Stephanie Twidale there, did you? You rendezvoused at the practice?

Professor Richard Boris Hill: We met – I can't remember whether it was outside on the pavement or in the waiting room. I can't remember the exact location. It was within the area of the practice; it was either on the pavement or upstairs in the waiting area.

Q. Was Dr Yinka African Bombata there when you got there?

Professor Richard Boris Hill: No. He arrived shortly afterwards. Professor Richard Boris Hill:

PAUSE:

Privileged dullards employed the world's language like DAME FAKA PATIENCE GOODLUCK JONATHAN or MODA as she was fondly called in OKRIKA. Mr Hut and Professor Richard Boris Hill employed the World's language like MODA FAKA

Q. When you conducted the inspection was Dr Yinka African Bomabata with you?

Professor Richard Boris Hill: Oh, yes.

Q. I want now to go to the detail of that report and it may be that you will be assisted by turning to divider 8 within that file that you have. Have you a first page which looks like this?

Professor Richard Boris Hill: Yes.

Q. First of all, have you seen this document before?

Professor Richard Boris Hill: I have seen the document, yes.

MR HUT: Did you compile this document or is this Stephanie Twidale's work?

Professor Richard Boris Hill: No. It's entirely Stephanie Twidale's work.

Q. When would you have seen this document, around the time she completed or some time long after?

Professor Richard Boris Hill: This is the draft report, I take it?

Q. Yes.

Professor Richard Boris Hill: That would have been emailed to me very shortly afterwards.

PAUSE:

The dialogue was in verbatim! Privileged dullards (Mr Hut and Professor Richard Boris Hill) employed the world's language like MODA FAKA or DAME FAKA PATIENCE GOODLUCK JONATHAN

Q. So you had an opportunity to look at it quite thoroughly.

Professor Richard Boris Hill: Oh, yes.

Q. We will look at the contents in more detail in a moment, but was there anything which you disagreed with or did you agree with the contents of the report?

Professor Richard Boris Hill: I don't think there was anything that I amended.

Q. First of all, and we will go back to the document if we need to, can I ask you about documentation.

Professor Richard Boris Hill: Yes.

Q. Under the Dentists Terms of Service is correct that there is a certain amount of documentation which a dentist should have available and is required to have available?

Professor Richard Boris Hill: There are certain things, yes, that you need to have on the premises. But the Terms of Service are not that specific in terms of what you should have. I mean, as long as on an inspection/visit if those documents are asked for, if they are not there at the time then in my capacity as a Dental Practice Adviser I would ask that they would be sent, or copies of them would be sent. For example, things like indemnity cover or CPD records. Quite often practitioners keep those things at home and so we would ask for those to be sent. We are not prescriptive and say, "You must hold those on the premises." Obviously there are certain things that need to be demonstrated, things like Employers Liability, things like a Health & Safety poster, those type of matters. But other documentation which is not required by law to be on the premises displayed in a place where the public are, then, you know, we will ask for that later.

Q. If we turn to p.3 within divider 8, you should have a piece of paper which is headed "Practice Inspection" and we have a grid. Do you see that there?

Professor Richard Boris Hill: Yes.

Q. Here we see "Document – required", then there is a column headed "Satisfactory" and then a column headed "Observations & Action discussed".

Professor Richard Boris Yes.

Q. Against the "Documentation – required" we have a cross against the column "Satisfactory". Is that right?

Professor Richard Boris Hill: Yes, I can see that.

Q. If we turn over the page where it says "See separate report", so our p.4 within divider 8, we see a list there under the heading of "52 Bromham Avenue".

"The following information was not publicly displayed:

a) Employers'/Public Liability ....

b) Practice Information Leaflets ....

c) Quality Assurance Certificate ...."

and between you, you have identified the source of the requirement for those things to be displayed, namely the Terms of Service.

Professor Richard Boris Hill: Yes.

Q. Under 2) we have:

"No written policies were available covering the following topics as required by various UK legislation, EU directives and professional guidelines:

a) Audit and Peer Review ....

b) Child Protection ....

c) Disability Discrimination Act ....

d) Clinical evaluation of radiographs ...."

Is that right?

Professor Richard Boris Hill: Yes

Q. And the source for the concern is there articulated. Then 3):

"The following documentary evidence was not available:

a) GDDDC certification ….

b) Defence society certification ….

c) Hepatitis B vaccinations ….

d) Evidence of recent CPR training for the nurse ….

e) Autoclave inspection certificate ….

f) Compressor inspection certificate ….

g) Evidence of Data Protection Registration ….

h) Evidence of installed equipment test certificates ….

i) Evidence of portable electrical appliance testing documents ….

j) Fire equipment maintenance contract ….

k) Evidence that all dental laboratories used are registered with the

MHRA ….

l) Contracts for disposal of clinical waste, sharps and hazardous waste.

m) No 'Duty of Care: Controlled Waste Transfer Notes' were available. The Dentist stated that these were not issued by the contractor who removed the clinical waste and sharps."

Just breaking off there, what is the issue about clinical waste and sharps that you were concerned about?

Professor Richard Boris Hill: It was to do with the transfer notes. A contractor is required to give the practitioner a transfer note to say that the material has been removed from the practice and what happens to it, so that it doesn't, for example, go into ordinary domestic waste landfill or something like this.

PAUSE:

In 2045, it became clearer that Dr Muscular Ugly-Ass Racist-Cougar was hired to create a follow-up for fabricated reports of July 22, 2004 and follow-ip of ndisclosed date, which were later withdrawn. Her brain was not good. She was a criminal who unrelentingly LIED under oath.

Q. What sort of thing would be within clinical waste?

Professor Richard Boris Hill: It depends. You would have your strong plastic boxes for needles and cartridges, used needles and cartridges, those type of ones. You would have yellow sacks for soiled tissues, gloves, that sort of thing. So they would be in different containers, but they would be removed by the same contractor, almost always removed by the same contractor.

PAUSE:

They create anything they liked and attach them to those they do not like. There was an annual Delivery Note.

In 2045, there was evidence that Mr Hut unrelentingly LIED under oath.

The white collar racist is craftier. He needs a cover in order to remove his mask.

Q. Moving on then:

"n) Clinical Governance and Quality Assurance Appraisal.

The Dentist was unaware of his responsibilities regarding setting up of a Quality Assurance system, submission of a summary to the PCT and displaying of the certificate."

From where did you get the information of the dentist's unawareness of his responsibilities. Can you remember?

Professor Richard Boris Hill: I can't honestly remember where we got that from. Stephanie would have asked the question, so I can't accurately or safely answer that one. I wouldn't remember.

PAUSE:

In 2045, it was obvious that the fabricated reports of 2004 were live and valid and their creator, Professor Richard Boris Hill was part of it corroboration; the creation of its successor.

Q. Moving on then:

"o) CPD records of the dentist …

p) Ionising radiation training records ….

q) Staff training and education …

r) Orientation programme for temporary staff …."

So that list (going down) shows things that should have been there, you would have expected to be there but were not.

Professor Richard Boris Hill: Yes, as I said, a number of documents, CPD documents and Professional Indemnity, you would expect them to be there for the inspection, but they could be provided later.

Q. I would like to ask you, please, about posters which were displayed in the waiting room. Can you remember there being an issue about posters being displayed in the waiting room regarding NHHHS treatment?

Professor Richard Boris Hill: Yes. I think there was one that we identified which mentioned about – the way I looked upon it was that it mentioned about composites, white fillings as against the amalgam mercury based fillings and to a hazard or it alluded, I think, to a hazard as regards mercury based fillings.

Q. Your concerns were such that there was a comparison drawn with the NHHHS. What were your concerns particularly about that?

Professor Richard Boris Hill: It's part of the Terms of Service for an NHS practitioner, a GDP, that you don't draw, if you like, derogatory comparisons between private and NHHHS dentistry.

Q. Was that your concern about this particular poster?

Professor Richard Boris Hill: Yes, it's that it might give that impression, that the patient would be better off with private treatment rather than NHHHS treatment.

Q. In terms of the comparisons that the poster was drawing, were they fair comparisons to draw?

A. It's a fine line; it's a very fine line between the two. I mean, if it's based upon, if you like, objective clinical data, then I would say it's fair. I'm not discussing that particular issue straight on in this case, but I'm saying if it's based upon objective, properly reviewed and accepted clinical data, then that would be okay. But if it's just perhaps more subjective and perhaps slightly more alarmist and it's not based upon objective data, then there is a risk that you are straying into that territory where you could be thought to be in breach of the terms of the NHS Terms of Service.

PAUSE:

In 2045, it became apparent that the poster in question had been there since 1996. Professor Richard Boris Hill had seen it on a number of occasions and had not complained.

Unbeknownst to Dr Yinka African Bombata, the inspection of February 22, 2007, the fabricated reports of July 22, 2004, was live, valid and accessible to the closeted white supremacists had come to artificially corroborate malicious racist fabrications.

PAUSE:

Parts of the administration of the LAW seem akin to organised RACIST CRIME; criminally DISHONEST, mediocre, and RACIST legal system (Part), run by the Anti-Christ, Closeted Racist Freemasons for the benefit of IMBECILES.

Q. Can I take you within the draft report to our numbering at p.6 at the very foot of the column which says "Waiting room". We see there an entry which deals with the waiting room poster:

"A poster was displayed which could give the impression that NHS treatment was inferior, and possibly dangerous.

Several posters were displayed, advocating the use of composite filling materials, and which could be misleading to patients regarding the safety of amalgam fillings."

Professor Richard Boris Hill: Yes.

Q. Was that the address you are addressing?

Professor Richard Boris Hill: The issue that I was actually relating to.

THE CHAIRMAN (Dr Shiv Chicken Massala India): Can I just clarify your answer there. It says "several posters" here on the documentation. Are you saying there were posters saying that composite was better than amalgam or it was dangerous? Can you run me through that?

Professor Richard Boris Hill: I can't remember exactly. I think you would have to ask Stephanie Twidale about that because she would have had the notes; she would have taken notes on that. I cannot honestly say, "Yes, I remember what was written"; you know, apart from the fact that I agreed with the report, I can't go further than that. It would be wrong of me to do so.

Mr Hut: That is fine. We will pick that up with Ms Twidale.

Professor Richard Boris Hill: Yes.

MR HUT: I would like to ask you next, please, about the autoclave. Did you have any concerns about the autoclave?

Professor Richard Boris Hill: Again, I can't.

Q. All right, we will come back to that if need be. Can I ask you then about the storage room. Do you remember a concern about the storage room, first of all?

Professor Richard Boris Hill: Yes, I think the main one, because everything's on the same level in the practice, our concern I think was the fact that it was unlocked and it could give access to clinical waste. It would be fine if it was locked, but it was the fact that it was unlocked. Now that might have been just an oversight at the time; you know, maybe on any other occasion the door was kept locked, but at that moment it wasn't and so it's an observation. You can't say that that was to be unlocked all the time.

Q. What do you recall being contained within the storage room that troubled you?

Professor Richard Boris Hill: I think it was the various sort of chemicals that were there, like x-ray developing chemicals and clinical waste and those sort of matters. Really the problem with such a situation, obviously, is if a child is unrestrained and the door is unlocked, then they can come into contact with hazardous materials in particular.

PAUSE:

Brainless nonsense!

Criminally DISHONEST, mediocre, and racist legal system (Part)

In 2045, it became apparent that Professor Richard Boris Hill visited the surgery earlier and did not see anything wrong with any room or any poster.

SLAVERY, peonage, and HOMOGENOUS administration of the LAW are RACE WARS; unilateral wars where ONLY EUROPEANS are/were 'armed'.

Q. If we look at p.6, again our numbering p.6 within divider 8 just below the middle of the page, we see an entry under "Storage room". Is that right?

"Unlocked room containing:

Clinical waste.

Chemicals, including those for x-ray processing.

Dental supplies including sharps.

There was public access to this room.

Some items were on open shelves, others in an unlocked cupboard."

Does that summarise the concerns you have just been addressing?

Professor Richard Boris Hill: Yes, clearly the points that were raised are the ones that are reported.

Q. Then coming on to the issue about instruments, if I may. Did you look at the instruments which Dr Yinka Afrucan Bombata had in his practice?

Professor Richard Boris Hill: We looked through the drawers where instruments were kept.

Q. What concerns did you have about your findings when you inspected the instruments in the drawers?

A. I think it probably was the quality of some of them, the fact that one or two of the flat plastic instruments had some cement adhering to them.

Q. Sorry, had?

Professor Richard Boris Hill: A little dental cement adhering to them.

PAUSE:

In 2045, it became apparent that at the inspection of February 2007, Professor Richard Boris Hill was not credible, as the fabricated reports of July 22, 2004, and the follow –up of undisclosed date were live, valid and accessible. Dr Muscular Ugly-Ass Racist-Cougar described the inspection of February 22, 2007, as the follow-up of the inspection of July 22, 2004 and its follow-up of undiclosed

In 2045, experts confirmed that Dr Muscular Ugly-Ass Racist-Cougar and Professor Richard Boris Hill were criminals as they unrelentingly LIED under oath; a criminally DISHONEST, mediocre, and RACIST legal system (Part).

MR HUT: If we go to p.8 within our divider 8, in the middle of the page we see an entry against Instruments:

"Several hand instruments had cement adhering to them, and were stored loose in drawers.

Endodontic hand instruments, apparently in use, were in poor condition.

Some surgical instruments were unbagged, and loose in drawers and cupboards. Several were rusty."

Does that help you in terms of remembering what you found?

Professor Richard Boris Hill: Yes, as I said, we found that some of the instruments were in a poor state.

Q. What is the issue then, the poor state of those instruments? What issue does that go to? What were your concerns as a consequence of the poor state of some of the instruments?

Professor Richard Boris Hill: I think it doesn't do much for patient confidence to have, you know, instruments with cement on them or rusty instruments or ones that maybe could break. If an instrument is rusty at all, it could break in someone's mouth.

PAUSE:

In 2045, it became apparent that Professor Richard Boris Hill had been to Dr Yinka African Bombata's practice on several occasions and he had never seen rusty instrument or instrument with cement. No one except Dr Muscular Ugly-Ass Racist-Cougar and Professor Richard Boris Hill saw rusty instrument and cement; when they did, the fabricated reports of July 22, 2004, and follow-up of the undisclosed date were live and valid. Their findings corroborated the fabricated reports of July 22, 2004 and follow-up of undisclosed date. They were all white.

Parts of the administration of the law seem akin to organized, racist crime.

Q. Is there an issue regards hygiene?

Professor Richard Boris Hill: Hm. This is a point which I have considered quite a bit since the inspection. Hypothetically, if they're put into bags; if they're autoclaved; if the instruments are autoclaved and the autoclave is checked with the marking strips then, theoretically, it should be okay, but.

125

I suppose what it does, it really relates to the way in which the instruments are dealt with by the chair side, the nurse, after the patient leaves the surgery and I think that was what we were moving towards, was: what does the nurse do when the patient leaves the surgery? Do they then take the instruments over to a dedicated sink, clean them, make sure they are free of cement and then move on from there? How does it operate? That's what we were looking at, you know, look at it as part of a wider picture.

PAUSE:

In 2045, it became apparent that Professor Richard Boris Hill and Dr Muscular Ugly-Ass Racist-Cougar unrelentingly lied under oath, and the fabricated reports they had come to corroborate were live, valid and accessible.

MR HUT: Sir, obviously Mr Hill has not finished yet and there are some areas still to go. It is now ten to eleven. Would like to take your morning break now or would you like to continue a little further?

THE CHAIRMAN (Dr Shiv Chicken Massala India): I did not know how long you were going to be. I was going to actually have a break after you finished, but if you are going to be a while, then we will have a break now.

MR HUT: We have still got a little way to go through the report, but I am very much in your hands, Sir.

THE CHAIRMAN (Dr Shiv Chicken Massala India): We have been going for a while, so I think the Committee will have a short break now. We will come back at ten past eleven. Mr Hill, you are still under oath, so you cannot discuss this case with anyone.

(Adjourned for a short time)

THE CHAIRMAN (Dr Shiv Chicken Massala India): Mr Hurst, please continue.

126

MR HUT: Mr Hill, can I take you now to our p.9 within divider 8 and ask you something about the entry "Mercury handling". You will see that is the second entry on p.9. What were your concerns about issues of mercury and amalgam?

Professor Richard Boris Hill: I think the main one really was the fact that there wasn't a tray around the amalgamator – that's the device which makes the amalgam which mixes together the mercury and the alloy. If a nurse, for example, is actually filling the amalgamator with the mercury, even if you use a little funnel it's very easily possible to spill a drop or two. If you had a tray surrounding it, then it can be caught. The tray has to have raised sides otherwise mercury, as we know, is in globular form and it will spill across the work surfaces.

Mr Hut: What is meant by an amalgam separator?

Professor Richard Boris Hill: It's basically – in effect what it does is it stops the amalgam from going into the water supply. This is one thing which is a fairly more recent requirement because an enormous – not enormous, a relatively large amount of waste amalgam was going down into the water supply and the cost of dealing with that by the water companies was quite prohibitive, so that's what happened there.

Q. Do you remember a concern about an amalgam separator on your inspection?

Professor Richard Boris Hill: No, I don't. That was beforehand.

PAUSE:

In 2045, it became apparent that Amalgam Separator was a new requirement; a year later, grants were provided for their purchase.

The BLACK that privileged dullards are more familiar with is the unnaturally selected and genetically reversed BLACK CARIBBEAN/ AMERICAN.

Genetic damage is the most enduring residue of European trade in millions of stolen human beings, including millions of stolen children.

Q. Can I come, please, to the x-ray unit at p.7 within our divider, "Clinical facilities – Radiographic equipment". You report:

"The surgery had an intra oral x-ray unit. There was no isolation switch …."

What was the issue here?

Professor Richard Boris Hill: The whole point really is so that you are out of range of the beam. Basically what we have in the practice in which I work is we have a switch outside the room so that we are something, like, about eight/nine feet away and outside a lead lined wall and nobody (apart from the patient) is exposed to that beam. If you have a hand held cable, hand held one with a switch, then, you know, you could be within the range of that beam.

Q. I think you talk about an "isolation switch". Is the isolation switch the same as the switch which is used to operate it?

Professor Richard Boris Hill: Yes.

Q. So the concern here being that the operator is potentially exposed to the beam. Is that right?

Professor Richard Boris Hill: Yes.

PAUSE:

Privileged dullards associate RACIST THUGGERY

In 2045, it became apparent that the isolation of mobile electrical equipment is a function of where it is plugged.

Professor Richard Boris Hill did not have any problem with the isolation unit at his previous visit.

Descendants of ALIENS with camouflage English names oppress the descendants of the robbed wth the yields of ROBBERY (STOLEN LIVES)

Q. And that over time can be potentially dangerous?

Professor Richard Boris Hill: It certainly can be. The accumulation of radiation is well known within the body and, okay, it's only a small x-ray machine, it's not a OPG, the large x-ray machine which takes the whole picture but, even so, over a long period of time you would expect that there will be absorption of ionising radiation.

PAUSE:

Dunce, racist professor! His spinal cord is his highest center.

"He who joyfully marches to music rank and file has already earned my contempt. He has been givn a large brain by mistake, since for him the spinal cord would surelt suffice." Albert Einstein

In 2045, it became apparent that Professor Richard Boris Hill had Alzheimer's; only lunatics tell lies under oath. Professor Richard Boris Hill unrelentingly lied under oath.

Q. Can I ask you about the flooring; the flooring was linoleum, is that right?

Professor Richard Boris Hill: Yes.

Q. If you could turn to p.9 of our numbering, we see there under "General conditions" concerns about the flooring.

Professor Richard Boris Hill: Yes.

Q. What were your concerns?

Professor Richard Boris Hill: It was the fact that we noticed that on the edges of the floor there was not a sealant; it wasn't sealed at the edge. The problem with that is if a hazardous substance, and we will use mercury as the example again, was to actually fall onto the floor, then it could find its way underneath the skirting board from which it would evaporate.

PAUSE:

In 2045, it was detected that some Bedford Professors were lunatics; their highest centre seemed to be their spinal cord. The lunatic professor implied that the alleged mercury will only evaporate when it manages to hide under the parapet or skirting board. Mercury is a viscous fluid. Those sitting before and besides the Professor were amongst the dullest adult population in the industrialised world.

Q. What about hygiene and cleanliness issues in relation to the flooring?

Professor Richard Boris Hill: I think we noticed there that the floor hadn't been thoroughly cleaned but, again, the surgery was not being used that day. I think, again, that's more of an observation. If the surgery had been used, then the whole thing may have been cleaned. It was just an observational point more than anything.

PAUSE:

'Thoroughly cleaned' – is a subjective term!

In 2045, it became apparent that the inspection and report of February 22, 2007 were the follow-up of the fabricated reports of July 22, 2004; they were deliberately created to corroborate it.

Q. So the issue really that concerned you about the flooring was the fact it was not sealed and, therefore, there was a risk ----

Professor Richard Boris Hill: There was a risk of perhaps a hazardous substance like mercury perhaps going onto the floor and then going under the skirting board where, of course, it would, as I said before evaporate. The hazard of evaporating mercury is well known.

PAUSE:

In 2045, it became apparent that Professor Hill's speculation about mercury was a brainless speculation, not only because mercury is in a sealed capsule that is used up once mixed. Furthermore, mercury is a viscous metal that will evaporate easier when not under the skirting board.

Q. That would be a hazard to staff potentially?

Professor Richard Boris Hill: The longer you are obviously in the room, the greater the hazard to yourself.

Q. Would it be a hazard to patients if they only attend occasionally and for a short period of time?

Professor Richard Boris Hill: It's very difficult to say. I am probably not qualified to make that point. The short time the patient is in the surgery it is unlikely that there would be a problem, you know, it is more a staff problem. As I say, I can't make a comment because I am not an expert in hazardous substances or toxicity.

PAUSE:

In 2045, it was apparent that Professor Richard Boris Hill spent 'donkeys' on 'Nit-picking' that was based entirely on SPECULATION. The 'meat' was that Professor Richard Boris Hill was a criminal who fabricated reports and unrelentingly LIED under oath.

Q. That is very fair. In terms of the decoration you considered it to be poor and not thoroughly clean. Is that right?

Professor Richard Boris Hill: I suppose it was rather tired, you would say, rather than poor. Obviously that doesn't reflect upon clinical standards.

Q. What about the cleanliness of the surgery, did you have a view as to the degree to which the surgery was clean?

Professor Richard Boris Hill: I thought the work surfaces and everything like that was perfectly acceptable. There would have been a note made otherwise to that effect but, if my memory is right, and it is quite a long time ago, I don't think there was anything there that concerned us on things like work surfaces, you know, clinical surfaces, chair, spittoon, etcetera, etcetera, within the clinical arena.

Q. In terms of cross infection, before we broke, earlier on in your evidence we looked at the certification that you would have expected to have seen. If we just go back to p.4 within our numbering of the report, you state there within section 3:

"The following documentary evidence was not available …."

and then:

"e) Autoclave inspection certificate."

What was your concern there?

Professor Richard Boris Hill: Well, under the Pressure Vessels Regulations, as it mentions there, it correctly notes the Regulations that are appropriate in that particular case is that a competent person, in other words a technician, is required to inspect and, if necessary, service an autoclave over an appropriate period. Now, the appropriate period is normally 12 months, but it is up to the competent person to actually then, if you like, recommend the intervals at which it should be carried out. If there isn't such certification, then it might be difficult to actually show and demonstrate that your autoclave is working effectively.

PAUSE:

In 2045, it became apparent that the certificate had been there since 1996 with no problem. Professor Richard Boris Hill and his kindred seemed to be nit picking and throwing flares; the 'MEAT' was that he was a CRIMINAL who fabricated reports and unrelentingly LIED under oath.

Q. We mentioned earlier on about your findings, that some of the instruments had some evidence of cement on them. Does that tie in in any way with the issues about the autoclave?

Professor Richard Boris Hill: No. For example, let's take the hypothetical situation of if you had a dental instrument which had some dental adhesive cement on it and that was put into an autoclave, then provided that you carry out the necessary steps, little marker strips to ensure that it was working properly, then, you know, that's not really the point.

PAUSE:

"If the theory does not fit the fact, change the facts." Albert Einstein

In 2045, it became apparent that a hypothesis is a hypothesis; only fact is SACRED. There was incontrovertible evidence that Professor Richard Hill was a RACIST and a CRIMINAL; he fabricated reports and unrelentingly LIED under oath.

Q. Thank you. In your statement you also deal with issues of certification, cross infection control certificate, which you considered to be out of date. That in fact has been accepted by Dr Yinka African Bombata. You deal with it at p.7 of the report, if that helps you (the top of p.7 in the middle of that first box). What was your view about that certification?

Professor Richard Boris Hill: This is the one which I think you are alluding to, paragraph 3 on p.7. Is that what we are looking at?

Q. Yes.

Professor Richard Boris Hill: I think we found that it was rather out of date.

Q. Were you able to work out how out of date it was?

Professor Richard Boris Hill: No. Stephanie Twidale thought that she had seen something similar before.

Q. She can explain it.

Professor Richard Boris Hill: She can explain that. She thought that it was something like that sort of date.

Q. You also again refer to an absence of documentary evidence that the nurse had had hepatitis B immunisation. I think that is covered in the matters we have looked at already. Page 8 of the report, at the foot of the page, Protection, about heavy duty gloves:

"No heavy duty gloves were available for the nurse to use whilst scrubbing instruments."

What was the issue here, Mr Hill?

Professor Richard Boris Hill: Going back to the point I made about what happens when the patient leaves the surgery and let's take it that there is a tray system of instruments which are then taken from the chair side to a dedicated sink – and there was a sink for that purpose. It is necessary then for the dental nurse to physically clean the instruments before they are then prepared for autoclaving. So because of the nature of many instruments, for example, you can have an instrument called an excavator which will have a sharp end, used normally to remove fine soft decay usually from the depths of the tooth, and that can be quite sharp. Unless you have those heavy duty gloves, it's possible that you could actually injure yourself. The requirement is that heavy duty gloves are provided for the dental nurse who is carrying out those duties to avoid those sort of injuries from occurring.

PAUSE:

In 2045, it became apparent that Professor Richard Boris avoided the question on Hepatitis B vaccination for the NURSE. They were nit picking. At the inspection, the fabricated reports of July 22, 2004 and follow-up of undisclosed date were live, valid and accessible.

Q. And heavy duty glove presumably best facilitate the thorough and proper cleaning of instruments.

Professor Richard Boris Hill: Yes, because the nurse would be more confident without, you know, thinking of the risk that she might be put to.

Q. Thank you. It is also right, as you have explained already, that you had an opportunity to review Stephanie Twidale's draft report that was sent to you. Is it right that you were content that it provided an accurate summary of the findings on your visit. You did not want to change anything or disagree with anything.

Professor Richard Boris Hill: No, I mean, we had followed the inspection sheet category by category and although Stephanie was leading on the issue, you know, physically, we verbally agreed on each point as we progressed. So I couldn't see anything there – I mean, there was nothing that I sort of even mentally noted that I wanted to actually change.

Q. So just then for completeness sake, I am not going to ask you to elaborate particularly, Mr Hill, but at p.6, for example, of the report there is a reference there to toilet facilities:

"No towels were available. No bins were available …

A cracked mirror ….

Although adequately clean, the decoration was tired and worn."

You agree with that finding.

Professor Richard Boris Hill: That's correct, yes.

PAUSE:

In 2045, it was apparent that at the inspection of February 22, 2007, the fabricated reports of July 22, 2004 and the follow-up of undisclosed date were live, valid and available; Dr Muscular Ugly-Ass Racist-Cougar had come to artificially corroborate the racist fabrications of July 22, 2004 and follow-up of undisclosed date.

Mr Hut: And at p.8, at the very top of the page, there is a reference to:

"The aspirator fitted to the dental unit had broken, and the dentist stated he was having difficulty getting it repaired. An alternative aspirator motor had been fitted to the unit, but this was insecurely standing on a cardboard box, and had no cover. The aspirator was venting directly into the surgery below the nurse's worktop."

Again, is that finding something that you would stand by?

Professor Richard Boris Hill: Yes. It really is about the effectiveness of the aspirator.

PAUSE:

In 2045, Professor Richard Boris Hill stood by the statement that Dr Muscular Ugly-Ass Racist- Cougar made.

Dr Muscular Ugly-Ass Racist-Cougar later withdrew from the position where she stood, which meant that Professor Richard Boris Hill would have moved with her.

What does effectiveness mean?

In 2045, it became apparent that shepherds knew that their sheep were morons; sheep did not know that shepherds were morons too.

Purified ROT!!

"Gentlemen, you are now about to embark on a course of studies which will occupy you for two years. Together, they form a noble adventure. But I would like to remind you of an important point. Nothing that you will learn in the course of your studies will be of the slightest possible use to you in after life, save only this, that if you work hard and intelligently you should be able to detect when a man is talking rot, and that, in my view, is the main, if not the sole, purpose of education." John Alexander Smith, Speech to Oxford University students, 1914

Professor Richard Boris Hill vocal cords seemed to be connected to his spinal cord, not his brain; he talked nonsense like a faulty automaton.

The world is dying!

Bedford's Judge Hayers could not spell and did not know the meaning of words; his children are likelier to be duller.

If the bottom of a whole were to descend to the basement, the top of that whole should fall to the bottom from whence the former bottom vacated. There will be change but there wouldn't be relative change because the distance between the basement (former bottom) and the bottom (former top) will remain unchanged. Contrariwise, if the bottom descends to the basement and the top refuses to descend to the bottom from whence the former bottom vacated, there will be a void, which could result in disharmony or, even, anarchy.

CHAPTER 8

In 2045, it became apparent that in a dialogue with a GIANT Austrian-like Dwarf (Professor BDA Midgeto Austria), Dr Muscular Ugly-Ass Racist-Cougar implicitly agreed that she was a dullard.

In 2045, the following dialogue was reviewed:

Prof BDA Midgeto Austria: Good afternoon. I do declare an interest that I do know who you are, but for the purposes of this meeting I need to ask you some questions about yourself. When did you qualify?

Dr Muscular Ugly-Ass Racist-Cougar: 1969.

Q. When did you become a Dental Reference Officer?

Dr Muscular Ugly-Ass Racist-Cougar: I have to count back. 11 years ago, so that is 1999, I think.

Q. 1997, if it was 11 years ago.

Dr Muscular Ugly-Ass Racist-Cougar: 1997, sorry that sounds right.

PAUSE:

A detailed review in 2045 revealed that Dr Muscular Ugly-Ass Racist-Cougar was a mathematical imbecile. In 2008, Dr Muscular was in her seventh decade; Alzheimer's disease is prevalent in her age group.

Q. What did you do between 1969 and 1997?

Dr Muscular Ugly-Ass Racist-Cougar: I spent my first 11 years working in the schools dental service and then the community dental service as a dental officer, then senior dental officer. Then an assistant area dental officer. I then went into general practice and opened a practice from scratch and kept that one and sold it after 11 years as a three surgery practice. That was purely NHS. 12 months before I sold that practice I opened up a second practice from scratch in my home village and sold that again as a 3 surgery practice, when I decided to join the dental reference service.

PAUSE:

Dr Yinka African Bombata ended up at the mercy of a brainless Dinner Lady or Lollipop Lady who seemed to have failed or nearly passed in almost everything and almost everywhere.

Q. So to summarise that it would be fair to ask you that you have had experience as a practice owner working within the general dental services?

Dr Muscular Ugly-Ass Racist-Cougar: Yes, I worked from 1980 through to 1997.

Q. From 1998?

Dr Muscular Ugly-Ass Racist-Cougar: From 19 –

Q. 78? You qualified in 1969?

Dr Muscular Ugly-Ass Racist-Cougar: Qualified in 1969, 11 years in the community which took me to 1980, then from 1980 through to 1997 that is 17 years, yes.

Q. You were experienced in working in the pre 1990 contract and the post 1990 contract, but not the 2006 contract?

Dr Muscular Ugly-Ass Racist-Cougar: That is correct.

Q. You describe to the Committee the changes to the way you worked, I think you were saying from just before the April 2006 contract and that has developed since then?

Dr Muscular Ugly-Ass Racist-Cougar: Yes.

Q. Between when you joined in 1997 and whenever it was in 2005 or 2006, did you undertake some practice inspections in those days?

Dr Muscular Ugly-Ass Racist-Cougar: Yes.

Q. In what context would they be undertaken?

Dr Muscular Ugly-Ass Racist-Cougar: Again when the Primary Care Trust asked for an independent inspection other than by their dental practice adviser.

Q. Would you be using some sort of check list for those inspections?

Dr Muscular Ugly-Ass Racist-Cougar: In the days when I first joined the Reference Service, no, there was not a full check list. The check lists started developing during that period. I can't remember when, in an endeavour to make sure that Reference Officer reports were, even though they were independent at least they were all running to the same, singing from the same song sheets basically. Particularly, when it became a question of trying to make sure that what we were asking for was similar to what the dental practice advisers were asking for, so the practitioners did not get conflicting opinions.

Q. Are you able to give the Committee a ball park type of figure of the number of practice inspections you would undertake each year?

Dr Muscular Ugly-Ass Racist-Cougar: Not a lot, probably about 3 or 4.

Q. So would it be fair from that to say that your experience may be somewhere in the region of 20 to 30 practices before you went to this particular practice?

Dr Muscular Ugly-Ass Racist-Cougar: Yes, probably.

Q. Thank you. My other question actually relates to the final questions put by the GDC's counsel. I am a little confused, I have to say, about this aspirator motor venting and the filter. If I say to you my understanding of an aspirator, the motor is just acting like a vacuum cleaner from the mouth, would that be your understanding as well, of what the motor does?

Dr Muscular Ugly-Ass Racist-Cougar: Yes.

Q. Therefore the "gunge", if we can call it that, would go from the mouth, and would go out, if it was a mobile unit, into a canister of some sort and in a non mobile unit it would be evacuated somewhere else out of the surgery, would that be correct?

Dr Muscular Ugly-Ass Racist-Cougar: Yes.

Q. I am not clear then what the relevance would be of a filter or not, on the motor. Why would you report, if the motor was actually sitting separately. I am not talking about the safety aspect of a motor sitting on the top of the cardboard box or not, that remains to be proved or otherwise by the Committee, but the actual output from the motor, what the difference would be of a motor sitting on a box or sitting inside the aspirator unit with a view to bacteria contamination being dispersed. Where would the filter fit in that?

PAUSE:

In 2045, it became apparent that the GIANT AUSTRIAN-LIKE DWARF was demented or, at least, he had started to dement. Alzheimer's is considerably more common than ordinarily realised.

Aspirator motors are fitted with replaceable bacteria filters. The GIANT AUSTRIAN-LIKE DWARF did not know that; was he a posh moron?

Dr Muscular Ugly-Ass Racist-Cougar: We did not consider the filter at all. That question has been asked of me this morning, so I have not, you know, the question of a filter did not arise. The more I am being questioned, you know I am thinking about and being asked about this, this morning, the more to be honest I am not positive in my own mind now that may be the motor itself in terms of it is or is it not going to vent noxious substances, let us be honest I am not sure now. I am getting more and more confused about this myself. We were certainly very unhappy about it, and we both felt at the time that where it was was (A) not appropriate, but (B) could be the source of infection. It may be that technically we are wrong on that, I would not like to comment, or put any further opinion on that other than to say it may be that if from an infection point of view it was not a problem, certainly from a safety point of view and appropriateness point of view we felt it should not be there. In terms of filters we did not actually pick up the question of filters, that is something that has come up this morning.

PAUSE:

In 2045, it became apparent that Mr Hut was confused. If Dr Muscular Ugly-Ass Racist-Cougar did not consider the filter at all, how did the dunce, closeted racist, white supremacist know that the Aspirator motor vented directly to the surgery room?

Oyinbo olodo!

Q. We need to be absolutely clear because this point has been raised previously before you gave the evidence. The only part now you are saying that you are clear in your mind that you are unhappy about was the safety aspect of where this thing was perched, if I can use that word, you did not use that word. If I say it was put on a cardboard box. That you are clear in your own mind you felt was unsafe?

Dr Muscular Ugly-Ass Racist-Cougar: Unsafe and totally inappropriate, yes.

142

Q. But you are not now clear whether in fact it posed a risk so far as contamination to patients by bacteria or viruses or other obnoxious substances?

Dr Muscular Ugly-Ass Racist-Cougar: I think at this stage I would wish to take technical advice on that before I wish to on oath comment further.

Q. OK. Thank you very much.

PAUSE:

In 2045, it became apparent that Dr Muscular Ugly-Ass Racist-Cougar understood the significance of testimony under oath. Irrespective of the implicitly declared understanding, she unrelentingly, criminally lied under.

****

CHAPTER 9

Mr Hut: In terms of the vent, it venting directly into the surgery below the nurse's work top, what was the issue there?

Professor Richard Boris Hill: Well, again, it was an efficiency matter, you know, the efficiency, the operating efficiency and also, you know, if you like, it could possibly overheat, the motor part could overheat.

PAUSE:

The vent must have been venting inefficiently!

"Well, again, it was an efficiency matter, you know, the efficiency, the operating efficiency and also, you know, if you like, it could possibly overheat, the motor part could overheat." Professor Richard Boris Hill

The Professor reasoned like an imbecile and expressed his reasoning worse than an imbecile.

White skin concealed DARK BLACK brain.

Mr Hut reasoned and expressed his reasoning like an automaton whose vocal cord was connected to his spinal cord; a white lunatic. Professor Richard Boris Hill responded to stupidity with more beautiful stupidity. They reminded one of the MODA FAKA from Okrika in the Niger Delta: Dame Patience FAKA Goodluck Jonathan or MODA FAKA.

Some people used guns to rain hell on the unarmed and defenceless world; lunatics thrive.

In 2045, Professor Richard Boris Hill had 'lost it'; he seemed intellectually disorientated and mentally imbalanced. Why should the motor part over heat? The lunatic Professor knew that those sitting before him were mentally subhuman. He talked rot with civilised decorum and delivered stupidity with the upper class English accent.

"There is no sin except stupidity." Oscar Wilde

Q. The next line says:

"The work surfaces were cluttered making cleaning difficult. The window sill was being used as an additional work surface. The paint on this was cracked, and was impossible to clean thoroughly."

Again, is that a finding with which you concur?

Professor Richard Boris Hill: Yes.

Q. At the very beginning of the draft report, on the second page, so our p.3 within our bundle, you have your grid, "Documentation – required" is considered to be not satisfactory; "Documentation – written policies" was satisfactory; "Premises" were considered unsatisfactory; "Clinical facilities" were considered unsatisfactory; "Resuscitation and drugs" were considered unsatisfactory; and "Resuscitation – sedation carried out" was not applicable. Then the draft report says this:

"Following implementation of action on all points listed in the following report, this practice would provide a safe environment for the provision of dental treatment."

Is that right?

Professor Richard Boris Hill: Yes.

Q. So in order for the practice to be safe the action points needed to be attended to.

Professor Richard Boris Hill: Yes.

Q. By that then, can the Committee take it that you had concerns about the safety of the state of the surgery?

Professor Richard Boris Hill: I think there were certain issues obviously that you've run through that needed to be addressed. This report would have gone to the PCT and I think if they'd had felt there was something which was unsafe at that time to treat patients in, then they would, I am sure, have taken urgent action. So it's a little relative, I'm afraid and

I can't really answer for the PCT on that point because I was not party to any discussion when that report was received. That would have gone to the Consultant in Dental Public Health who would then have advised the Authority, the directors and senior managers of the Authority if there had been need to do that. I was not aware of any such discussion or I was never told of any discussion.

Q. But issues which have been identified in the report relate to staff issues. Is that right?

Professor Richard Boris Hill: Yes.

Q. Patient issues?

Professor Richard Boris Hill: Patient issues in the sense that we have discussed some of those in terms of autoclaves, this type of thing, you know, Pressure Vessels Regulations, compliance with that. We have talked about mercury spillage, so some of those are issues which could affect patients.

Q. And public issues as well, for example, access to the store cupboard and clinical waste and so on.

Professor Richard Boris Hill: Yes. As I mentioned before, you can only see on a visit – you can only report on a visit what you see. Now, it may well be (and I would urge caution on this) that that door was locked on every other occasion. I know that when we arrived at the practice Mr Bamgbelu wasn't there, he arrived a little later; but the nurse was there and it may have been – I mean, I'm speculating now; I am trying to be as fair possible – that the nurse had actually unlocked that door that morning because there were no patients coming into the practice. So to be scrupulously fair, you can't say, you know, that would have been there all the time unless you had a fly on the wall camera or something. In the interests of total fairness, you have to say it may have been different at other times.

Q. In the report you identify issues of cleanliness, for example, the cluttered and unclean surfaces and so on.

Professor Richard Boris Hill: The point really there is if you've got various materials on your work surface it is more difficult to keep it clean rather than putting them away in little cabinets and that sort of thing. It is a problem. I think if you have a well trained nurse, then that can be dealt with; I don't think that's a problem. But, yes, it was that, the fact that, you know, if you've got a lot of things on there it's more difficult to keep them clean. It's not a matter which I think, you know, is concerned with patient safety.

PAUSE:

In 2045, it became apparent that superiority based on superior skin colour was the secret supreme virtue; apartheid by stealth.

Q. The inspection visit ended, I think you have assessed it as being about half past two. Before the visit ended, there was a time of summing-up between you, Dr Muscular Ugly-Ass Racist-Cougar and Dr Yinka African Bombata where you discussed some of the areas. Is that right?

Professor Richard Boris Hill: Yes. In all fairness, it was actually Stephanie Twidale and Ola Bamgbelu. She would present the findings back to him. I was not particularly involved in that discussion.

Q. Then, as you have already explained, you received this draft for you input some time after it had been compiled by Ms Twidale.

Professor Richard Boris Hill: Yes.

Q. You later learnt that in fact the second part of the visit was not actually to take place, so you did not go back on any second visit.

Professor Richard Boris Hill: Yes. I mean, there had been no decision taken on how the second visit, which would have been the record card inspection and the patient examination part of it, was going to be carried out; whether or not I would be involved had yet to be decided.

Q. It is also right to say that you did not see any response yourself from Dr Yinka African Bombata to the provision of the draft report.

Professor Richard Boris Hill: No.

Q. Thank you very much indeed, Professor Richard Boris Hill. If you would just wait there.

PAUSE:

The standard was too low.

NEWEST APARTHEID: Subjugated, diverse merit (HOMOGENEITY) in the administration of the English LAW

THE CHAIRMAN (Dr Shiv Chicken Massala India): Thank you. Mr Moore, would you like to cross examine Professor Richard Boris Hill?

****

CHAPTER 10

Professor Richard Boris Hill cross-examined by MR DAVID MOORE:

Q. Mr Hill, I am going to go back over some of the matters you have been giving evidence about. I am sorry to trawl through these again. Can I go back to the very beginning just to establish the position about when you first came into professional contact with Dr Yinka African Bombata. I think in answer to a question you mentioned the year 1994.

Professor Richard Boris Hill: Yes.

Q. Can you recall that he first started Grove Place in fact at the end of 1995?

Professor Richard Boris Hill: I don't have a record of that. No, I don't have a record of that, no.

Q. But you would not have been in contact with him before his arrival at Grove Place.

Professor Richard Boris Hill: No. We had a previous practitioner who established the practice and was there for quite a short time. I think it was probably about a year and a half she was there. As I say, I don't have the details; that would be kept in the records.

PAUSE:

In 2045, it became apparent that Professor Richard Boris Hill was either guessing or telling incompetent lies.

Q. I am sure this can be matter of agreement but just to establish the principle, you would not have come into contact with Dr Yinka African Bombata before he arrived at Grove Place.

Professor Richard Boris Hill: No, certainly not.

Q. But your recollection is that would have been some way back in 1994.

Professor Richard Boris Hill: As I recollect it, but if I'm wrong on the date then, you know, I would certainly concede that.

PAUSE:

In 2045, it became apparent that Professor Richard Boris Hill unrelentingly lied under oath; he made almost everything up. Homogeneity in the administration of the law seemed to guard mendacity.

Q. The issue of visit and inspection, I think that you use the words interchangeably. I think you also conceded that although you use and your colleagues may well have used the words interchangeably, there was in fact a substantive difference. Would you accept that it was appropriate to use the word "inspection" when there was an element of formality and policing involved.

Professor Richard Boris Hill: I think that's probably a pretty good description rather than an informal approach which would be a visit.

Q. And in contrast to an informal visit approach, an inspection would involve formal notice being given to the practitioner and the template check list being sent to him in advance to identify the areas that would be inspected.

Professor Richard Boris Hill: We didn't in those early days actually have a template, that followed on later. We would not have a template. Inspections didn't begin within the GDS, let's say, routine inspections didn't begin until 1992. It was up to each (then) Family Health Service Authority to devise its own approach towards it.

Q. But using that distinction that you have drawn, as far as your attendances (let me put it neutrally for the moment) at his practice in 1996/1997 you would classify those as informal visits rather than formal inspections.

Professor Richard Boris Hill: Yes. I would describe them as support and mentoring activities.

Q. Before I come to the particular details of the visits in 1996 and 1997, can I ask you this – we will come back to it globally as we go through, I think is probably the best way to do it. Let us go to the 22 January 1996. We can see that behind tab 12. When you made your visit in January 1996 the problems you identify are set out there as 1, 2 and 3.

Professor Richard Boris Hill: Yes.

Q. Is it fair to say the only cross infection issue raised was under paragraph 3, the presence of a Kavoklave in the premises?

Professor Richard Boris Hill: Yes. The others are supplementary, I think we have described them.

Q. The carpet on the floor was a safety issue.

Professor Richard Boris Hill: A safety issue. Not a patient ----

Q. Not a cross infection issue.

Professor Richard Boris Hill: No, not at all.

Q. And similarly the quality of the cabinetry, you have described the risk of, again, grooves.

Professor Richard Boris Hill: That's right. It is sort of an observational point which would be addressed not necessarily as a matter of urgency.

PAUSE:

In 2045, it became apparent that an Australian Caucasian woman ran the Practice from 1993 to December 1995. That's 3 years, not 1 year. Like Dr Muscular Ugly-Ass Racist-Cougar, Professor Richard Boris Hill seemed to be a mathematical imbecile.

Q. This report which you have made would that have been prepared by you after you left the practice from your records?

Professor Richard Boris Hill: Yes.

Q. That report would not have been sent to the practitioner, but what would have been sent to him was the letter you wrote to him on 2 February which we see behind tab 13.

Professor Richard Boris Hill: That's right. The report on the practice visit would go to the Health Authority to the appropriate manager. At this stage we were looking to see if we could find some monies to support the practice development.

Q. You outlined what was necessary to be done. You said you were looking to identify some monies to support the practice development. As I think you pointed out, he had taken on this practice from its founder, the lady who had been there a year and a half before.

Professor Richard Boris Hill: That's right. What had happened was that we felt that Dr Yinka African Bombata had a problem with it because I think she had used quite cheap fittings. He was new to being a practice principal and not only that, he inherited a very large patient list. The problem at the time was that under the 1990 Dental Contract those patients within a certain time frame – and for an adult at that time it was two years and it was subsequently reduced to fifteen months – would be entitled to attend

152

the practice to have NHS dentistry. So he had something which I believe was not far short of about 4,000 patients who had been registered by the previous practitioner and that's a very, very onerous task for anybody who is coming into practice as a principal for the first time. You are having to deal with the clinical needs of your patients; you are also having to deal with all the administrative functions and you are coming new to those. I know that Dr Yinka African Bombata had worked in hospital extensively and had gained a lot of experience and he had also worked as an associate, I believe in South Wales, but it's a very different job coming into a practice like that where perhaps, perhaps, it had been less than efficiently operated in the past. So that's one of the reasons why we recommended that the patient list should be reduced. Now, obviously that cannot be done straight away.

PAUSE:

In 2045, it became apparent that Dr Yinka African Bombata was admitted to the Bedford Dentist List of December 18, 1995. He started work there on January 8, 1996. He was visited by Professor Richard Boris Hill on January 22, 1996. He was asked to make some changes; he did, and promptly. In pursuance of corroborating the lies of a white supremacist more than a decade later, he was punished for his inheritance of a decade earlier.

"How is it that we hear the loudest yelps for liberty among the drivers of Negroes?" Dr Samuel Johnson

"Slavery is now no where more patiently endured, than in countries once inhabited by the zealots of liberty."

"Of black men the numbers are too great who are now repining under English cruelty."

Q. But he took steps to deal with it.

Professor Richard Boris Hill: He took steps. He was very cooperative and he took steps. I think what Ola was doing, he was trying to do his very best for his patients. He didn't want to turn people away; he wanted to see them if necessary, you know, to treat them, but with that such large number it was very difficult. I wouldn't want to treat that number of patients or to have the responsibility for it.

Q. Thank you. You came back, as we know, in April. We have got that behind tab 14. He had purchased the autoclave which you identified as the SES 2000.

Professor Richard Boris Hill: That's correct.

Q. And the Kavoklave which was now being used as a back up machine. Just help us with a little bit of background of the Kavoklave. Are Kavoklaves still manufactured and sold in this country?

Professor Richard Boris Hill: Yes, they are. Yes, they are. It's a sort of, if you like, a little like a pressure cooker. It's quite a small machine. If a practice is not particularly busy, then a Kavoklave is probably reasonably okay. As I said, my problem with the earlier ones – and I remember talking to a Dental Reference Officer about this at the time – was that you could break into the cycle. But when you've got a busy practice, as this was, then a standard autoclave, the SES 2000, etcetera (there are others available) is certainly necessary. It just makes your job or the nurse's job a lot easier because you can autoclave a lot of instruments at the same time.

PAUSE:

In 2045, it became apparent that Professor Richard Boris Hill fabricated reports and unrelentingly lied under oath.

"If a practice is not particularly busy, then a Kavoklave is probably reasonably okay." Professor Richard Boris Hill

Sterilisation is 'all or none'.

If Kavoklave is good, it cannot also be bad. Professor Richard Boris Hill was not an expert, and Dr Yinka Bombata's predecessor had used a Kavoklave at the practice for several years.

"RECORD OF PRACTICE VISITS: BEDFORD PCT. DENTIST: Dr Yinka African Bombata. ADDRESS: Greys Dental Practice 52 Bromham Drive, Bedford. Visit Date: JULY 2004. CONCERNS: No risk assessment, no CoSSH, A Kavoclave type autoclave was present in the surgery. This type of autoclave should not be used as the cycle can be broken into before sterilisation is complete. No other member of staff were present at the visit so could not be questioned as regards the methods of cross infection control used by practice."

The report was a merciless, RACIST FABRICATION. It was withdrawn albeit more than four years later, October 16, 2008

HOMOGENEITY or subjugated, diverse merit in the administration of the LAW is the NEWEST APARTHEID.

"A Kavoclave type autoclave was present in the surgery. This type of autoclave should not be used as the cycle can be broken into before sterilisation is complete. No other member of staff were present at the visit so could not be questioned as regards the methods of cross infection control used by practice." Professor Richard Boris Hill

HABAKKUK: If some of one's ancestors were EVIL TERRORISTS; merciless, RACIST murderers, armed robbers and human being thieves (Stealer, carrier and seller of grabbed people), it'd be naïve not to expect mendacity to be part of one's inheritances.

Q. You certified at the end of your inspection in April that the premises could be considered satisfactory.

Professor Richard Boris Hill: Yes.

Q. And complied with the Terms of Service. You then came back in July following some further complaints that had been received. We have got the report of the visits you made behind tab 15. It mentions there:

"This was part of an ongoing visiting programme that had originally identified deficiencies with the practice. These had mostly concerned infection control and cleanliness issues."

Is that a reference to the specific items you have flagged up in your January visit?

Professor Richard Boris Hill: Very much, yes. That is directly related.

Q. And as far as those issues were concerned, you confirmed in July that those issues had been addressed and dealt with.

A. Yes. There had by this stage been a marked improvement in the practice from when Dr Yinka African Bombata bought it. It was then at that stage a safe practice, a safe environment in which patients could be treated.

Q. Can I ask you now the global question I was going to ask you a little earlier. Covering all the visits you conducted in 1996 and 1997, the only infection control issue that you identified on the ground was the Kavoklave issue and by the time you went back in July that had been dealt with by the purchase of the autoclave.

Professor Richard Boris Hill: As I said, I am sure that we could have a number of people who were experts in dental cross infection control and a number would say they are perfectly good.

I just have this thing about a busy practice and this is why we suggested the SES or the Little Sister which is an alternative, why we suggested that should be used. It's really the busyness of the practice and really the fact that it's much more convenient to use one of those large autoclaves rather than the slightly messier technique of a Kavoklave, where you put your instruments into little plastic boxes and then feed them into the machine. It's much easier to put them on trays and straight into the front loading SES autoclave.

Q. That is ease of use.

A. It is.

Q. And the ability to clean many more instruments at one particular time.

A. Yes.

Q. The specific issue I think you raised of being able to break into the cycle before the completion of the cycle of sterilisation, is that still current with the Kavoklave machines?

Professor Richard Boris Hill: I'm not aware of it with the present Kavoklave ones. I am not aware of it. It's not – I did once have a Kavoklave myself, but that was one of the early ones. But I'm not aware whether it's possible to break into the cycle today.

Q. Then you went back in April 1997 (behind tab 19) and by that stage a new surgery had been fitted.

Professor Richard Boris Hill: Yes.

Q. Can you help us here with the Kavoklave. In putting in a new surgery had the Kavoklave disappeared by that stage?

Professor Richard Boris Hill: I think it was in a different room, but it was there obviously as a back up.

I don't have a problem with that. If you've only got one autoclave, then what happens if it breaks down?

Q. I think again, if I can take this globally, the cleanliness issues that you identified on your first visit back in January had these by this stage been dealt with?

Professor Richard Boris Hill: Yes. It was far better.

Q. Thereafter you said that from time to time you would make informal visits to the practice at short notice and have pastoral chats with Mr Bamgbelu. I think you raised an illustration of the issues that you would help him with were staff improvements and administration.

Professor Richard Boris Hill: Yes. Those were the two major issues. There was also an issue that we thought would be appropriate and that was some communications training which we thought would be a useful thing to undertake. I talked to our Education and Training Adviser at the time at the then Health Authority about organising some sort of course.

PAUSE:

In 2045, it became apparent that Professor Richard Boris Hill was being cross- examined about alleged 1996 incidents, in 2008, which seemed aimed at corroborating the sensational allegations by Ms Bishop's Cathedral of 2007.

Organised crime!

Q. But no infection control and cleanliness issues.

Professor Richard Boris Hill: No. We found that those sort of earlier problems which had largely been inherited had been overcome very well.

Q. Coming on then to the report that you have put before the Committee, we see it behind divider 20, and although the description of the exhibit on p.1 is of a "Practice Inspection Report", again, I think you have described it in your evidence as a routine visit.

Professor Richard Boris Hill: Yes. I mean, normally our procedure nowadays for inspection is very much a team approach; so there would be a minimum of two of us and often three of us. The other two would come from the PCT so they could actually then discuss issues which are in their ambit, largely contractual matters and that sort of thing. So it would be face to face and the PCT could then interchange information with the practitioner. That is really what I would today call an inspection.

Q. What you have got here then is a repeat of a 1996/1997 style visit but by this stage you have got – I think you described it as a Department of Health form.

Professor Richard Boris Hill: Pro forma.

Q. Pro forma.

Professor Richard Boris Hill: Yes, as I said before, it was devised, I believe, jointly by the Department and the General Dental Services Committee as then was.

Q. While Dr Yinka African Bombata accepts that these informal visits continued, he has difficulty in accepting that this particular visit took place on 2 April 2003.

Professor Richard Boris Hill: 2003.

Q. It may not be of very serious import, but I would like you to help us in this regard. If I can take you to divider 21, where we have got an email from you to the PCT in the form of John Hooper, Charlotte Dowling and Sue Gregory:

"Please find attached the record of practice visits that you were chasing up. Sorry for the delay! …."

Just dealing with the issue of delay, please, can I show you an earlier email. I cannot take you to the bundle; I am going to have to give you another document. I wonder if this could be circulated. (Same done)

THE CHAIRMAN: We will call that D2.

MR MORRIS: This was an email from Sue Gregory to your good self and Charlotte Dowling back on 18 May 2005 and, as it is new to us, if I can just read it:

"Dear Charlotte and Richard,

Vicky Harrison (my colleague in Northamptonshire) has telephoned me with some continuing concerns about Mr Bamgbelu's other practice on her patch. Most of these relate to cross infection control and include disposing of clinical waste in general waste. I know that we had a number of concerns about his practice in Bedford and he had both money and support to get things right.

Please can you let me know if we have any outstanding concerns and when his practice was last inspected.

On a related issue, he has tried to get another dentist on the Northants list …."

I do not think that need concern us. So that was you being emailed in 2005 and talking about a number of concerns about his practice in Bedford. Was your understanding of that going back to the 1996/1997 episodes?

Professor Richard Boris Hill: Yes.

Q. And as you said, money had been forthcoming and he had put in a completely new surgery.

Professor Richard Boris Hill: Absolutely. It was a perfectly modern surgery.

Q. He had upgraded the surgery.

Professor Richard Boris Hill: Yes.

Q. I think there was a bit of a delay because your effective reply to that I think was the email we have got behind tab 21, is it not, in September 2006, so a year passes?

Professor Richard Boris Hill: Yes.

PAUSE:

In 2045, it became apparent that if Professor Richard Boris Hill told the truth when he stated that the reports were in the Practitioner files and accessible, Mr John Harper would not have asked him for them, and if the reports existed, it would not have taken 3 weeks to produce them; the reports were fabricated, and they were later withdrawn.

Q. You are apologising for the delay. You include the synopsis of visits. These are the synopsis of visits that you recall that you carried out. We can see that on p.3 onwards.

Professor Richard Boris Hill: Yes. These are the ones that we would have undertaken.

Q. You say "we" ----

THE CHAIRMAN (Dr Shiv Chicken Massala India): I am sorry, I just need to clarify this. Are you saying that this is the response to that email? This is your response to that email?

Professor Richard Boris Hill: I am not sure if it is. There's a long delay and I'm not sure that that would have actually been ----

THE LEGAL ADVISER (Mr Acromegaly Bonehead Mason): Mr Morris, might I make this point, that in the request one in 2005 it appears to be referring to Dr Yinka African Bombata, but the sense (and this is without prejudice, obviously) of the response in 2006 appears to be a reference to numbers of practices. Therefore, there must actually have been a request to Professor Richard Boris Hill for some sort of detail of all his practice visits and the two cannot be related because one is specific and one is general, all his practices. I would say that without prejudice to anything Professor Richard Boris Hill says. It seemed odd that you put it in that way.

MR DAVID MOORE: I think that is a fair comment. It may be an unfair way of putting it to Mr Hill.

THE LEGAL ADVISER (Mr Acromegaly Bonehead Mason): I did not want to stop you, but it did appear to be in another direction.

PAUSE:

In 2045, it became apparent that Mr Acromegaly Bonehead Mason lied or he was confused when he stated:

"In the request one in 2005 it appears to be referring to Dr Yinka African Bombata, but the sense (and this is without prejudice, obviously) of the response in 2006 appears to be a reference to numbers of practices. Therefore, there must actually have been a request to Professor Richard Boris Hill for some sort of detail of all his practice visits and the two cannot be related because one is specific and one is general, all his practices. I would say that without prejudice to anything Professor Richard Boris Hill says. It seemed odd that you put it in that way."

Brainless nonsense!

Dr Yinka African Bombata was not aware of the 2005 correspondence. He was not contacted directly or indirectly about any concern, and he was not aware about the 2003 and 2004 reports.

The request for reports in 2005, which were the 2003 and 2004 reports concerned only Dr Yinka African Bombata. The request for report in 2006 concerned only Dr Yinka African Bombata.

Only Mr John Harper asked for report, and only Dr Soft Ugly-Ass Wrinkling – Cougar responded to the request:

"Subject: RE DRS Visit -

John [that is John Harper]

I know that Richard has done practice visits to Dr Yinka African Bombata in the past, he will need to let you have the details."

Dr Soft Ugly-Ass Wrinkling-Cougar."

The response to the request by Dr Soft Ugly-Ass Wrinkling-Cougar confirmed that the request concerned only Dr Yinka African Bombata

MR DAVID MOORE: Yes. (To the witness) I think I ought to show you another email and, I am sorry, I do not think it is copied in our bundle. I have not had it copied in order to hand up. Can I just show it to my learned friend and then, if he is content, I will just read it out. (Same done)

Sir, it was exhibited but it does not appear to be in your bundle. We will have copies made of it, but so as not to delay matters I will read it to you. It is not particularly long. It is from Dr Soft Ugly-Ass Wrinkling-Cougar, dated 15 August 2006 to John Hooper, Sue Gregory (again), Richard Hill and a copy to Mrs Do-Little Fake-Ass.

"Subject: RE DRS Visit – Dr Yinka African Bombata

John [that is John Harper]

I know that Richard has done practice visits to Dr Yinka African Bombata in the past, he will need to let you have the details."

Dr Soft Ugly-Ass Wrinkling - Cougar."

I am sorry, I am taking this out of order. The original message is this:

"From: John Harper ....

Sent: 15 August 2006 ....

To: Dr Soft Ugly–Ass Wrinkling-Cougar; Professor Richard Boris Hill

Cc: Mrs Do-Little Fake-Ass

Subject: DRS Visit – Dr Yinka African Bombata

Dr Soft Ugly-Ass Wrinkling Cougar/Professor Richard Boris Hill

Dr Muscular Ugly-Ass Racist-Cougar called us a few weeks ago about DRS visits and Mrs Do-Little Fake-Ass prioritised Dr Yinka African Bombata's practice. Stephanie has been in touch a few times as her colleagues had highlighted issues from a similar practice in Northants and they would like to review report etc. etc. prior to visiting.

She also wanted to know if there has been a dental inspection there at all and I did not know the answer …. Cue Professor Richard Boris Hill have you carried out an inspection at this practice. Please could you advise Dr Muscular Ugly-Ass Racist-Cougar when she contacts you, and would it be possible to see our reports so we can be more proactive with any other queries."

I will show the witness that. (Same done) (To the witness) I do not want take an unfair point, but going back to the May 2005 email, can you recall when and what your response might have been to that?

Professor Richard Boris Hill: I don't have any record of a response. There might have been an oral response, but there was certainly nothing in writing.

Q. And if it was an oral response, can you recall what the nature of that was? Please do not guess if you have absolutely no recollection.

Professor Richard Boris Hill: I daren't guess. No, I have no idea.

PAUSE:

The response was deducible.

"MODA FAKA! I do not have reports. I will cook something up." Professor Richard Boris Hill

Q. But looking at the records that we do have, would it be fair to surmise this, that following the original concern back in 1996/1997 you had been keeping informal contact with Mr Bamgbelu ----

Professor Richard Boris Hill: Yes.

Q. ---- and there had been no continuing cross infection control/cleanliness issue?

Professor Richard Boris Hill: There had been nothing brought to my attention. We were happy – well, I was happy that things had stabilised and I was not informed of any complaints through the complaints department of the PCT that there were concerns. I am sure I would have been informed because what happens is if there is a typical number of complaints on a particular issue, let's say a number of people phone over a period of time saying the surgery was dirty or the practitioner was not wearing gloves, this type of thing, you see a pattern emerge and then I would be asked by the PCT to visit the practice and carry out a formal inspection in that situation. That's normally along with a colleague, so it's a proper and formal procedure. But I have no record of being told that there were any concerns.

Q. Coming back then to divider 21, it would appear much more likely that that email was a response to that email of August 2006. I am grateful, happy to be corrected on that. But then we look at the synopsis of visits that you compiled and we see the relevant one on p.3 to Mr Bamgbelu at the new premises at Bromham Road dated July 2004 with concerns set out there. I think it is right that in fact that was an error on your part.

Professor Richard Boris Hill: It was an administrative error which we acknowledge.

Q. So (a) there was no visit in July 2004.

Professor Richard Boris Hill: No, it was April 2003 which we discussed was, again, a pastoral type of visit.

Q. And (b) the concerns listed there were not relevant to Dr Yinka African Bombata's practice.

Professor Richard Boris Hill: Not at all.

Q. They were another practice.

Professor Richard Boris Hill: They were another practice that did not refer to him. It did in error, but it was not about him.

PAUSE:

In 2045, it became apparent that Mr David Moore invited Professor Richard Boris Hill to agree that there was a visit to another practice in Bedford on July 22, 2004; he lied. The reports were fabrications. They were withdrawn albeit after more than four years.

Q. But, unfortunately, that synopsis was sent off to the Bedford PCT in the form of Mr John Harper, Mrs Do-Little Fake-Ass and Dr Soft Ugly-Ass Racist-Cougar

Professor Richard Boris Hill: Yes, although I don't think they acted upon that as regards the Dental Reference Service visit. I think these were required more so for the Health Care Commission which is why there was a whole series. Prior to this, a few months earlier, I carried out a similar exercise for another area that I also advise, because they had an imminent visit from the Health Care Commission.

PAUSE:

In 2045, in became more apparent that Professor Richard Boris Hill lied under oath when he stated that his maliciously, racially motivated fabricated reports were unrelated to the inspection of February 22, 2007.

Mr John Harper asked for the reports because Dr Muscular Ugly-Ass Racist-Cougar wanted to review them before visiting the surgery of Dr Yinka African Bombata.

Dr Soft Ugly-Ass Wrinkling-Cougar promised to share concerns in the reports with Dr Muscular Ugly-Ass Racist-Cougar

Mrs Do-Little Fake-Ass stated under oath that the fabricated reports were the reason why Professor Richard Boris Hill was asked to assist Dr Muscular Ugly-Ass Racist-Cougar with the inspection. Dr Muscular Ugly-Ass Racist-Cougar stated that she had several discussions with the NHS about the fabricated reports. The reports were later withdrawn albeit four years after the alleged visit of July 22, 2004.

Q. Just in terms of the April 2003 visit, I think you have mentioned the Health Care Commission and you were asked to provide details of all your practice visit reports back in 2006.

Professor Richard Boris Hill: Yes.

PAUSE:

In 2045, it became apparent that the only disclosed request was the one by Mr John Hooper of August 15, 2006; it concerned only Dr Yinka African Bombata.

Q. At that time I think some of your inspection visit reports were missing.

Professor Richard Boris Hill: Two or three were missing. The reason was and the reason I suspect why that was missing was because we had moved office, I had moved office in 2002, 2004 and 2006 and the problem is that I work for one session a week and I am at the office quite often only once every other week; the other time I'm on the road visiting. What happens is that when there's a move, other people are responsible for putting all my files into boxes and then re-filing them at the other location simply because I'm not there.

PAUSE:

Tortuous gibberish!

In 2045, it became apparent that three reports were missing and they all belonged to Dr Yinka African Bombata: The real report of July 22, 2004 was missing; its handwritten draft was found. The April 02, 2003 was missing; its hand written draft was also missing. The follow-up report of the July 22, 2004 report was also missing; the handwritten draft report was found. The April 02, 2003 report was later found; its handwritten draft was never found. The July 22, 2004 was never found. The follow-up report of the July 22, 2004 was never found.

Q. So when we look at the 2003 report that we have behind tab 20, it had got lost and is it the case that this is a contemporaneous document ----

Professor Richard Boris Hill: Yes.

Q. ---- or might it have been a document reconstituted from memory following the loss of an earlier document?

Professor Richard Boris Hill: This would have been contemporaneous. Well, when I say contemporaneous, what I would do, without support, would be to make some notes and then complete it normally the next day. This was carried out of an evening. We try to be flexible. Most of our inspections/visits are carried out at lunch time and most practitioners are happy for that; it means that we can actually have myself and one or two PCT members of staff visit as well so that we can have, if you like, a holistic approach to the whole practice, not just seeing if people comply but trying to sort of find ways in which we can support the practitioner in the future. So it is a multifaceted approach. In this particular case, we visited in the evening because Mr Bamgbelu was finding that much more convenient. I don't know whether that was because he was at dual locations he could only make it in the evening, but we would normally do it lunch time. Unfortunately, in those circumstances you do not get any support because people finish at 5 o'clock and I go straight from practice. I finish in my practice probably mid-afternoon and then I arrange for that visit to be carried out in the evening.

PAUSE:

Tortuous gibberish!!

In 2045, it became apparent that the 'MEAT' of the matter related to the fact that Dr Yinka African Bombata was never given the 2003 report, and it was disclosed to him after he had been charged with the alleged concerns raised in the report about six years after the alleged visit of April 02, 2003.

Q. So this visit that you have documented here behind tab 20, you would have had this pro forma with you, would you?

Professor Richard Boris Hill: Yes, I would take it with me.

Q. Because you now have this pro forma, would there be any need to make any notes?

Professor Richard Boris Hill: I would make sort of relevant notes which are not covered by these, sort of anything to do with dentist problems, worries, that sort of thing, concerns.

PAUSE:

In 2045, it became apparent that Professor Richard Boris Hill found his handwritten relevant notes and used them to reconstitute the reports of July 22, 2004 and its follow-up of undisclosed date.

"I would make sort of relevant notes which are not covered by these, sort of anything to do with dentist problems, worries, that sort of thing, concerns." Professor Richard Boris Hill

"In 2006 the Healthcare Commission carried out a visit to Bedford and I was asked to provide all my practice visit reports. While collating this information, I noticed that some inspection reports were missing, which included an inspection of Dr Yinka African Bombata's practice on 02.04.2003. Around that time my department and it is possible that some reports had been lost during the move. I did locate some of my draft handwritten notes and referred to these to prepare my inspection report dated 22.07.2004 for Dr Yinka African Bombata's practice which at the time, I understood to be a correct and accurate record of my inspection. Following another move to different premises, I went through some of my files and found my correct inspection report dated which is exhibited to my September 2008 statement as RWH11." Professor Richard Boris Hill

In 2045, it became apparent that it was impossible to reconstitute reports with handwritten drafts, which recorded other matters

Criminally DISHONEST, mediocre, and RACIST legal system (Part), run by the ANTI-CHRIST, CLOSETED RACIST FREEMASONS for the benefit of IMBECILE (adults with the basic skills of a CHILD).

Q. It is really just the date, as I said, that is a concern because Mr Bamgbelu's recollection is that on that date, 2 April 2003, certainly in the evening he would have been in his Wellingborough practice.

Professor Richard Boris Hill: As I said, we cross referenced it with our database which their Contracts Manager was able to do to corroborate that date, otherwise it would have been changed on the database.

Q. Just dealing with the issues that you have raised. You talked about disabled access and that would obviously be apparent from your conversation with him. You make a note about the autoclave which you confirm was present plus Kavoklave as backup. Again, Dr Yinka African Bombata's recollection is that by that stage he did not have the Kavoklave, but by that stage he would have had two autoclaves at Bedford.

Professor Richard Boris Hill: Yes, there were two autoclaves there.

Q. Making the need for the Kavoklave backup rather redundant.

Professor Richard Boris Hill: Which, of course, we are only concerned with the fact that there is a well maintained inspected autoclave. So it may be that it was a second autoclave and was wrong in the detail, but certainly the practice has two autoclaves.

PAUSE:

In 2045, it became apparent that part of the administration of the law was akin to organised crime. Experts found that the 2003 report like the 2004 reports was a retrospective RACIST fabrication, which was never disclosed to Dr Yinka African Bombata until after he was charged with the content of the report, almost six years after the alleged visit; peonage or legal terrorism.

CHAPTER 11

A perfect lie is impossible because reasoning and vision are unbounded. Incompetent dishonesty is oftener guarded by direct or indirect terrorism.

Reasoning and vision are unbounded; if Christ is infinite, He must be who He says He is.

Q. I think we can now move on to 2007 and you were taken through the draft report that we have behind tab 8. Again, I think you said this was part of a routine process that came in following the introduction of the new contract.

Professor Richard Boris Hill: That's correct, yes. Just to reinforce that point, all practices who actually hold a new GDS contract are required over the three year cycle to be visited by the Dental Reference Service and to undertake the sort of checks that I mentioned previously, to wit, the inspection of the premises, patient check, record check. So it's a routine one which everybody has to undertake and it's one that well over a year ago we had a visit in our practice. I found it a very useful exercise; somebody else coming in and being totally objective is a great way of learning. It's a peer review exercise in a sense.

PAUSE:

In 2045, it was detected that what was very different was that at the inspection February 22, 2007 the fabricated reports of July 22, 2004, and the follow-up of undisclosed date were live and valid. In that year, it was also found that the fabricated reports were withdrawn albeit more than four years after they were originally created.

Q. I think your recollection is that when you arrived on the premises Dr Yinka African Bombata had not yet arrived and you were met by the practice nurse.

Professor Richard Boris Hill: Yes. He arrived shortly afterwards, if my recollection is entirely true, but am pretty sure that was the case.

Q. I am not going to go through all the issues that have been canvassed with you by Mr Hut on behalf of the GDC because a number of the issues form part of allegations that have been admitted. Can I just take you to one issue which is the display of an out of date and altered infection control certificate. I think that was a certificate that was present in the waiting room, on the waiting room wall. Is that correct?

Professor Richard Boris Hill: I think that's correct.

Q. It had been altered in as much as its date was missing. Is that your recollection? I think that is certainly the suggestion.

Professor Richard Boris Hill: I think that was the suggestion. I mean, it was not something that I picked up on myself, I must admit. It was something that I had my attention drawn to, so I can't really say what date it would have been. It's simply, you know, something which I think Dr Muscular Ugly-Ass Racist-Cougar put in her report and it was noticeable that there had been something cut from beneath it. But I have no idea what the age of the document was.

MR DAVID MOORE: I want you to have a look, please, at a couple of photographs, Mr Hill. (Same handed) Again, Sir, I apologise, I do not the moment have copies for the Panel, but I will certainly have these circulated. These were taken at the Bedford premises literally a few days ago.

(To the witness) That is a specific picture, Mr Hill, and it is really whether or not you identify the premises, first of all, as being the Bedford premises?

They only concern the corridors, but there is a view into the surgery, the treatment room.

Professor Richard Boris Hill: Yes, I can identify that as the relevant surgery.

Q. Before I pass it round, could I just show you that first, which is a picture of a framed certificate. (Same handed) Is that the sort of certificate that features in the report as being out of date, the altered infection inspection control certificate?

Professor Richard Boris Hill: If I can just refer to that.

Q. I think it is p.7.

"A copy of certification was displayed that stated the entire staff had attended a course of training on cross infection control – the date had been cut off, and the document proved to be about ten years old."

Professor Richard Boris Hill: I mean, this would be certainly evidence of an infection control training programme.

Q. I think the date on it is 1998, which would make it about ten years old.

A. So I would expect that to be really updated. I would expect staff to undertake ----

Q. That is clearly old.

Professor Richard Boris Hill: Yes.

Q. And if staff had changed in the meantime it would not be an accurate reflection that all current staff had completed that programme.

Professor Richard Boris Hill: That is absolutely correct. Most practices tend to have quite a high staff turnover. You would expect it to be updated. That's all I would suggest.

Q. Do you recollect whether that framed certificate was up on the wall not in the waiting room but in this entrance hall when you visited?

Professor Richard Boris Hill: I certainly have a memory of that document, of that poster. As I said, I am sure it was not in the waiting room, but it was present.

Q. Just to be accurate, that document, you are sure you have a recollection of it. This one has a date on it.

Professor Richard Boris Hill: Yes.

Q. Do you recollect this one with the date on it being there?

Professor Richard Boris Hill: I don't recollect the date. My memory is not as good as that, but I recollect the document.

Q. Just before I hand the bundle round to the Panel, can I just show you another photograph in relation to the storage room that you were talking about. Can you identify the door to the storage room on that?

Professor Richard Boris Hill: If my memory is correct, I think this was the door to the storage.

Q. I think that is the door that has got "Private" marked on it.

Professor Richard Boris Hill: It has; it has got "Private" marked on it.

Q. And, as you said, on that day when you visited there were no patients there; it was unlocked; and you did not know whether that was standard or not or whether it was usually locked.

Professor Richard Boris Hill: That's right. As I said, being completely honest about the whole situation and fair, my feelings are it might have been on that day only with the nurse present in the practice dealing with patient telephone conversations, maybe booking patients. There were no patients on the premises and it might have been left open for access purposes. So I am not going to say that that was a regular occurrence because we don't know.

I think that's a fair statement to make, that we can't tell.

Q. Just looking at that, there is another door immediately adjacent to the door into the storage room that we see in that photograph, is there not?

Professor Richard Boris Hill: The door here?

Q. Yes.

Professor Richard Boris Hill: The door which then leads towards the surgery.

Q. If that door is open, fully open, it would completely hide the door to the storage room.

Professor Richard Boris: If it were fully opened in this direction, yes.

Q. Yes, because it is the direction it opens in.

Professor Richard Boris: The problem is if it's not locked – and I know it's hypothetical; I'm not saying it wasn't locked as a routine regular basis – an inquisitive child perhaps could access that door. Children of a certain age can find their way anywhere and it's one issue that we have with the most conscientious of practitioners. Dr Yinka African Bombata has given a lot of thought about the layout of his practice, but one thing that people often miss is children and hazardous things and they can find them. On most – I say most, on a good number of visits and I've noticed, you know, over this year so far that we've found that even amongst, you know, corporate bodies, that we find there is something which is dangerous and accessible and practitioners haven't really given much thought to it. So that's my worry about it. There have been cases in the past involving GDPs and also the General Medical Practice, I believe, in West London once, where a child put a hand into a used needle box and obviously then the whole trauma about testing for HIV comes into focus. So it's a little hobby horse of mine really, I think. But I'm not saying that that door was permanently unlocked.

PAUSE:

Purified rot!

In 2045, it became apparent that at the inspection of February 22, 2007, the fabricated reports of July 22, 2004 and the follow-up of undisclosed date were live, valid and accessible.

New Apartheid: subjugated, diverse merit in the administration of the LAW; it conceals and propagates racial bias

Q. Thank you. I wonder if that and one other copy could now be circulated so that the Panel can have a look at these photographs before they fade from memory.

THE CHAIRMAN: Mr Moore, the issue about the infection control certificate and Charge 13 (c) has been admitted, has it not?

MR MOORE: Yes, it has.

THE CHAIRMAN (Dr Shiv Chicken Massala India): This is an admission.

MR MOORE: Yes, it is.

THE CHAIRMAN (Dr Shiv Chicken Massala India): I just wanted to check that.

MR MOORE: Can I just make plain what Dr Yinka African Bombata's case on that issue is, that the certificate about which criticism is made, it was a copy of that that was on the wall in the waiting room. The certificate that you see there in the photograph in a frame was out in the corridor leading to the entrance. (Photographs circulated)

THE CHAIRMAN (Dr Shiv Chicken Massala India): We will call that D3. We will give it a number.

MR DAVID MOORE: Thank you.

THE CHAIRMAN (Dr Shiv Chicken Massala India): Please continue, Mr Moore.

MR DAVID MOORE: Inadequate toilet facilities is documented at p.6 of the report. Mr Bamgbelu's recollection is that when you visited there were towels available and bins were available, but he accepts that there was a cracked mirror over the bath. Have you any comment about that?

Professor Richard Boris Hill: I can't recollect the situation in terms of having a memory of it outside of this.

Q. Beyond this record you cannot say.

Professor Richard Boris Hill: No, beyond the record it's impossible to say.

Q. I understand. As far as the flooring is concerned, you identified no seals at the edges in some parts.

Professor Richard Boris Hill: Yes.

Q. But as far as cleanliness is concerned, although there had not been a thorough clean that day, it was a day when no patients were being seen.

Professor Richard Boris Hill: Absolutely. There was nobody attending the practice, no patients attending the practice. I mean, as I mentioned earlier, I think that without patients coming to the practice it was not a serious issue at that moment. It may have been that the nurse at the end of the day after we had left the practice was going to do a thorough cleaning of that surface. Obviously at the time we were busy in all parts of the practice, so it wouldn't have enabled her to have got on with that job.

Q. Can you just help us with this: as you went round conducting this visit and, as you said, Ms Twidale was the lead inspector, so to speak, you accompanied her, was Dr Yinka African Bombata with you as you went round?

Professor Richard Boris Hill: Oh, yes.

Q. What is your recollection of Mr Bamgbelu's input as you went round?

Professor Richard Boris Hill: He was very helpful. He would, you know, show everything that was there. He wasn't hiding anything. He was, you know, being very useful as a guide around the practice.

Q. Was he in any sense being difficult or obstructive?

A. No. I have known Dr Yinka African Bombata all these years and I wouldn't call him obstructive in any way. He's a very open person and he would show everything in the practice that we requested.

Q. Did he dispute any of the findings that Ms Twidale identified?

Professor Richard Boris Hill: I recall there was a discussion, but then if you have two professional people discussing various requirements one may come to one conclusion and one to another. There's some very grey areas, of course. I would describe any – how should we describe it – sort of disagreement as there was as simply discussion and that's how I would put it.

Q. You commented on the need for heavy gloves for scrubbing instruments that a nurse might require. Again, Dr Yinka African Bombata would say that heavy gloves were available in the premises. I do not suppose, again, you can go beyond what is in the report.

Professor Richard Boris Hill: No, I can't go beyond that.

Q. Can we move on to the x-ray unit switch which you deal with. It is on p.7 of the report.

"There was no isolation switch for the unit outside of the main beam area. The unit was plugged into a switched socket, located behind the nurse's work station."

Dr Yinka African Bombata's recollection was on the day in fact it was not plugged in at all. Again, I do not suppose you can assist.

Professor Richard Boris Hill: No. The problem is really trying to interpret someone else's narrative. Now, I don't know whether that meant the unit was generally plugged into a switched socket as a matter of course or whether it was plugged into that socket at that time.

Q. Can you help us with this: was it a mobile x-ray unit?

Professor Richard Boris Hill: Yes, it was.

Q. On wheels.

Professor Richard Boris Hill: Yes.

Q. With such a unit would it be possible with the electric cable, the power cable, to have the unit plugged in next to a patient with the power cable going to a switch or a plug well outside the x-ray beam area?

Professor Richard Boris Hill: The beam area, yes.

Q. In case of a problem, if the operator was standing or somebody was available to stand next to the plug, the whole machine could be switched off without that person going within the beam area.

Professor Richard Boris Hill: Yes, as long as they are outside the area of the beam and they had that facility, that can be carried out.

Q. So if that were the scenario to the use of the mobile x-ray unit, you would not call that an unsafe operating procedure.

Professor Richard Boris Hill: If that was implemented, I think it would be something that we would consider to be satisfactory.

Q. Just dealing with the aspirator, please. The aspirator was capable of working, was it not, because of the alternative motor that had been fitted to the unit?

Professor Richard Boris Hill: I believe that was the case.

Q. So although it required an extra motor, as an aspirator it was actually working.

Professor Richard Boris Hill: It was functional.

Q. It was functional.

Professor Richard Boris Hill: The vent is described as venting directly into the surgery below the nurse's worktop. Obviously that is an internal venting of the gases that might come out of it.

Professor Richard Boris Hill: Yes.

Q. If that vent had a filter on it, that would prevent, would it not, any risk in terms of health?

Professor Richard Boris Hill: Oh, yes, if there was filter there.

Q. Were you able to check whether or not there was a filter in place?

Professor Richard Boris Hill: No, we didn't turn the machine over but, as you rightly say, it was functional.

PAUSE:

Ignorant Professor!

In 2045, it was apparent that the professor was a dunce who knew very little about the aspirator motor.

Q. You have described work surfaces being cluttered. The report says at p.8:

"The work surfaces were cluttered making cleaning difficult."

Did you notice whether the work surfaces were in fact unclean?

Professor Richard Boris Hill: No, I don't think there was any indication that they were unclean. I think you would have to be present in a session where patients were being treated, sort of anonymously, if you like, invisibly, to be able to see what was actually happening, if those surfaces were being cleaned thoroughly. It's just that where there are a lot of instruments on the surface, it does make it more difficult for the nurse to really thoroughly clean those surfaces. But I don't think there was any indication in this report that they were dirty.

Q. It is accepted that there were some instruments stored loose in drawers and that they should have been bagged. Dr Yinka African Bombata does not recollect there being rusty instruments or instruments with cement on them. Again, can you go beyond what is in the report in relation to that?

Professor Richard Boris Hill: I don't think I can. As I said, I have no written report on that, so I have to go along with this.

Q. Thank you very much, Mr Hill. I have no further questions.

THE CHAIRMAN (Dr Shiv Chicken Massala India): Thank you, Mr Morris. Mr Hut, can I just ask you about Charge 10 (b) of the inspection on 9 May 2005. I do not know, unless I have missed it, have you asked Mr Hill about anything to do with that particular charge?

MS HARLEY: That is Northampton.

MR HUT: I think you have the answer, Sir. There are witnesses who deal with Northampton.

THE CHAIRMAN (Dr Shiv Chicken Massala India): I am grateful. That is the one that I thought we had not heard anything on, but I appreciate that. Thank you very much.

MR HUT: Not at all, Sir, but thank you for raising it.

PAUSE:

Schooled courtesy is not the evidence of veracity or sincerity.

In the 2045, in became apparent Dr Shiv Chicken Massala India unrelentingly LIED under oath. His brain was not good. Everything about him seemed to be an act.

Re-examined by MR HUT

Q. Mr Hill, back to me. I hope I will not keep you very long. You were asked questions and in the course of your answers you explained how you yourself in fact had been inspected by the Dental Reference Service only this year. You found it very helpful to have somebody come in.

Professor Richard Boris Hill: It was actually last year.

Q. Sorry, last year, thank you, and be thoroughly objective. It was a peer review process, you said.

Professor Richard Boris Hill: That's right. It is Quality Assurance, but it takes the form of peer review because you have a colleague, probably unknown to yourself, who comes in and reviews your performance, your practice, your record keeping and feeds back information which you can then input into the way you organise your practice.

Q. So as a professional person you welcome objective constructive criticism and can alter your practice accordingly.

Professor Richard Boris Hill: Yes. What we do in our practice, we go beyond that, we do certainly a yearly appraisal. It's quite easy for us because there are six of us working part time and we split into groups of two generally to do the record check and then call in a few patients who are agreeable to come in and that type of thing.

PAUSE:

In 2045, it became apparent that what Mr Hut omitted to say to his kindred was that at the inspection of February 22, 2007, the fabricated reports of July 22, 2004 and the follow-up of undisclosed date were live, valid and accessible. He also forgot to say that his kindred, Professor Richard Boris Hill fabricated the reports. He, also, did not say that the withdrawal statement of the incompetent fabrications were fabrications.

In 2045, experts detected the following statement of October 16, 2008 by Professor Richard Boris Hill:

I, PROFESSOR RICHARD BORIS HILL make this statement supplemental to my statement dated September 23, 2008. I attach as Exhibit SRWH1 a copy of my report dated July 22, 2004, I attach a synopsis of practice visits that makes reference to a practice visit to Dr Yinka African Bombata's practice at 52, Bromham Drive, Bedford. The document is incorrect in recording that the inspection took place in 2004. No such inspection in fact took place. In 2006 the Healthcare Commission carried out a visit to Bedford and I was asked to provide all my practice visit reports. While collating this information, I noticed that some inspection reports were missing, which included an inspection of practice on April 02, 2003. Around that time my department moved and it is possible that some reports had been lost during the move. I did locate some of my draft handwritten notes and referred to these to prepare my inspection report dated July 22, 2004 for Dr Yinka African Bombata's practice which at the time, I understood to be a correct and accurate record of my inspection. Following another move to different premises, I went through some of my files and found my correct inspection report dated which is exhibited to my

September 2008 statement as RWH11. The contents of the July 22, 2004 and the April 02, 2003 report differ. The reason that the contents differ is because the hand written notes I used to prepare the July 22, 2004 also had a reference to a difference and dates and notes were mixed up. Having reviewed the documents, it became clear to me that the July 2004 was created in error. The contents of the April 02, 2003 report is an accurate reflection of the inspection done at the time and I stand by the contents of the same. I did not undertake any further inspections at Dr Yinka African Bombata's practice between 2003 and 2007. The content of the synopsis of the practice was correct at the time, but the reason why it does not make reference to the April 02, 2003 inspection is because that report was not found at the time of creating the synopsis of practice visits and reference to the July 22, 2004 visit was inserted. When I undertake practice visits, I take rough notes and write up the report at a later date, usually a couple of days afterwards in order to keep the report as contemporaneous as possible. I attach as Exhibit SRWH2 an anonymised list of consolidation practice visits confirming that practice was visited on 02.04.2003. This list has been signed by Mr J BREADBERY, Primary Care contract Manager at Bedford 23.09.2008 confirming that an inspection did take place on 02.04.2003. I confirm that the facts stated in this witness statement consisting of 2 pages are true to the best of my knowledge information and belief.

PAUSE:

In 2045, it became apparent that Anti-Christ, Closeted Racist Freemasons were the true rulers of the whole world; politicians come and go, FREEMASONS never leave.

Like the Pharisees, Anti-Christ, Closeted Racist Freemasons seemed oblivious to the overriding importance of genetics and the fact that they do not have control of it. The deluded self-appointed experts and shepherds could not discern that reasoning and vision are unbounded, and if Christ's is infinite, He must be who He says He is.

In 2045, it became apparent that on October 16, 2008, Professor Richard Boris Hill that he belatedly realised that the alleged visit of July 22, 2004 report and, implicitly, the follow –up of undisclosed date were fictitious; they were, extra-ordinarily created from hand-written draft, which recorded other matters.

Incompetent mendacity is part of lunacy.

In 2045, it became apparent that there was no other request for reports other than the request by Mr John Harper. Professor Richard Boris Hill stated that there was an impending Health Care Commission visit to Bedford in 2006, he did not specify the exact day. He was asked to provide all his reports; he did not state who told him to do so. No one stated that he was asked to provide reports for the alleged Health Care Commission visit to Bedford. While he was collating his report, he noticed that 2 or 3 of his reports were missing, which included those of Dr Yinka African Bombata. He found handwritten draft for another visit only a year later in 2004, presumably a follow-up. He used the handwritten draft, which he stated under oath recorded other matters – to reconstitute the July 22, 2004 reports and the follow up of undisclosed date.

Pretty Extraordinary!

Purified cowardice!

Like the Pharisees, the soft underbelly of the Anti-Christ, Closeted Racist Freemasons is the intellect of the individual member.

In 2045, it became apparent that Professor Richard Boris Hill expected a single report of April 02, 2003 to be similar to the report of July 22, 2004 and its follow-up of undisclosed date; a brainless nonsense by a crooked Professor that seemed guarded by the Anti-Christ, Closeted Racist Freemasons.

In 2045, brainless Professor stated that he stood by the report of April 02, 2003. Why should whatever he stood by be relevant or important? He similarly stood by the reports of July 22, 2004 and the follow-up of undisclosed date; they were withdrawn more than four years after the alleged visit of July 22, 2004.

"The content of the synopsis of the practice was correct at the time, but the reason why it does not make reference to the April 02, 2003 inspection is because that report was not found at the time of creating the synopsis of practice visits and reference to the July 22, 2004 visit was inserted." Professor Richard Boris Hill

Brainless nonsense!

What a tortuous gibberish that seemed guarded by the Anti-Christ, Closeted Racist Freemasons.

Professor Richard Boris Hill couldn't find a single report of April 02, 2003 and he inserted two reports from 2004: the report of July 22, 2004 and follow-up of undisclosed date.

Brainless nonsense!

Those regularly spun are amongst the dullest adult populations in the industrialised world. Professor Richard Boris Hill seemed guarded by the Anti-Christ, Racist Freemasons.

Q. In terms of the draft report as a result of your visit with Ms Twidale on

22 February 2007, do you consider it to have been a fair and accurate summary of the findings that you reached that day?

Professor Richard Boris Hill: I think it is. There may be some sort of semantics involved in what particular words or phrases might mean, as I mentioned earlier on, but overall I think it's, you know, a fair record.

PAUSE:

Fair indeed!

Parts of the administration of the law seemed akin to organised crime.

In 2045, it became apparent that at the inspection of February 22, 2007, the fabricated reports of July 22, 2004 and the follow up of undisclosed date were live and valid. The inspection and report of February 22, 2007 were created to corroborate the fabricated reports of July 22, 2004 and the follow-up report of undisclosed date.

Homogeneity or subjugated diverse merit in the administration of the LAW is the NEWEST APARTHEID.

Q. There is nothing obviously with which you disagreed because you were invited to provide your comments.

Professor Richard Boris Hill: Yes.

PAUSE:

In 2045, it became apparent that the agreement between Professor Richard Boris Hill and Dr Muscular Ugly-Ass Racist-Cougar was based on mendacity and mediocrity.

Dr Muscular Ugly-Ass Racist-Cougar stated that she did not have any contact with Professor Richard Boris Hill prior to the inspection of February 22, 2007. Professor Richard Boris Hill said that he had contacts with Dr Muscular Ugly-Ass Racist-Cougar prior to the inspection of February 22, 2007. Dr Muscular Ugly-Ass Racist-Cougar stated under oath that she did not have any contact with Professor Richard Boris Hill.

Professor Richard Boris Hill and Dr Muscular Ugly-Muscular Racist-Cougar seemed intellectually disorientated and mentally imbalanced.

Q. When the inspection was going on you explained in your evidence-in-chief that you were going round with Dr Yinka African Bombata as you did it.

Professor Richard Boris Hill: Yes.

Q. And between you, you were pointing out the things which were of concern. Is that right?

Professor Richard Boris Hill: I think that was the case, yes.

Q. That was the general idea.

Professor Richard Boris Hill: Yes, the idea was that you would go down the sheet, the pro forma, and the Dental Reference Officer will make comments or notes on the sheet pertaining to if there are areas which perhaps she or he would believe have not being complied with.

Q. In a sense, perhaps we can put it this way, there are different scenarios, but one would be where you go round in almost complete silence with a clipboard and a pen and you make notes, you go away and then maybe some time later the dentist finds out what you found. At the other end of the scale, you go round with your colleague, you discuss what you are looking at, why you are looking at, what your findings are, what your concerns are and the dental practitioner is there listening to all of that. Is that right?

Professor Richard Boris Hill: That's correct, yes.

Q. And that is what happened in this case.

Professor Richard Boris Hill: I am sure that's happened in this case. My way of dealing with visits is, you know, it is consensual. I never wanted to be the clipboard box ticker because nobody learns from that. You only learn from, again, it is peer review; it's actually feeding back information to people. It's only that way that any of us can improve.

PAUSE:

Those regularly spun by privileged dullards are amongst the dullest adult populations in the industrialised world.

In 2045, it was apparent that at the inspection of February 22, 2007, the alleged visit report of April 02, 2003 was live and valid, and the reports of alleged visits of July 22, 2004 and the follow-up of undisclosed date were also live, valid and accessible. Dr Yinka Black was not aware of any of the reports. So, the alleged feed-back that Professor Richard Boris Hill spoke about did not take place.

Q. The idea, of course, also is that any concerns that you raise as you find them are then able to be discussed with the dental practitioner at that time because the dental practitioner may have something to say about the concern which has been identified.

Professor Richard Boris Hill: Oh, yes. It is a two-way street. Because somebody goes into a practice and does, you know, let's say for want of terminology, an inspection, it doesn't mean to say that they are always right.

Q. And if the dentist who is being inspected has an observation to make, a comment or query on a potential finding of the inspectors, then that observation may well find its way into the report. Is that right?

Professor Richard Boris Hill: I would expect it to do so.

Q. So if, for example, a dental practitioner said, "Well, I appreciate you have a problem about X, but may I explain the reason you have a problem with X is that in fact I have yet to do Y and I will correct Z tomorrow", then that would be something which will go into the report, will it not?

Professor Richard Boris Hill: I am not certain that I can probably agree with that entirely. This type of report is something which is peculiar to the Dental Reference Service and something which until that time I was not obviously familiar with; it goes much, much further than what I would normally do. I don't know how Dental Reference Officers are trained, you know, I'd come to this party a bit late, as it were. I don't know how they're trained and I don't know whether they are told to actually put in comments or to make it as dry a report as possible, shall we say that, one which just contains what they see, what they observe and how that complies.

Q. If we just look at the very first page of the report, which is our p.2 within divider 8, there is a section which says "Synopsis of visit". Do you see that there, Mr Hill?

Professor Richard Boris Hill: Yes.

Q. The second paragraph within the 'Synopsis of visit" says:

"There were many areas requiring attention, and a full report of deficiencies follows. For each entry, the relevant legislation or guidelines is listed for reference. Dr Yinka African Bombata stated that several of the missing documents were in fact at his other practice."

And then there is another comment after that. We see there Mr Bamgbelu is stating that several of the missing documents were in fact at his other practice. Is that an example where in the course of the inspection the issue about arguably or potentially missing documentation was raised with him and he gave a response which has been recorded and noted.

Professor Richard Boris Hill: Yes. I mean, I think that is obviously a statement of fact, isn't it, but, as I said, if I go on from that, again, there is a difference obviously between DRS inspections and PCT inspections, the kind that I carry out. In those circumstances, if I carried out one of our inspections and there was certain paperwork missing, then we would ask for copies of that to be sent to us so that we could compile it. I do not know how the DRS operates in that sense and it might not be particularly appropriate or practical for those to be sent on to a Dental Reference Officer.

PAUSE:

In 2045, it became apparent that the 'MEAT' was that the inspection February 22, 2007, was a follow-up of dishonest fabrications: the report of April 02, 2003; July 22, 2004 and the follow-up of undisclosed date.

Parts of the administration of the LAW seemed akin to organised RACIST crime.

Homogeneity or subjugated, diverse merit in the administration of the LAW seems to be the NEWEST APARTHEID

Q. Just turning then, if I may, to three areas you were specifically asked about. You were asked about issues generally of cleanliness and you very fairly made the point that there were no patients at the practice that day and it could be that the nurse would do a clean at the end of the day in anticipation of the surgery receiving patients the next day. Is that something that Mr Bamgbelu said to you as you walked round carrying out your inspection? Did he say words to that effect to you that you can remember now?

Professor Richard Boris Hill: No, and I wouldn't actually expect that to be said.

Q. You were asked questions about the x-ray unit and the switch. A scenario was put to you in a sense about the portability of the x-ray unit, if I can summarise it in that way, and you said the scenario then would not be unsafe. Again, can you remember now whether when concerns were addressed about the x-ray unit whether Mr Bamgbelu said to you and your colleague, "Ah, well, it's moveable; it's just been moved and ordinarily the plug is in another position"?

Professor Richard Boris Hill: Again, I couldn't fairly state whether that was the case.

Q. In relation to the vent, you were asked questions about whether if a filter was attached to the vent it would have an effect as regards risk. Again, you gave your very fair answer, that you did not turn the machine over to check but a filter would make a difference and the machine was functional. Again, can you remember now whether Dr Yinka Africa Bombata mentioned anything about a filter being on the vent when you were carrying out your inspection?

Professor Richard Boris Hill: Again, my memory does not lead me to that. I can't recall that.

CHAPTER 12

PAUSE:

In 2045, it became apparent that Mr Hut was thoroughly dull. He couldn't have acquired such level of dullness from nature; he must have been born with it. Professor Richard Boris Hill did not say that Dr Yinka African Bombata was asked about filter. Dr Yinka African Bombata was swamped with mediocrity by brainless white supremacists.

Professor Richard Boris Hill was ignorant about the workings of the aspirator motor. He related the location of the aspirator motor to its location; he related it to efficiency. Brainless nonsense!

He reasoned with his spinal cord and spoke like an automaton. Dr Muscular Ugly-Ass Racist-Cougar confirmed under oath that she was confused about the workings of the aspirator motor.

Closeted Racist, White Supremacists hate blacks, but only secretly. When they see an opening, they dive into it.

Q. Did you ever receive any feedback yourself from Dr Yinka African Bombata addressing any of these criticisms in this report.

Professor Richard Boris Hill: Myself, no, I didn't receive any communication.

Mr Hut: Thank you. Those are my questions.

THE CHAIRMAN (Dr Shiv Chicken Massala India): Thank you, Mr Hurst.

MR MOORE: Sir, I am sorry to rise, but there is one matter I should have put and I failed to put. May I be permitted to put it on the basis that if my learned friend wants to further re-examine that he, of course, may?

THE CHAIRMAN: Legal adviser?

THE LEGAL ADVISER: Sir, if Mr Morris has omitted or wishes to put something further that is permissible.

MR MOORE: It does not arise out of questions. It is something I should have put during cross-examination.

THE CHAIRMAN: Are you happy with that, Mr Hurst?

MR HUT: Yes, Sir.

PAUSE:

Excessive, incessant schooled or fake courtesy has nothing to do with veracity and sincerity.

"Some people think that incompetence is the same thing as sincerity." Quentin Crisp, paraphrased

Further cross-examined by MR DAVID MOORE

Q. Professor Richard Boris Hill, just this: when I was asking you about the nature of the conversation that took place between you Dr Muscular Ugly-Ass Racist-Cougar and Dr Yinka African Bombata when you went round, you were asked whether there were any disagreements and you said that there were discussions, I think was the way you put it.

Professor Richard Boris Hill: Yes.

Q. Did you get the perception as you went round that Dr Yinka African Bombata thought that Dr Muscular Ugly-Ass Racist-Cougar was being a bit nit picking in relation to certain matters?

Professor Richard Boris Hill: I think that Dr Yinka African Bombata put his point of view. That's being, I know, a little bit – you know, every practitioner has a right to discuss with a Dental Reference Officer, a Dental Practice Adviser, where they think they are right and one of us is wrong. I wouldn't go as far as saying it was nit picking, no. I think there were maybe from time to time – (pause) – robust discussion is probably a reasonable way of putting it.

PAUSE:

In 2045, it was apparent that unbeknownst to Dr Yinka African Bombata, on February 22, 2007, Professor Richard Boris Hill and Dr Muscular Ugly-Ass Racist-Cougar had come to do a follow-up of deliberately fabricated reports of April 02, 2003; July 22, 2004 and the follow-up of undisclosed date.

Parts of the administration of the LAW seemed akin to organised crime.

Homogeneity in the administration of the LAW is an instrument of war.

Subjugated, diverse merit in the administration of the LAW is the NEWEST APARTHEID.

Q. Thank you, Professor Richard Boris Hill.

THE CHAIRMAN (Dr Shiv Chicken Massala India): Thank you, Mr Morris. Mr Hurst, is there anything you wish to come back on from that?

MR HUT: No, thank you, Sir.

THE CHAIRMAN (Dr Shiv Chicken Massala India): Professor Richard Boris Hill, there will be some questions from the Committee at this stage.

It may be helpful for you to know who is on the Committee. There are three dental members of the Committee. I am one of them and Professor B.D.A. Midgeto Austria, on my far right, is another one; Dr Flat-Fat-Ass Irish-Dunce, on my far left, is also a dental member. Dr King-Prawn Fried-Rice Dogeater and Ms Typically English-Mademoiselle Always-dull are lay members. We will start with Professor B.D.A. Midgeto Austria

Chief Justice: Dr Shiv Chicken-Massala India

Judge 1: Professor B.D.A. Midgeto Austria

Judge 2: Dr Flat-Fat-Ass Irish-Dunce

Judge 3: Dr King-Prawn Fried-Rice Dogeater

Judge 4: Ms Typically English-Mademoiselle Always-dull

Independent Legal Assessor: Mr Acromegaly-Dickhead Mason

CHAPTER 13

In 2045, the cross examination of Professor Richard Boris Hill by THE COMMITTEE was revisited.

Professor B.D.A. Midgeto Austria: Thank you. Good afternoon, Mr Hill.

A. Good afternoon.

Q. Can I, first, take you back to the 1990s visits/inspections. We do not need to refer to the papers. I am just checking generally. You started in 1994 as a Dental Practice Adviser.

A. 1991.

Professor B.D.A. Midgeto Austria: 1991.

A. November '91, I think.

Professor B.D.A. Midgeto Austria: And you were doing inspections during the 1990s or visits.

A. Yes. The nature of it changed. When I was first appointed – and it was originally for a six month period because the FHSA didn't know whether they had any future funding; it was a trial – I visited every practice within the FHSA's area and the reason was that as we were moving to the beginning of a more managed service, the General Manager of the FHSA wanted to know what was going on out the field. As we all know, in those days there was very little contact apart from registration and administration between practitioners and the FHSA, so I did a whole visit of practice, got the views of practitioners and then fed it back, did a whole report and fed it back to the FHSA. So the nature changed from then to post April 1992 when the Terms of Service 1992 Regulations gave the Authority the power of actually going into a practice and carrying out an inspection or visit giving reasonable notice. So the nature changed, yes.

Professor B.D.A. Midgeto Austria: You have answered my next question, actually. Moving on from 1992, I think you said, and I just want to clarify this, your visits were pastoral and you did not actually have a check list.

A. No, we didn't in the early days.

Professor B.D.A. Midgeto Austria: Round about when did you start a check list?

A. We had a pro forma from about the end of '92, but that pro forma was really more descriptive. I suppose the first check list, if you want to describe it thus, was the DH, the GDSC one, which is the current inspection sheet.

Professor B.D.A. Midgeto Austria: So you did not actually use any guidance or pro forma centrally produced from those early days until the 2003 one?

A. It wasn't centrally produced. It had been produced, you know, by the FHSA and the local dental committee. Obviously it was run past the local dental committee to say, you know, "Are you happy with this?" so that they had shared ownership of the programme. As the years have past obviously legislative requirements have increased dramatically, particularly with European legislation coming into play. So it is more, I would say today more a box ticking exercise than it used to be. But I think that's the nature of the beast; that's the nature of general dental practice. You know, one of the things that I found, certainly in the mid-1990s, that sort of time, with older practitioners was they would ask me the question: "Why is this necessary?" and I would say to them, "Look, the world has changed; the world is changing and there is so much more, particularly with Health & Safety Regulation, that you have to comply with." If we showed this list to a GDP from 30-odd years ago, I don't think they would have believed it but, as I said, there has been that drift towards formality, box ticking – I hate the terms because it acts as a barrier between the practitioner and yourself.

Professor B.D.A. Midgeto Austria: Can I take you to section 20, p.4. You have already given evidence and been asked questions about the three items that you have written, but there are some of those that are not ticked, that you have not made any note about.

A. Yes.

Professor B.D.A. Midgeto Austria: Should we read anything into that?

A. Not at all. Not at all. If there's something which does not comply or there is not compliance, then I would write it in to the box.

Professor B.D.A. Midgeto Austria: So the fact that "Fire equipment maintenance" and the "National Inspection Council" is not ticked, that is not particularly of relevance.

PAUSE:

Parts of the administration of the LAW seemed akin to organised RACIST CRIME.

In 2045, it became apparent that Professor B.D.A. Midgeto Austria was too dull to discern the fact that the April 02, 2003 report was exhumed on September 23, 2008, almost six years after the alleged visit. The report was revealed to Dr Yinka African Bombata on October 21, 2008 after he had been charged with its content. That would be considered to be legal terrorism in BOBBY'S ZIMBABWE!

Homogeneity in the administration of the LAW seems to be a tool of LEGAL TERRORISM.

A. That's not relevant.

Professor B.D.A. Midgeto Austria: Thank you. Now if we turn to tab 8, p.9, I would like to just discuss with you what you found about clinical waste. I am not entirely clear about the description:

"Open bins were present attached to the rear of the dentist's and nurse's work station, each containing a white plastic bin liner." I think I understand that, but maybe if you could describe that a bit more and then I will ask my question from that.

Professor Richard Boris Hill: Yes. Once again, I have to keep returning to this point and I know it's sort of tiresome, but it's the fact that I'm relying very much on memory whereas the report, I was putting input into the report but was not responsible for its drafting. So I think probably that's a question that would be better put to Stephanie Twidale rather than myself. I don't think I could give you a very good answer.

Professor B.D.A. Midgeto Austria: But given that you have been a few times, I think it is legitimate to ask the next question.

A. Fine.

Professor B.D.A. Midgeto Austria: Did you ascertain what happened to those white plastic bags (if that is confirmed) when they left the surgery? In other words, what other arrangements were there for the storage of clinical waste? Where did they go? I am aware that the respondent will give us his view, but what did you see?

A. I felt that it went – you know, it was then bagged and went into the cupboard which we discussed before and that cupboard would hopefully be secured and then it would be collected by a subcontractor.

Professor B.D.A. Midgeto Austria: You have just used the words that it would be "bagged", but would it be your understanding from that visit and your memory that those white bin liners would go into a yellow bag or something else before they went into the storage cupboard?

A. That was my understanding.

Professor B.D.A. Midgeto Austria: Would that be an acceptable practice in a dental practice?

A. That they would go into a yellow bag?

Professor B.D.A. Midgeto Austria: That they would have clinical waste bags in the surgery of any kind and then at the end of the day or whenever (that is irrelevant) they were taken and put into a yellow bag and then put for storage.

A. Obviously it's better if you have a rigid container into which, you know, you would put all your waste so that it's well protected rather than just bags.

Professor B.D.A. Midgeto Austria: In your experience of visiting many practices have you seen on other occasions where, if I give you an example, I am not allowed to lead you, but there is a sort of hole in the worktop, for instance?

A. Yes.

Professor B.D.A. Midgeto Austria: Particularly Spaceline used to use that design, a hole in the worktop into which the clinical waste went which had a small bag underneath it and then the dental nurse would have to take the small bag at the end of the day and put it into the yellow bin. Is that something you have seen in other dental practices?

A. I can't say that I have for a long time, no. That type of arrangement, I can't recall – I was trying to run through – I can't recall.

Professor B.D.A. Midgeto Austria: So do I perceive from that answer that the generality now is when you go into a dental practice you expect to see yellow bags in rigid containers, perhaps one or two rigid, or however many, somewhere in the surgery?

A. Somewhere which is safe, somewhere perhaps on a worktop. We had an issue with this with a particular practice a few weeks ago where they were, okay, rigid containers, but on the floor round the back of the nurse's chair. So in a safe place away on a worktop if you can.

Professor B.D.A. Midgeto Austria: Thank you.

THE CHAIRMAN (Dr Shiv Chicken Massala India): Thank you. Ms Harley, any questions?

PAUSE:

In 2045, it became apparent that privileged dullards isolated a Negro and artificially created jobs for themselves. The open bin was rigid and it was built-in with a compact dental unit. In 2007, it had been there for more than a decade. Professor Richard Boris Hill had seen it on several occasions. He had never complained about it. Yellow bags were supplied by the contractor. The 'MEAT' was the fact that they had come to corroborate fabricated reports; a follow-up of fabrications. Mr David Davis, the Cameroonian said that Dr Muscular Ugly-Ass Racist-Cougar and Professor Richard Boris Hill would have been jailed had they been black.

Ms Typically English-Mademoiselle Always-dull: Yes. I am a lay member. Would you explain to me the significance of the instruments being stored loose in the drawer, please.

A. Yes, it's a bone of contention in a way, I think. Can I just return to that so I can just read it through, read the narrative? Can you indicate which page?

THE CHAIRMAN (Dr Shiv Chicken Massala India): It is on p.8.

A. There we are.

Ms Typically English-Mademoiselle Always-dull: The fact that they were unbound and loose in the drawer.

A. Ah, yes, surgical instruments. These are forceps; these are elevators, what are used for extractions and minor oral surgery, for example. The normal procedure is that they are then placed into bags, autoclaved and then put into drawers or boxes. In my practice we put them in boxes after they've been autoclaved; but they're bagged, first of all, cleaned, bagged, autoclaved and boxed.

PAUSE:

In 2045, it became more apparent that Professor Richard Boris Hill fabricated reports and unrelentingly LIED under oath. Mr David Davis, the Cameroonian stated that he would have been jailed had he been black. Forceps were too big for the drawers. Ms Typically English-Mademoiselle Always-dull and Professor Richard Boris Hill were confused.

Ms Typically English-Mademoiselle Always-dull: So does the fact that they were loose suggest that they had not been autoclaved?

A. It doesn't; it doesn't necessarily mean that, but what it can mean is that it's more difficult to prove that they have been. So whilst not saying that they weren't, not at all, it is simply that.

Ms Typically English-Mademoiselle Always-dull: Because I think you said that the cement on them, if they had been autoclaved, then it would not be a problem that there was cement left on them. Did I understand that right?

A. I mean, you know, you have to clean. The cement has to be cleaned off. The point that I was trying to get across was that at the end of every patient visit, what happens to the instrument is they must be scrubbed before they are then autoclaved.

Ms Typically English-Mademoiselle Always-dull: I am sorry, I just need to understand this: so when they were scrubbed by the nurse in the sink, that is when you would except the cement to come off.

A. That's right.

PAUSE:

In 2045, it became apparent that Ms Typically English-Mademoiselle Always-dull seemed very dull. Cement on forceps! How? She seemed naturally very dull, even duller than Dr Samuel Johnson's Sherry.

"Sir, he was dull in company, dull in his closet, dull everywhere. He was dull in a new way, and that made many people think him GREAT. He was a mechanical poet." Dr Samuel Johnson

"Why, Sir, Sherry is dull, naturally dull; but it must have taken him a great deal of pains to become what we now see him. Such an excess of stupidity, Sir, is not in Nature." Dr Samuel Johnson

Ms Typically English-Mademoiselle Always-dull and Professor Richard Boris Hill seemed thoroughly confused. The legal process seemed to be a racially motivated legal lynching of a Negro by aliens with camouflage names.

Ms Typically English-Mademoiselle Always-dull: Then they would be bagged, autoclaved and you say you would expect to see them in the drawer in their bags.

A. Certainly what we referred to here were surgical instruments and that is specific for those, you know, you bag those up. I mean, you are not, you know, necessarily going to bag mirrors, probes and things like this, but surgical instruments, yes.

Ms Typically English-Mademoiselle Always-dull: And these were surgical instruments.

A. Yes. It's not very specific, is it? It just says "some surgical instruments". I would interpret that in the generic in the sense that it's a mixture of forceps, elevators, etcetera.

Q. Thank you very much.

PAUSE:

The standard was too LOW!

Significant decline in educational standards is incompatible with competent administration of the LAW.

Privileged dullards were speculating about nonsense; legal terrorism.

In 2045, it became clearer that forceps were too big for the drawers. Professor Richard Hill fabricated reports and unrelentingly LIED under oath.

Ms Typically English-Mademoiselle Always-dull seemed to be a brainless moron. Her superior white skin colour seemed to conceal her dark black brain. She seemed irreversibly confused. In 2045, some people state that in 2008, she acted like someone who had accepted brown envelopes.

In 2045, the firm opinion of experts was that Ms Typically English-Mademoiselle Always-dull was a lunatic or lunatic-like; she was very powerful. In an ideal world, the lunatic or lunatic-like Mademoiselle should have been knocked down.

Powerful LUNATICS deserved to be KNOCKED DOWN.

"If a madman were to come into this room with a stick in his hand, no doubt we should pity the state of his mind; but our primary consideration would be to take care of ourselves. We should knock him down first, and pity him afterwards." Dr Samuel Johnson

In 2045, it became apparent that in a dialogue with Professor B.D.A. Midgeto Austria, Dr Muscular Ugly Ass Racist Cougar admitted that she was a dunce and didn't understand the workings of an aspirator motor. Irrespective of this fact, Ms Typically English-Mademoiselle Always dull asked Dr Muscular Ugly-Ass Racist-Cougar stupid questions about a subject that she did not understand.

In 2045, the dialogue between Professor B.D.A Midgeto Austria and Dr Muscular Ugly-Ass Racist-Cougar was revisited.

Professor B.D.A. Midgeto Austria: I am not clear then what the relevance would be of a filter or not, on the motor. Why would you report, if the motor was actually sitting separately. I am not talking about the safety aspect of a motor sitting on the top of the cardboard box or not, that remains to be proved or otherwise by the Committee, but the actual output from the motor, what the difference would be of a motor sitting on a box or sitting inside the aspirator unit with a view to bacteria contamination being dispersed. Where would the filter fit in that?

A. We did not consider the filter at all. That question has been asked of me this morning, so I have not, you know, the question of a filter did not arise. The more I am being questioned, you know I am thinking about and being asked about this, this morning, the more to be honest I am not positive in my own mind now that may be the motor itself in terms of it is or is it not going to vent noxious substances, let us be honest I am not sure now. I am getting more and more confused about this myself. We were certainly very unhappy about it, and we both felt at the time that where it was was (A) not appropriate, but (B) could be the source of infection. It may be that technically we are wrong on that, I would not like to comment, or put any further opinion on that other than to say it may be that if from an infection point of view it was not a problem, certainly from a safety point of view and appropriateness point of view we felt it should not be there. In terms of filters we did not actually pick up the question of filters, that is something that has come up this morning.

PAUSE:

In 2045, it became apparent that Dr Muscular Ugly-Ass Racist- Cougar was a closeted racist, ignorant fool; they did not consider filter at all. If they did not consider filter at all, what was the basis of the Cross-infection issue apart from the Negro being a Negro?

Oyinbo olodo!

Professor B.D.A. Midgeto Austria: We need to be absolutely clear because this point has been raised previously before you gave the evidence. The only part now you are saying that you are clear in your mind that you are unhappy about was the safety aspect of where this thing was perched, if I can use that word, you did not use that word. If I say it was put on a cardboard box. That you are clear in your own mind you felt was unsafe?

A. Unsafe and totally inappropriate, yes.

Professor B.D.A. Midgeto Austria: But you are not now clear whether in fact it posed a risk so far as contamination to patients by bacteria or viruses or other obnoxious substances?

A. I think at this stage I would wish to take technical advice on that before I wish to on oath comment further.

Professor B.D.A. Midgeto Austria: OK. Thank you very much.

THE CHAIRMAN (Dr Shiv Chicken Massala India): Thank you. Ms Typically English-Mademoiselle Always-dull?

Dr Muscular Ugly-Ass Racist-Cougar was questioned by Ms Typically English-Mademoiselle Always-dull

Ms Typically English-Mademoiselle Always-dull: I am a lay member.

A. Yes.

Ms Typically English-Mademoiselle Always-dull The aspirator vent itself, could you comment on where that was situated? Not the motor, it is the actual venting of the aspirator?

A. To be honest I am not sure. We accepted the aspirator system as incorporated into Mr Bamgbelu's set of cabinetry which was all very self contained and I am assuming it was all in there. What we were concerned about was this replacement motor, the actual aspirator itself we accepted the system. I am not sure where it was.

PAUSE:

In 2045, experts queried whether Ms Typically English-Mademoiselle Always-dull was dementing or demented, as she was there in November 2008 when Dr Muscular Ugly-Ass Racist-Cougar stated under oath that she was clueless about the workings of an aspirator motor.

"I think at this stage I would wish to take technical advice on that before I wish to on oath comment further." Ms Muscular Ugly-Ass Racist-Cougar

Irrespective of the unambiguous statement by Dr Muscular Ugly-Ass Racist-Cougar, seemingly, dementing or demented Ms Typically English-Mademoiselle Always-dull asked questions about aspirator motor as if she had already accepted payment to ask questions, which she did not which to give back.

"Not the motor, it is the actual venting of the aspirator?" Ms Typically English-Mademoiselle Always-dull

What idiotic Nonsense by an intellectually impotent NONENTITY. The thoroughly dull Mademoiselle did not know that only the aspirator motor vented.

Parts of the administration of the law seemed akin to organised, racist crime.

Ms Typically English-Mademoiselle Always-dull: You do not feel there were any problems associated with where the aspirator itself was venting?

A. We had no concerns over the original equipment as it was set up had his motor not broken and he had been unable to have it repaired. I don't think we would have raised any queries.

PAUSE:

In 2045, it became apparent that homogeneity or subjugated diverse merit in the administration of the LAW is the NEWEST APARTHEID; it subjugates and propagates racial bias.

"We had no concerns over the original equipment as it was set up had his motor not broken and he had been unable to have it repaired. I don't think we would have raised any queries." Dr Muscular Ugly-Ass Racist-Cougar

In 2045, the statement was found to be meaningless. She did not understand the workings of the aspirator motor.

The aspirator motor vented through a bacteria filter. The vent and bacteria filter were visible and on top of the aspirator motor. The cretins were very ignorant but they were white and privileged; descendants of mere agricultural labourers who were immeasurably transformed by the yields of STOLEN LIVES

****

THE CHAIRMAN (Dr Shiv Chicken Massala India): Thank you. Dr King-Prawn Fried-Rice Dogeater?

Dr King-Prawn Fried-Rice Dogeater: My question is also about instruments. I am a lay member too. Can you clarify something for me. Would you say if you find an instrument with dried up cement it is a sign that they have not been cleaned properly after use and that is why it is still there?

A. Yes. You would expect that to be cleaned first and the nurse would carry that function out, as we mentioned before, in the sink, the dedicated sink where they can be cleaned before they are autoclaved. It's not exactly a patient confidence booster to see cement on instruments.

PAUSE:

Parts of the administration of the law seemed akin to organised RACIST crime.

In 2045, it became apparent that prior to the inspection of February 22, 2007, which was conducted by Professor Richard Boris Hill and Dr Muscular Ugly-Ass Racist-Cougar, no one had seen rusty instruments or instruments with stained cements in the surgery of Dr Yinka African Bombata. No patient had ever complained about rusty instruments or instruments with cement. There is conclusive evidence that Dr Muscular Ugly-Ass Racist-Cougar and Professor Richard Boris Hill unrelentingly LIED under oath.

In 2045, it became apparent that the ONLY evidence of rusty instruments or instruments with cements was the oral evidence of Dr Muscular Ugly-Ass Racist-Cougar and Professor Richard Boris Hill. There was conclusive evidence that they lied. The 'MEAT' of the matter was CROSS-INFECTION, which the closeted, white supremacists seemed to artificially create. In 2005, Dr Soft, Ugly-Ass Wrinkling-Cougar asked for reports; Dr Yinka African Bombata was not contacted directly or indirectly or in any way whatsoever. No reports were provided in 2005. On August 15, 2006, Mr John Harper asked Professor Richard Boris Hill for reports on behalf of Dr Muscular Ugly-Ass Racist-Cougar. It took Professor Richard Boris Hill 3 weeks to produce the reports, which he released on September 06, 2006. He spun the cretins that were around him that the reports that he produced 3 weeks after they were requested – were in the Practitioner's files and accessible to the Ugly-Ass Racist-Cougars who controlled him. Homogeneity in the administration of the LAW is the pillar of LEGAL TERRORISM.

In 2045, it became apparent that what the privileged dullards couldn't think is – if Professor Richard Boris Hill carried out a visit on April 02, 2003 and he found concerns, and there was no evidence that he gave Dr Yinka African Bombata the report or shared the concerns with him, and if Professor Richard Boris Hill conducted another visit of July 22, 2004 and carried out a follow-up on an undisclosed date, and, again, he did not give the reports of the alleged visits to Dr Yinka African Bombata, it would be extraordinary, unless it were a malicious setup, if Dr Yinka African Bombata was not contacted when the adverse reports laden with cross infection issues were released more than two years after the alleged visits of July 22, 2004, on September 06, 2006. Furthermore, when the she-she-man looking man, Professor Richard Boris Hill was asked to accompany Dr Muscular Ugly-Ass Racist-Cougar, he implied that he was reluctant to do so and did so only on the insistence and orders of his superiors.

In 2045, it became apparent that the inspection of February 22, 2007 was dishonestly fabricated to corroborate the fabricated reports of July 22, 2004 and follow up of undisclosed date. Dr Muscular

Dr King-Prawn Fried-Rice Dogeater: So normally if these instruments are cleaned thoroughly after each use, then you should not see any cement?

A. No. That should be gone.

Dr King-Prawn Fried-Rice Dogeater: The rusty instruments, these instruments are not stainless steel, they rust.

A. Yes, they do and the only place really for a rusty instrument is to throw it away.

Dr King-Prawn Fried-Rice Dogeater: If they are still there that means perhaps they could be used on patients.

A. I mean, what happens is that, you know, part of the autoclaving process produces condensation, produces dampness, instruments are put into sinks while they're being cleaned and, of course, you know, rusting occurs, but it's the time to get rid of them.

Dr King-Prawn Fried-Rice Dogeater: Are you in a position to tell me, these instruments that were found loose in these drawers, I suppose they were all mixed together with other instruments in use.

A. I can't honestly say if that was the case. I mean, if you are referring to the ones that were said to be rusty ----

Dr King-Prawn Fried-Rice Dogeater: Yes, because they were found loose in this drawer. So you cannot tell me whether they were mixed with other instruments in current use?

A. I can't recollect. I can't really – you know, I would not like to say that.

Q. Fair enough. Thank you very much.

PAUSE: In 2045, it became apparent that Dr King-Prawn Fried-Rice Dogeater was not aware that Professor Richard Boris Hill was a criminal who had lied unrelentingly under oath and audaciously but incompetently fabricated reports. Had he been aware that Professor Richard Boris Hill was a RACIST CRIMINAL who was seemingly, guarded by the FREEMASONS, he might've had a different view. No one else had seen a rusty instrument or instrument with cement. No else had complained about rusty instrument and instrument with cement. The only evidence of rusty instrument and instrument with cement was the say-so of Professor Richard Boris Hill and Dr Muscular Ugly-Ass Racist-Cougar. Again, Dr King-Prawn Fried-Rice Dogeater did not know that Dr Muscular Ugly-Ass Racist-Cougar and Professor Richard Boris Hill were criminals who unrelentingly lied under oath, and Professor Richard Boris Hill fabricated reports. Furthermore, at the inspection of February 22, 2007, the incompetently created racist fabrications were live, valid and accessible, and they had come to corroborate the fabrications. In fact, Dr Muscular Ugly-Ass Racist Cougar described the inspection of February 22, 2007 as the follow-up of the fabrications of July 22, 2004 and follow-up of undisclosed date. The cements and rusts were racist fabrications, which were used to corroborate racist fabrications of July 22, 2004 and follow-up of undisclosed date. The racist fabrications of July 22, 2004 and follow-up of undisclosed date were later withdrawn, albeit more than four years after the alleged visit of July 22, 2004, on October 16, 2008.

HOMOGENEITY or subjugated diverse merit in the administration of the LAW seems to be the NEWEST APARTHEID; it conceals and propagates racial bias.

THE CHAIRMAN (Dr Shiv Chicken Massala India): Thank you. Dr Flat-Fat-Ass Irish-Dunce

Dr Flat-Fat-Ass Irish-Dunce: I was just wondering, as a general dental practitioner would you have been happy to work and see patients in Dr Yinka African Bombata's practice?

A. When are you referring to?

Dr Flat-Fat-Ass Irish-Dunce: At any time during the period would you have been happy or not been happy?

A. Certainly in those days in the nineties and early part of two thousands, particularly in the Grove Place practice, I would have been happy. I would have been quite happy in those days to have been treated there because one thing that we did have at the then Health Authority was that quite a lot of patients were referred to Dr Yinka African Bombata for minor oral surgery. He is experienced in that field and we received back, you know, glowing compliments; patients were very happy with what they had received; the work was well carried out painlessly and so let's balance it out. We had the compliments. There were the complaints, but we felt largely that they were based upon (1) communication issues (2) staff issues and (3) having too many patients to deal with. But once he got to grips with the practice, you know, we did have that good positive feedback.

Dr Flat-Fat-Ass Irish-Dunce: So that was in the 1990s. And from 2000 onwards?

PAUSE:

In 2045, it became apparent that 2000 backwards was brainless nonsense. Dr Flat-Ass Irish-Dunce was, indeed, a DUNCE.

A. I think it was when we did the 2007 inspection which was a very, very thorough inspection. It goes much, much further than what the PCT would do, where there were these issues highlighted. I don't know whether it was working in two locations; it may have had a bearing on that but, obviously, the report, okay, there were disputed areas in the report, but even so they are significant.

Dr Flat-Fat-Ass Irish-Dunce: So you would have had concerns working there?

A. Yes, at that stage I would.

Dr Flat-Fat-Ass Irish-Dunce: Thank you.

PAUSE:

Parts of the administration of the LAW seemed mediocre and institutionally racist.

Dr Flat-Fat-Ass Irish-Dunce seemed to be a dunce.

SHOCKING!

"Why, that is, because, dearest, you are a dunce." Dr Samuel Johnson

In 2045, it became apparent that Dr Flat-Fat-Ass Irish-Dunce was too dull to consider the following:

Professor Richard Boris Hill was invited to state that following the inspection of February 22, 2007, he would have been concerned with treating patients at Dr Yinka African Bombata's Practice. Dr Muscular Ugly-Ass Racist-Cougar who was the hired 'assassin' was the 'chief inspector'; she was a neighbour and very close friend of Dr Flat Fat-Ass Irish-Dunce.

In 2045, experts confirmed that Professor Richard Boris Hill and Dr Muscular Ugly-Ass Racist-Cougar were RACIST criminals who unrelentingly LIED under oath, and Professor Richard Boris Hill fabricated reports. Criminals who tell lies under oath and who fabricate reports will do anything. The February 22, 2007 report was artificially created to corroborate the fabricated reports of July 22, 2004 and the follow-up of undisclosed date. If cross-infection was a GREAT issue in February 2007 and beyond, why did he did Professor Richard Hill contact Dr Yinka African Bombata (indirectly) about 2 months (April 2007) after the discovery was discovered, and why was he ordered to continue to treat his patients in exactly the same situation for 3 further months?

Reductio ad absurdum!

Oyinbo Olodo (imbecile Caucasian)!

Exceedingly dull, intellectually impotent nonentities seemingly propped up by the yields of STOLEN LIVES.

In 2045, it became apparent that Dr Flat Fat-Ass Irish Dunce was a Dunce whose higher centre was in her spinal cord; she seemed to have been given a BIG BRAIN for NOTHING. The following are among what the dunce and ugly, Flat Fat-Ass Irish Dunce couldn't think:

"I think it was when we did the 2007 inspection which was a very, very thorough inspection. It goes much, much further than what the PCT would do, where there were these issues highlighted. I don't know whether it was working in two locations; it may have had a bearing on that but, obviously, the report, okay, there were disputed areas in the report, but even so they are significant." Professor Richard Boris Hill

In 2045, it became apparent that it was the 2007 inspection, which was the follow-up of the visits and fabricated reports of the July 2004 and the follow-up of undisclosed date, which concerned Professor Richard Boris Hill. The she-she-man like man (Professor Richard Boris Hill) implied that the significant cross-infection issues that he detected in July 2004, which remained unresolved at a follow-up of undisclosed date and, implicitly remained a concern when the reports resurfaced or were refabricated, on September 06, 2006 were not a concern; REDUCTIO AD

ABSURDUM. The professor seemed to be an incompetent liar. If some of one's ancestors were THIEVES (stealer, carrier, and seller of millions of kidnapped AFRICANS), MENDACITY should be part of one's genetic inheritances.

If, and only if, some of one's ancestors were merciless evil TERRORISTS, racist murderers, armed robbers and thieves (stealer, carrier, and seller of human beings), it would be naïve not to expect mendacity to be part of one's genetic inheritances.

In 2045, it became apparent that the July 22, 2004 report and follow-up of undisclosed date were racist fabrications, and the February 22, 2007 report was created by Dr Muscular-Ass Racist-Cougar and the creator of the fabricated reports of 2004, in pursuance of corroborating them (reports of 2004).

Homogeneity or subjugated, diverse merit in the administration of the LAW seems to be the NEW APARTHEID.

Reasoning and vision are unbounded, ONLY Christ's is infinite. Christ is the ONLY living God; He is ALLAH, the God of Mohammed.

CHAPTER 14

THE CHAIRMAN (Dr Shiv Chicken Massala India): I have a few areas I want to explore. First of all, you said you work two/two and a half days in practice. Is that within the NHS?

A. That's NHS today. I used to work part time in what was largely a private practice, but over the last I think seven/eight years it's been largely NHS.

Q. Can I just take you back to what I would call the early visits in the mid-nineties and you have a series of visits that you did which were done within three or four month gaps.

A. Yes.

Q. I think in your evidence you said the first one on 22 January was following a complaint. Were these complaints relating to the premises from patients?

A. They were that and I think they were also, again, communication problems, that sort of thing. I think really, as I said, it was very much based upon the fact that Ola Bamgbelu was having to come to a practice as a single handed practitioner as a principal for the first time and I think probably, you know, the stress builds and a lot of them were in terms of that sort of thing.

PAUSE:

In 2045, it became apparent that in 2008, cretins went back to 1996 to exhume mummified lies to corroborate incompetent RACIST DISHONESTY by Ms Bishop's Cathedral Wollaston, more than a decade later. Dr Yinka African Bombata was admitted on to the Bedford Dentist List on December 18, 1995. He started work there on January 08, 1996. His practice was visited two weeks later, on January 22, 1996. Seemingly, white supremacists needed something to corroborate the incompetent, mendacious allegations by Ms Bishop's Cathedral Wollaston.

Q. You went back again in April of that year as a follow up.

A. Yes.

Q. And then you went back again in July following a further complaint. You also said that was part of the ongoing visit programme.

A. That's right.

Q. Was that a decision that the PCT made at time to keep going every three/four months to this practice?

A. I think what they did, once things had settled down, then the strategy that was decided upon by the Health Authority was to actually have a more mentoring and more supportive framework for the visits rather than it being – we have talked about the distinction between inspection and visits. They were really visits and, as I mentioned I think earlier on, much earlier on, the way in which they would deal with it would be to monitor complaints. In those days it was easier because, of course, today we have sort of internal resolution; in those days the complaints would come directly to the Health Authority, so they could keep a good record on that.

Q. So there were no concerns initially apart from the three identified in the first visit which were rectified fairly soon after.

A. Yes. What had happened very early on, there had been a whole series of complaints, but the numbers did soon fall and you mentioned after those three, yes, I was not informed by any relevant person at the Health Authority that there was a concern with the number of complaints.

Q. We seem to have a gap after that from 1997 and then the next inspection was in 2003. Why was there a gap? Was there a reason? Did you feel things were fine and there was no need for pastoral support?

A. After that time (1997) these were pastoral visits, informal visits which were I said supportive; in those days it was much less formal. Today I think under something like a Performance Management Strategy, which of course we have jointly with the LDC, it's likely that we carry it out in that way; in fact since we now have the strategy generally in which myself and an LDC member will together visit a practice where there are concerns and deal with it in that way – to start with, anyway.

Q. So even at that stage it was still pastoral, but it is a bit more structured in the sense that you have got a tick box that you have described from the Department of Health 2003.

A. Yes.

Q. You also said in answer to Professor B.D.A. Midgeto Austria's question that you had a right of entry.

A. Giving reasonable notice.

Q. Giving reasonable notice, so even though it is like a pastoral type thing, it is still expected; the practitioner expects you to come along.

A. Yes. The basis of that one was when the move from Grove Place to Bromham Road took place, so in that sense we pay a visit anyway just to see what it's like or the equipment's life; if it's serviceable; if it's safe.

PAUSE:

In 2045, experts were surprised that in 2008, privileged dullards revisited 1996 seemingly in pursuance of corroborating the evidence of Mrs Bishop's Cathedral Wollaston. Experts detected that Ms Bishop's Cathedral Wollaston unrelentingly LIED under oath.

Q. Can I take you to the last visit (February) which you did jointly with Stephanie Twidale.

A. 2007.

Q. That is what head of Charge 13 is actually based on. Were you surprised by the findings when you went to inspect?

A. Yes, I was because prior to that things had gone very well; in fact there had been a turn around in the practice. I know that there were certain staffing issues and

I think there had been quite a large turnover of staff. I think with a single handed practitioner being on the premises perhaps not all the time, that can be a problem. But that's just my sort of musing on the subject; I don't know. But I was, yes.

Q. It is just the evidence that the Committee has in front of it, you paid a visit to that practice in 2003 and there were not any serious issues ----

A. No.

Q. ---- apart from the risk assessment and the documentaries and then four years on there seems to be, well, you said it yourself, you would not work there in that practice. There seemed to be a real deterioration in what was found. Do you think that is because of the nature of the inspection, in other words, if you had done an inspection as thoroughly in 2003 you may have found the same deficiencies because you were looking at similar areas? Do you generally feel that there was a big deterioration in the standards within that practice?

A. I think it might be a mixture of the two in a way. I mean, as we have seen, the DRS inspection takes five or six times the amount of time that the PCT one does and it is necessarily intended to be a policing role, a very, very thorough policing role.

Q. But you were still looking at similar issues though.

A. We were looking at similar issues but not as extensive, not quite as much in depth and we have to separate what the purpose of those are. We carry out the two very much these days in tandem in the three year cycle. That would be carried out normally first; the PCT visit would be first and then later on – this is the strategy we have adopted over the last couple of years – we would follow on from that.

Q. Just as an example and, I am sorry, I just need to clarify this in my own head as to the way the inspections were done because the Quality Assurance statement that needed to be displayed, you had ticked the box and said that it was there and it was fine.

A. Yes, that was fine.

Q. And three years on, now does that mean there was no statement on the wall when that visit happened or did you look at other things?

A. Yes, we looked at other things. We looked at it in the generality. In other words, you know, is Clinical Governance being observed? Things like, for example, CPD; things like compliance with quality of treatment; things like a complaint system; all those things in place that actually go to make up the whole ambit of good Clinical Governance. I think what was intended, but this never actually happened, was that the PCTs (and I think that's the point of that particular box) would actually every year give practices that were complying with their Clinical Governance requirements a certificate. It was intended that obviously there would be a greater development of Clinical Governance, much more so than actually has happened so far, with Clinical Governance officers actually working with practices. I think a large part of that – we do have somebody that does that, but very part time and has to actually deal with GPs and every other health professional. So what it was going to be, it was going to certainly be, you know, a much more structured system with certification, re-certification each year. But so far that hasn't happened.

Q. Just one last question: the last visit again with Stephanie Twidale you said in your evidence it was suggested to you that you go along. Is it unusual for you to accompany a Dental Reference Officer?

A. I've never been asked before.

Q. Do you know why you were asked? Did you ask why you were asked?

A. I've no idea. I think probably – the answer I think I was given was, you know, to represent the PCT. It was really the fact that it would be between the two of us, that was myself as Dental Practice Adviser and Sue Gregory as Consultant in Dental Public Health. Sue has many other duties; she is incredibly busy, so she asked if

I would go and carry it out.

Q. I am grateful. I am sorry, there is an additional question from Professor B.D.A. Midgeto Austria.

Professor B.D.A. Midgeto Austria: Clearly from the answers you have been giving us, you had a good working relationship the respondent during the last ten years or so. Have you experienced any personally insulting or degrading behaviour or dismissive behaviour to you in any of your visits?

A. No. Dr Yinka African Bombata has always been open, welcoming and helpful. There has never been anything that can possibly approach that sort of description.

THE CHAIRMAN (Dr Shiv Chicken Massala India): Thank you very much. I think those are all the questions we have. There may be some questions arising from our questions. I will ask Mr Hurst first.

MR HUT: Thank you, Sir.

Further re-examined by MR HUT

Q. You were asked questions about the instruments and about the cement which was still attached to some of the instruments and you said you would have to clean off the cement; they have to be scrubbed before they are autoclaved. Does it then follow that if they are not scrubbed before they are autoclaved they have not been cleaned properly?

A. I think that's a fair assessment.

Q. You were asked about the bagging of surgical instruments and you said it is accepted wisdom to bag surgical instruments. Wisdom going to what? Why is it wise to bag your surgical instruments?

A. Well, so that you can demonstrate that they are perfectly sterile. The bag ----

Q. So if you have an unbagged – I am sorry, I interrupted you. Go ahead.

A. The bag will actually have a little mark on there which then, you know, once autoclaving is complete, once the cycle is complete satisfactorily, then it will indicate from the colour change that that is okay.

Q. So an unbagged instrument may not be a sterile instrument.

A. It may not be. I will return to the point I made earlier, if you were challenged it would be more difficult to demonstrate so.

Q. But leaving aside the question of challenging for now, the point about bagging them is to keep them sterile?

A. Oh, yes.

Q. And, therefore, if they are not bagged there is a risk that they are not sterile.

A. It depends where they are put and depends how you actually store them. In drawers, for example, and it depends how long it's going to be before you use them, but surgical instruments I would say, you know, you need to bag.

Q. In order to keep them sterile. In terms of the cleaning of instruments, you explained it would be the nurse who would clean them and scrub them. If they are not, however, kept clean and although it may be the nurse's job, it still follows, presumably, that it is the dentist's overall responsibility to ensure that the instruments are clean?

A. Yes. I mean, the dentist is obviously responsible for the action of their staff, albeit vicariously at times.

Q. Thank you.

Vicarious responsibility!

PAUSE:

Vicarious responsibility!

Brainless Nonsense! Mediocre, Dishonest and Racist Descendant of Thieves: stealer, carrier, and seller of bodies

In 2045, experts concluded that Professor Richard Boris Hill and Dr Muscular Ugly-Ass Racist- Cougar unrelentingly lied under oath. Reverend Cameroon stated that they were likelier to be jailed had they been black.

"Michael Jackson would have been jailed if he'd been black." Jo Brand

In 2045, experts corroborated the fact that Professor Richard Boris Hill criminally fabricated reports.

THE CHAIRMAN (Dr Shiv Chicken Massala India): Mr Morris, is there anything?

224

MR DAVID MOORE: Yes, please, Sir.

Further cross-examined by MR DAVID MOORE:

Q. I just want to follow on really from Ms Brady's question. I think you said at Grove Place you would be happy to be treated there. We know, I think, or do you accept, that Mr Bamgbelu moved from Grove Place to Bromham Road in 2000 and, thereafter, your informal visiting continued? Prior to the concerns that were apparent to you in 2007 when you came to that, would you have been happy to be treated there at Bromham Road?

A. I certainly would, yes.

Q. The Chairman asked you whether it was possible that the less formal shorter visits that you were conducting prior to the full inspection in 2007 might have meant that you were not picking up on some of the concerns that were being raised in 2007. Just on that issue, looking at the Department of Health form that you had and said that you used in 2003 behind tab 20, just help us, please, and I am sure you have given the answer already, when did those forms come into use by you?

A. They would have been – I'm trying to actually establish it in relation to other events because there was never actually a date on the form actually put there by the Department. I would have said – and don't take this with any complete accuracy – it was 2002. I would have said it was then when we did this type of form, when we had this for the first time. I may be wrong, but I can't be absolutely certain.

Q. In relation to that form, would there have been any entry that you had made or any box that you ticked indicating compliance where you had not satisfied yourself you were entitled to make that entry?

A. No.

Q. Just help us, please, with the open bins that is described on p.9 of the report at divider 8. You were asked a question by Mr Kravitz about that.

The unit that Mr Bamgbelu had in relation to the waste in his surgery was a Cacan (C-a-c-a-n) unit. Does that mean anything to you?

A. It's not one that I am generally familiar with, no. I mean, I have seen the equipment, but it's not one which I generally have familiarity.

Q. But the bins that were there in the surgery were in a unit and as far as you could see were only used for non domestic waste.

A. Yes, clinical waste.

Q. Thank you very much.

PAUSE:

Ignorant descendant of merciless, racist murderers and human being THIEVES.

In 2045, experts concluded that the inspection report of February 22, 2007 was deliberately created to corroborate the fabricated reports of July 22, 2004 and the follow-up of undisclosed date.

If some of one's ancestors were merciless, racist, murderers, cowards, armed robbers and HUMAN BEING THIEVES, mendacity should be part of one's inheritances - HABAKKUK

What was the value of a criminal (Racist Perjurer) witness who unrelentingly LIED under oath?

THE CHAIRMAN (Dr Shiv Chicken Massala India): Thank you very much, Professor Richard Boris Hill. I know it has been quite a long morning. Thank you very much for coming to assist us.

PAUSE:

Imbecile Member! Imbecile Indian!

In 2045, experts found that Professor Richard Boris Hill and Dr Muscular Ugly-Ass Racist-Cougar unrelentingly lied under oath; their dunce Indian, with very high title, also lied under oath. The findings of the experts revealed that Professor Richard Boris Hill criminally fabricated reports.

THE CHAIRMAN (Dr Shiv Chicken Massala India): The Committee will now rise for lunch. It is quarter to two now; we will return at quarter to three.

(Luncheon adjournment)

CHAPTER 15

Chief Justice: Dr Shiv Chicken-Massala India

Judge 1: Professor B.D.A. Midgeto Austria

Judge 2: Dr Flat-Fat-Ass Irish-Dunce

Judge 3: Dr King-Prawn Fried-Rice Dogeater

Judge 4: Ms Typically English-Mademoiselle Always-dull

Independent Legal Assessor: Mr Acromegaly-Dickhead Mason

THE CHAIRMAN (Dr Shiv Chicken Massala India): Yes, Mr Hut, would you care to continue.

MR HUT: Sir, I am not sure whether this is an appropriate time for us to canvass another matter?

THE CHAIRMAN (Dr Shiv Chicken Massala India): Yes, there is a declaration of interest on two of the witnesses by two of the members of the Panel which I will allow the members to first make and then invite views from both sides on that. Professor B.D.A. Midgeto Austria

Professor B.D.A. Midgeto Austria: Yes. I would like to make a declaration of interest that I did serve on a Committee at the BDA with Dr Muscular Ugly-Ass. I am trying to assess how long ago; it was somewhere between 15 and 20 years ago. We have no particular professional relationship and I have not had anything other than a passing hello contact with her during the last 15 to 20 years. I personally do not perceive I have any conflict of interest.

PAUSE:

Mediocre Dwarf; Missing Link! Thoroughly mediocre and confused!

In 2045, experts decided that CONFLICT OF INTEREST should have been 'all or none', as crooks who fiddle expenses get to the top at the BDA in Bedford Massachusetts.

THE CHAIRMAN (Dr Shiv Chicken Massala India): Thank you very much, Professor BDA Midgeto Austria. Dr Flat-Fat-Ass Irish Dunce.

Dr Flat-Fat-Ass Irish Dunce: I have known Stephanie Twidale for 12 years. We live in villages that are adjacent to each other by five miles and we both own practices in those villages. During the time she owed her practices, we shared emergency cover for our patients which was not arranged by us, which was arranged by the managers. She has been my Regional Dental Officer since I started that practice about 12 years ago which led into her being my Dental Reference Officer; and she has inspected both of my practices in August of this year.

I also know Kevin Atkinson, who I have known for seven years professionally. We are both Vocational Dental Practitioners on the same scheme and during that seven years I have had educational and social contact with him on a very regular basis

THE CHAIRMAN (Dr Shiv Chicken Massala India): Thank you, Dr Flat-Fat-Ass Irish Dunce. Can I invite views now from both parties on that.

PAUSE:

Deceit!

Incompetent art incompetently imitates life. Crooked Freemasons' Justice

MR HUT: Sir, I think probably it is very much more a matter for Mr David Moore.

THE CHAIRMAN (Dr Shiv Chicken Massala India): Mr David Moore.

MR MOORE: Sir, your learned Legal Adviser (Mr Acromegaly Dick-Head Mason), kindly alerted me to the declaration of interest that Dr Flat-Fat-Ass Irish Dunce was going to make and outlined roughly what that was to be. I have not had a chance to discuss Professor BDA Midgeto Austria declaration. If I may just have a short word with Dr Yinka African Bombata?

PAUSE:

In 2045, experts decided that the problem with Dr Flat-Fat Ass Irish Dunce transcends 'conflict of interest' as she seemed to display some of the clinical manifestations of Alzheimer's disease.

In 2045, experts revisited the 2008 dialogues between Dr Flat Fat Ass Irish Dunce and Ms Bishop's Cathedral Wollaston. The dialogue revealed that the highest centre of Dr Flat-Fat-Ass Irish Dunce was her spinal cord, which meant that she had been given a big brain for nothing.

"He who joyfully marches to music rank and file, has already earned my contempt. He has been given a large brain by mistake, since for him the spinal cord would surely suffice. This disgrace to civilization should be done away with at once. Heroism at command, how violently I hate all this, how despicable and ignoble war is; I would rather be torn to shreds than be a part of so base an action. It is my conviction that killing under the cloak of war is nothing but an act of murder." Albert Einstein

In 2045, experts re-examined a dialogue in 2008:

DR FLAT-FAT-ASS IRISH DUNCE: When you went to the maxillofacial department did you have any idea of the qualifications that the surgeons there might have? Did you know whether or not they were primarily medical, dental, both, either?

MS BISHOP'S CATHEDRAL WOLLASTON: No, not really. At the time, looking back in hindsight now you think "Why didn't I do this, why didn't I do that?" but at the time I was in absolute pain, I couldn't see out of one eye; I had children to care for, I couldn't drive, I couldn't eat, I couldn't go to work; I was in a right mess really. So you don't always think in the way that you would if you are in full health.

PAUSE:

"When you went to the maxillofacial department did you have any idea of the qualifications that the surgeons there might have? Did you know whether or not they were primarily medical, dental, both, either?" DR FLAT-FAT-ASS RACIST COUGAR

Reductio Ad Absurdum!

Meaningless, Brainless Nonsense!

****

THE CHAIRMAN (Dr Shiv Chicken Massala India): Yes, by all means.

MR DAVID MOORE: (After conferring with Dr Yinka African Bombata) We do not have any concern about Professor BDA Midgeto Austria's connection with Dr Muscular Ugly-Ass Racist-Cougar, but there is concern about Dr Flat-Fat-Ass Irish Dunce's connection with Dr Muscular Ugly-Ass Racist- Cougar and, indeed, with the Scottish Professor (Postgraduate tutor).

In relation to the connection with Dr Muscular Ugly-Ass Racist-Cougar, it would appear to be clear from the declaration (for which, of course, we are extremely grateful) that she has had professional dealings with her both in the context of shared emergency cover and also in relation to Dr Muscular Ugly-Ass Racist-Cougar being her RDO and then subsequently her Dental Reference Officer, having conducted an inspection earlier this year. As a result of that professional contact, inevitably Ms Brady has additional information over and above that which is available in evidence given by Dr Muscular Ugly-Ass Racist-Cougar to this Panel with which to come to a conclusion and make judgments about Dr Muscular Ugly-Ass Racist-Cougar. I think it would be asking the impossible for her to exclude that information which must be or should be extraneous to this hearing when coming to consider the evidence that Ms Twidale is going to give and, of course, in some significant respects Dr Muscular Ugly-Ass Racist-Cougar evidence is challenged by Dr Yinka African Bombata

In those circumstances, it appears to me, as I said, it would be impossible to expect Ms Brady to put to one side any views which she understandably would have formed about Ms Twidale as a professional person and colleague.

A similar submission really is made in relation to her connection with the Scottish Professor (Postgraduate tutor), which stretches over seven years and comprises both the professional sphere and a social sphere. Clearly, again, she has information about a GDDDC witness which is really extraneous to a consideration of that witness's evidence by this Committee. Again, it would appear, in my submission, impossible to invite her or to expect her fairly to put that information to one side when coming to draw conclusions about Scottish Professor's (Postgraduate tutor) evidence. Again, that evidence will be challenged in some significant respects.

That being the case, it would appear to me and it would be my submission that there must be an appearance of perceived bias (I am not suggesting actual bias, but perceived bias) which in all the circumstances would, in my submission, make it impossible to continue with her on your Committee and at the same time ensure a fair trial of these allegations.

PAUSE

Brainless tortuous gibberish by a descendant of thieves: stealer, carrier, and seller of human beings.

Peonage: They created jobs for white privileged lawyers and others within the legal system of one of the least literate countries in the industrialised world.

In 2045, experts wonder why Mr David Moore wanted Dr Yinka African Bombata to reject his white kindred openly in his presence. If he had truly desired to know what the only NEGRO in the process truly felt, he should have asked him in secret. Anti-Christ closeted RACIST FREEMASONS agree things in secret, they are then played out in the open as if they were live and real; incompetent art incompetently imitates life.

PEONAGE: Homogeneity or subjugated, diverse merit in the administration of the LAW seem to be the NEWEST APARTHEID

****

THE CHAIRMAN (Dr Shiv Chicken Massala India): Thank you, Mr David Moore. Mr Andrew Hut, have you got any view?

MR HUT: Sir, I cannot properly oppose any such application. These are all points which are properly made by the defence, it seems to me. So it is a matter between you and the defence. We in effect remain neutral.

THE CHAIRMAN (Dr Shiv Chicken Massala India): Thank you, Mr Hut. I shall now invite our Legal Adviser to give us his advice on the matter.

THE LEGAL ADVISER (Mr Acromegaly Dick-head Mason): Sir, you have heard what Mr Moore has to say, having heard Dr Flat-Fat- Ass Irish-Dunce's (built like a very heavy barn door), declarations. It is a matter for the Panel to consider. The test in very broad terms where the issue is of potential bias is it is important that the matter is heard before an independent and impartial tribunal. The case in particular I would advise you about is that of the English case of Porter v Magill [2002] 2 AC 357. Essentially the test is whether a person who is an informed bystander who, as it were, knows the facts, would consider that the Registrant, Dr Yinka African Bombata in this case, could have a fair hearing bearing in mind essentially what Ms Brady has declared.

The issue is this: that, in particular, you may think that she having undergone an inspection of her practices earlier this year, which is exactly the issue that you are considering with regard to the witness Dr Muscular Ugly-Ass Racist- Cougar in relation to Dr Yinka African Bombata, the question is whether or not any views or matters that Dr Flat-Fat-Ass Irish Dunce may have in mind or may have formed about Dr Muscular Ugly-Ass Racist-Cougar, whether she would be able to put those to one side or whether they would inevitably be brought to bear when considering the issues in this case and, therefore, whether it is possible for her to simply consider the evidence that she hears in this case and put out of her mind any views she may have formed or any matters that she may consider relevant, whether she would be able to do that. In the end it is a matter for you but, as I say, the test is whether the fair minded and informed observer having all the facts in front of them would consider that there was a real possibility that the tribunal would be biased in the sense that Dr Flat-Fat-Ass Irish-Dunce has the information that she has.

I should also say this, that it is important – and I think it is a matter that you, Sir, should make clear – if this is the position, that Dr Flat-Fat-Ass Irish Dunce has not expressed to any member of the Committee any views she may already have formed about Dr Muscular Ugly-Ass Racist-Cougar so that the Committee has no, as it were, advance opinion expressed by Dr Flat-Fat-Ass Irish Dunce about this witness. I think it is important that that matter is made clear if it be the case that Dr Flat-Fat-Ass Irish Dunce has not expressed any views about the witness. The similar points applies to the Scottish Professor (Postgraduate Tutor). He is clearly somebody Dr Flat-Fat-Ass Irish Dunce knows well professionally and, she has said, socially for some seven years. Again, would she be able to approach his evidence in an unbiased fashion and, again, might she in the course of any discussions you were to have express views that she had formed about Mr Atkinson as it were outside of this arena?

Those are all matters Dr Flat-Fat-Ass Irish Dunce and indeed the Committee should consider. As I say, the test is the question of whether the fair minded and informed observer having considered the facts would conclude that there was a real possibility that the tribunal was biased. That essentially is the test. That is the advice I would give.

I have to say that I do not have in front of me the particular section or paragraph in any schedule of any Act which indicates that this Committee would not be able, were you to come to that view, to continue with four and you would still be quorate, butI believe that to be the position. That is a matter, if necessary, that can be explored further.

So that is my advice, unless either party would wish me to say anything further or to correct anything I have said.

THE CHAIRMAN (Dr Shiv Chicken Massala India): Is there anything from the Legal Adviser's advice?

MR MOORE: No, thank you, Sir.

MR HUT: No, thank you, Sir.

PAUSE:

Schooled or fake courtesy is deceit.

In 2045, experts confirmed that Mr Hut unrelentingly LIED under oath. Mr Cameroon implied that he was likelier to be jailed had he been BLACK.

THE CHAIRMAN (Dr Shiv Chicken Massala India): My understanding is that we can continue with four as long as there is a dental member present, which there is. That is my understanding. We will look at that if we reach that point. Can I ask all parties to withdraw while the Committee considers the submission, please.

THE STRANGERS THEN, BY DIRECTION FROM THE CHAIR, WITHDREW

AND THE COMMITTEE DELIBERATED IN CAMERA

STRANGERS HAVING BEEN READMITTED

DETERMINATION

THE CHAIRMAN (Dr Shiv Chicken Massala India) : Following declarations of interest made by Dr Flat-Fat-Ass Irish-Dunce and Professor B.D.A. Midgeto Austria, the Committee has heard a submission by Mr David Moore, on behalf of

Dr Yinka African Bombata, that on the basis that Dr Flat-Fat-Ass Irish Dunce knows the witnesses Dr Muscular Ugly-Ass Racist-Cougar and the Scottish Professor (Postgraduate Tutor), there is a possibility of perceived bias if she continued to sit with the Committee. Mr Hut, on behalf of the Council, did not argue against the submission.

Mr Moore did not submit that Professor B.D.A. Midgeto Austria should step down because of his limited knowledge of Stephanie Twidale. The Committee has also accepted the advice of the Legal Adviser.

PAUSE:

Conflict of interest should be all or none.

Things are agreed prior to hearings they are played out in the open as if they were live and real.

Parts of the administration of the law seem akin to organised crime.

****

The Committee has considered that there is a possibility of there being a perception that the Committee might be biased if Ms Brady continued to sit on the Committee. The Committee, in particular, noted that Ms Twidale's evidence concerned a practice inspection carried out on Mr Bamgbelu's practice and that Ms Brady has recently had an inspection of her practices by Ms Twidale. It also noted the connection that

Dr Flat-Fat-Ass Irish Dunce has had with Dr Muscular Ugly-Ass Racist-Cougar over the past 12 years when Dr Muscular Ugly-Ass Racist-Cougar was her Dental Reference Officer and that they shared emergency cover. It also considered that Dr Flat-Fat-Ass Irish Dunce knows Scottish Professor (Postgraduate Tutor) well.

It is felt that Dr Flat-Fat-Ass Irish Dunce would find it difficult to consider the evidence in this case without bringing her personal knowledge to bear and that, therefore, it is appropriate if she stands down.

The Committee would want to make it clear that Dr Flat-Fat-Ass Irish Dunce has expressed no views about either witness to the members of the Committee.

Can I ask Dr Flat-Fat-Ass Irish Dunce to leave, please. Thank you very much.

(Ms Brady left the room)

CHAPTER 16

The BLACK that some Europeans (Americans) are more familiar with is the unnaturally selected and genetically reversed BLACK AMERICAN and BLACK CARIBBEAN.

"Many Scots masters were considered among the most brutal, with life expectancy on their plantations averaging a mere four years. We worked them to death then simply imported more to keep the sugar and thus the money flowing. Unlike centuries of grief and murder, an apology costs nothing. So what does Scotland have to say?" Herald Scotland: Ian Bell, Columnist, Sunday 28 April 2013

In the European plantations of The Americas and The West Indies, the brightest Africans were very, very rebellious and they objected to indefinite slavery; they demanded DEATH or LIBERTY. The civilized European Christians deselected them; they were all slaughtered. The BLACK genetic pool was weakened.

"Give me liberty or give me death." Patrick Henry

Of the rest of the kidnapped and stolen Africans, the bright but placid Africans refused to breed on HELL ON EARTH (Slave Plantations), as they realised that the owner of the Cow owned its Calves; they did not want to make the EVIL CIVILIZED CHRISTIANS richer, and, more importantly they did not want to leave children on HELL on EARTH. Their genes were lost for eternity, and BLACK genetic POOL was further weakened.

Of the remainder, the European selected the prettiest for their personal use. They became Mulatto slave babies' factory. The Ugly Africans and/or those Europeans didn't fancy, were deliberately paired up and bred for labor.

Genetic damage is the most enduring residue of European Commerce in millions of Stolen Africans.

Genetics is the Holy Grail: Reasoning and vision are unbounded, if Christ's is infinite, He must be who He says He is.

ONLY the Divine Y chromosome is exceptional, extraterrestrial and immortal.

ONLY Christ is God; He is ALLAH, the GOD of MOHAMMED.

Lightning Source UK Ltd.
Milton Keynes UK
UKOW04f0824150817

307313UK00001B/112/P